No Offense Intended

ALSO BY BARBARA SERANELLA

No Human Involved

No Offense Intended

BARBARA SERANELLA

HarperCollins*Publishers*

HarperCollins books may be purchased for educational, business, or sales promotional use. For information please write: Special Markets Department, HarperCollins Publishers, Inc., 10 East 53rd Street, New York, NY 10022.

FIRST EDITION

Designed by Elliott Beard

Library of Congress Cataloging-in-Publication Data
Seranella, Barbara.
    No offense intended / Barbara Seranella. — 1st ed.
      p. cm.
    ISBN 0-06-019212-7
    I. Title.
    PS3569.E66N64   1999
    813'.54—dc21   98-42409

99 00 01 02 03 ❖/RRD 10 9 8 7 6 5 4 3 2

Acknowledgments

I'd like to thank all the police personnel—active, retired, and otherwise—for taking the time out of their busy schedules to assist me, with special mention to Deputy Mike Blackwood, Investigator Patricia Brookman, and Deputy Rick Simms of the Riverside County Sheriff's Department, Mike Walker, formerly of the LAPD and the Oregon Sheriff's Department, and Deputy Tom Rice of Josephine County, Oregon.

I am also deeply indebted to my agent, Sandy Dijkstra, and her fine staff; my editors at HarperCollins, Carolyn Marino and Marjorie Braman; my publicist, Jackie Green; and the wonderful, supportive world of independent and mystery bookstores: Mysterious Bookshop West in Beverly Hills, Mysteries to Die For in Thousand Oaks, Mystery Annex/Small World Books in Venice Beach, Mysterious Galaxy in San Diego, Coffee, Tea, and Mystery Book Shoppe in Westminster, Dutton's Books in Brentwood, Mystery Ink in Laguna Beach, Book Carnival in Orange, Bay

Acknowledgments

Books in Monterey, A Clean Well-Lighted Place in Cupertino, San Francisco Mystery Bookstore, Latitude 33 Bookshop in Laguna Beach, M is for Mystery in San Mateo, Village Books in Pacific Palisades, Little Professor Bookstore in Temecula, The Poisoned Pen in Scottsdale, and all the other privately owned and operated book merchants devoted to the written word, writers, and readers. Thank you for treating us all with respect.

And lastly, to all the children I've had the honor to love and foster, in order of appearance: Jeremy Seth, Solo, Michera, Maryanne, Cameron, Jamie, Shannon, Carrie, and Savannah.

1

"**N**o offense," the plumber began.

Munch sighed. Why did people always feel the need to warn you before they said something stupid? She looked up from the carburetor she was working on and gave the man in the stained overalls her full attention.

"But don't you think that working on cars is kinda, I don't know, unfeminine?"

She lifted out the float assembly on the quadrajet. "Yeah, I worry about it all the way to the bank. What kind of gas do you burn in this thing?"

"Whatever," he said. "Why?"

She shined her droplight into the float chamber. "You're full of shit here." She kept her face straight, knowing the double entendre would be lost on this Neanderthal. It was 1977, for God's sake. Didn't he realize that barefoot and pregnant went out with the sixties? "This is going to take at least a half a day," she said. "In fact, it would be better if you left it overnight." She looked over his shoulder and spotted Happy Jack, the owner of Happy Jack's Auto Repair. "Hey, Jack. You wanna write this guy up? He needs a carb overhaul."

Jack grabbed a clipboard and headed their way. "You got a visitor," he said, jerking his thumb over his shoulder. Her boss's expression told her that he didn't approve. She followed his gaze and understood why.

Munch's visitor leaned against the fender of a blue Chevy pickup. The truck was fairly new: a '74 model, perhaps even a '75. Sleaze was doing well, it seemed.

His mother had named him Jonathan Garillo, but on the street he was known as "Sleaze John." The last time she'd seen Sleaze was when he was driving for Sunshine Yellow Cab out of Venice. That was a year ago—in another life. Driving a cab had been just the vehicle for Sleaze's other various vocations: pulling cons on tourists, ripping off dopers trying to score, running numbers for bookies unwise enough to trust him.

"Thanks, Jack," she said, climbing down from the milk crate she stood on when she worked on trucks. "This won't take long."

Leaving Jack to write up the plumber, Munch made her way over to where Sleaze waited. The truck's idle stumbled as she drew closer. The bearded stranger in the passenger seat glanced at her briefly and then looked away. She stuck her grease rag in her back pocket and approached them warily.

"What do you want?" she said.

"What happened to hello?" he asked.

"Hello. What do you want?"

"You got a light?" A Cheshire cat grin stretched his full lips. He was clean-shaven and a brunette this week, which complemented

2

his even white teeth and thickly lashed eyes. There was a time when she had thought him quite the fox.

She pulled out her lighter, automatically reaching for the pack of Camels in her shirt pocket.

With her lighter in his hand, he pointed to her cigarettes and, almost as an afterthought, asked her for a smoke.

Same old Sleaze. She shook her head, wondering what this visit would cost her.

He lit both their smokes and exhaled a "Thanks."

She caught his hand before her lighter disappeared into his pocket.

"What are you doing here?" she asked.

"I've missed you."

"Sleaze—" She glanced at the man riding shotgun, noting his long sleeves and dark sunglasses. A faded blue jail tattoo crossed the man's left jugular vein. She recognized the insignia of the Aryan Brotherhood: a pair of jagged lightning bolts that formed the letters SS. The man crossed his arms over his chest and rocked back and forth.

The truck's idle stuttered again and then resumed an even pace. "Hear that?" Sleaze asked. "What do you think that is?"

"If you want work done, you're going to have to leave it. I'm backed up right now," she said, aware of Jack hovering protectively just out of earshot.

"I'm in kind of a hurry, too," he said. He looked around, then dropped his voice. "Actually, I'm in a little bit of a jam."

Munch noticed that the gas cap of the truck was painted blue. She reached out and touched it. The surface was tacky. She leaned in the open window and saw the ignition wires dangling under the dash, their insulation stripped and two of them twisted together. The passenger moved a hand to his cheek and kept it there. The gesture was fine with her; she didn't want to remember him either. She pulled the rag from her back pocket and carefully wiped off all the surfaces she remembered touching.

"I don't want any part of this. I could get revoked for just talking to you."

"Since when did you pay attention to court orders?" he asked.

"Since I got a year suspended. I've changed, Sleaze. Don't mess this up for me."

He appraised her from under half-closed lids. "Yeah, I heard you got religion. I'm real proud of you. Are you happy?"

"Yes, of course." The words came out too quickly.

He raised an eyebrow, making him look a little like Clark Gable. Had he picked up the defensiveness in her tone?

"You look really good. I was going to say something."

She snorted. "Spare me. You want to do something nice for me? Just get out of my life." She kicked the tire of the truck. "And take this with you."

"Hey, don't be like that. We've got too much history."

"Forget it. It's like you said. History. What happened and what didn't happen was . . . for the best. Neither one of us wanted to be dragging a kid around." She looked at his face to confirm that this was the truth, but she couldn't read him.

"Aren't we at least friends?" he asked.

"I never had friends, Sleaze, just using partners." She looked pointedly at his travel companion.

"So that's it, huh? The rest of us are just shit on your shoes?" His tone and expression were accusatory, like she was some sort of traitor to the cause. But there was no cause, she thought angrily, just a bunch of loaded assholes trying to justify their existence.

"I'm just trying to tell you that I've got something good going here," she said. "I don't want to mess it up."

"I'm not looking to mess you up."

"I have a disease, John. I have to be careful."

"What are you talking—disease?"

"I'm in remission from alcoholism and drug addiction. I can't be around anyone still using."

How could she make him understand? She wasn't sure herself. She was spouting program dogma at him, all the tools of defense she had learned. Maybe it would be easier if he just got mad at her.

"And that's how you want it?" he asked.

"That's the way it has to be."

"What about Deb?" he asked. "And Boogie? I thought he was your ace boon coon."

"I haven't heard from them in almost a year. I don't even know where they are."

"They're up in Canyonville."

"Where's that?"

"Oregon. Pretty country if you don't mind rain."

This news made her pause. "She made it, huh?" Moving to the country had been their mutual dream. The country was a place for fresh starts, cleaner living, a good place to raise Boogie. "You got a number for her?"

Sleaze reached into his pocket and drew out his wallet. "Just a sec. You got a pen?"

She handed him her pen. He walked over to the counter and picked up several of the shop's business cards. Behind her, Jack frowned.

Sleaze flipped one of the cards over, wrote the word "Snakepit" and copied down a number from his wallet with an

Oregon area code. "She doesn't have a phone at her house," he said, "but you can usually reach her here."

"Snakepit?"

"It's a bar in Canyonville."

"Is she doing all right?"

"She's got an ol' man."

"There's a surprise." Deb always had an old man. She always fell passionately in love for life with each of them and cried buckets when they left. Munch envied her that—her depth of passion.

"He's an asshole," Sleaze added.

Her face twisted in a wry smile. They were always assholes, especially after Deb was done with them.

"I did some business with him," Sleaze said. "He tried to get over on me."

"Uh-huh." She didn't need to ask for any particulars. Nothing he said or she asked would move the conversation any closer to the truth. Sleaze had a way of explaining things that neatly sidestepped any culpability on his part. The other guy was always wrong and usually a step too slow. "I have to get back to work. Just tell me what you want, Sleaze."

He glanced back nervously at his companion in the truck. "Like I said, I'm in a little bit of a jam. Nothing serious. It should blow over soon."

"And I'm supposed to do what?" she asked.

"I just wanted to see you," he said, watching traffic as if he were waiting for something. "It's been so long." He reached over and touched her cheek. "Too long."

She pulled back. It was time to end this exchange.

He wasn't the first to come around from her old life. She'd found a simple formula for getting rid of the others: her ex-using partners who had somehow managed to sniff her out, sensing some prosperity not their own that might be available for leeching. They'd come to her with hard-luck stories, told with sorrowful faces and sincere tones. Maybe they thought getting clean and sober had somehow affected her memory. That she wouldn't spot their games since she was no longer on the pitching side. She had learned that it was easier to indulge them: listen to their bullshit and agree about the unfairness of the world. Then she'd loan them money—sometimes a twenty (she'd gone as high as fifty)—and they would promise to pay her back as soon as they "got on their feet." The ones who owed her never came back. The money she "lent" was a small price to pay to ensure that they wouldn't return.

"How much would it take to get out of this jam?" she asked, reaching for her wallet. She carried her wallet in her back pocket, like a man would. Maybe the plumber was right. She looked over in his direction and found Jack watching her. He tapped his watch. "I've got to get back to work," she said.

Sleaze saw her go for her wallet. He probably wasn't even aware that he had licked his lips. "I've got a kid," he said, "a little girl."

She felt a lightning bolt streak between her gut and heart. He always knew how to find the soft spots. Hadn't he been the one who taught her how to isolate the mark and single out the vulnerabilities? She tried to think if there were any way he could know about the scarring within her body, how it had rendered her infertile. She had spoken of it at meetings, so it wasn't exactly privileged information. But the meetings that she attended were here in the San Fernando Valley. Had he somehow heard?

"Good for you," she said. "Who's the mother?"

"Karen."

"That broad who worked at the phone company?" Another mark, Munch remembered. Karen was always good for a twenty

7

that Sleaze would collect on her lunch break while Munch waited in the front passenger seat of the taxi with the meter off.

"Yeah, that's the one."

She felt an uncomfortable flash of heat shoot up the back of her neck. It was time to play "Name That Emotion." Emotions were a new thing, another dubious gift of sobriety. Before, they'd never been an issue. Before, if anyone had cared to ask at any given time how Munch was feeling or what she was feeling, she would have had only two possible answers: good or sick. Sobriety opened up a whole new range.

Those first few months, her sponsor, Ruby, had driven her crazy asking her how she was, what was she feeling. Finally Munch had told her: She was pissed off. Then Ruby had patiently explained that anger wasn't an emotion. It was a reaction. Get past the anger, Ruby said. It was a shield, a coat of armor.

Munch looked at Sleaze. He had a kid. He and Karen had a kid. How did that make her feel? She didn't have to think too long.

Ruby said that one day maybe Munch might adopt. That was another of those nebulous in-the-future things that Ruby was always promising. Like getting married one day. Munch told her that yeah, that might happen, but first she needed a date.

"So what do you want from me?" she asked.

"I want you to meet my kid," he said.

"What about Karen?"

"Karen's dead. She OD'd." His eyes clouded. If she didn't know better, she'd think he really felt bad. This realization annoyed her. More jealousy? she wondered.

"I've been staying in Venice," he said. "You're going to laugh when I tell you where." He held up an oval rubber key fob with the number 6 stamped on it. A single door key dangled from the stainless steel ring.

"What? Back at the Flats? Many happy memories there."

"There's a few, you can't say there isn't. The truth is I haven't been home in a few days."

"Too hot?" she asked.

He grinned that infuriating I-know-I've-been-bad-but-I'd-probably-do-it-again grin at her. She had to fight herself to not respond with a smile of her own. How did he get his eyes to twinkle like that?

"So who's watching this kid of yours now?" she asked.

"A neighbor."

"Does this kid have a name?" She felt herself being sucked into his bullshit. *Forget the kid's name,* she told herself, *forget misplaced loyalties to old running partners.* She wasn't a part of that world anymore. The war was over. She had surrendered.

"Asia."

"Asia?" she echoed, shaking her head. What kind of name was that? She turned to step away from him. She had work to do. She didn't need this shit.

He followed her as she walked back to the Cadillac she'd been working on, the one with the leaking water pump. She was conscious of her walk and how it didn't wiggle. Steel-toed boots didn't lend themselves to sexy walking.

"Actually," he said. "There is one other thing."

"I'm sure there is." She squeezed her arms around the radiator shroud of the Cadillac to get to the four bolts that held the fan on. She knew she would pay for this action later. Soap and water wouldn't completely wash out the bits of fiberglass that would embed in her arms. She'd be itching for days.

Sleaze leaned over a fender, ingratiating himself under the hood.

"I just need you to take the baby over to my sister's and pick up a few things at the apartment. Mostly just the baby's stuff—clothes, her car seat, a couple toys."

She paused, feeling that tug between two worlds, and thought about Venice Beach—the place that used to be home. Nostalgia filled her as she remembered all the old haunts: the boardwalk, the circle, Hooker Hill, Sunshine Cab. There was a time when she knew who she was and what she was about. Think harder, she told herself, think about the misery attached to that old life—the running, the constant fear, the hopelessness.

"I don't go to Venice," she said.

"I'm not asking you to stay there," he said. "Just a quick pit stop. You'll be in and out in two minutes."

"What about your sister? Have Lisa go to Venice."

"I'm kind of overextended with her," he said.

"You mean she's fed up with your bullshit."

"No," he said. "The thing is, there's these guys—"

"Don't tell me any more. I don't want to know."

She put her cigarette between her teeth to free her hands as she worked the ratchet. Smoke filled her eyes and she squinted, feeling her face scowl. She stopped working and threw away the butt.

"But you'll come?" he asked, dangling the key.

She looked at him for a long minute, framing a reply.

"You're my only hope," he said.

"Don't do me like that. I'm not anyone's only hope. I didn't get sober to keep digging losers out of holes. Whatever you've gotten yourself into, that's your problem. I can't get into any of that."

"You've changed."

"That's what I've been trying to tell you."

"You didn't use to be so cold."

She wanted to say that wasn't it. She was anything but cold. All her using career she had wound her feelings into a hard knot and stored them in a place deep inside her. A place so dark and barren that nothing and no one could get to them. She had hoped that eventually all that was vulnerable would shrivel and die, free her from the pain of life. But it hadn't gone like that. Now that she was going to live, she had to tread carefully. He would never understand that her reprieve was a daily thing, so instead she said nothing. Let him think what he would.

The fender lifted slightly when he stood. Through the reflection of the Caddy's windshield, she watched him climb into the cab of the truck and then shake his head like he was disappointed. He said something to his passenger and the other guy nodded and said something back.

It pissed her off. Who the hell did he think he was, passing judgment on her? He was the one who fucked up, right?

Her knuckles slammed into the cold steel of the engine block as the socket slipped off the bolt she was loosening. Now look what he'd made her do. She felt tears well up in her eyes.

Feelings sucked.

When she looked down she saw he had left the key on the fender.

2

Munch spent the next two hours sweating over the Cadillac. Three bolts had broken off inside the block. One shop teacher at an extension class she had taken at West Valley College called it electrolysis when two metals such as aluminum and steel bonded inseparably. Although she had liked the sound of the word, how it rolled on her tongue, part of her always felt that it was too benign a term to assign to a condition that always gave her so much grief.

"Rust never rests," she said aloud as she pried the leaking water pump loose from the motor with a large screwdriver. Earlier in the day she had explained to the owner of the Cadillac that the bearing supporting his impeller shaft had failed. Any other mechanic might have just said that the water pump was broken and let it go at that, but she loved explaining to people what was wrong with their cars, especially when it gave her the opportunity to sound out the words always ringing in her head.

The broken bolts in the Cadillac added an additional forty-five minutes to the job. Forty-five minutes that she didn't have to spare. Why did this sort of shit always seem to happen on Fridays? she wondered.

She sweated as she worked. Her uniform clung to her back. Beads of perspiration fell from the tip of her nose, flattening when they hit the cross-brace of the frame. The thermometer mounted on the Caddy's sideview mirror read ninety-two degrees. This was her first autumn in the Valley. It was a year of firsts—one right after the other. Ruby said to think of it as an adventure.

And were all adventures this lonely? Munch wondered. She didn't mean to seem ungrateful. But what did you do with the many hours of the day? When every moment of your life was spent pursuing drugs and the ways and means to get more and then suddenly that all ended? You don't use anymore. Great. You're going to live. Now what? What do you do with yourself when you're not busy with work or on your way to another meeting? What about Sunday at 3:00 P.M.? Whom do you talk to when you have a foot in two worlds and you can't relate to anyone?

These things take time, Ruby always said. You didn't get screwed up in one day; you won't get better all at once, either. Sometimes Ruby would point out that Munch was still young, which Munch supposed was meant to be comforting in some way.

Another bolt felt like it wasn't going to give. She sprayed it with penetrating oil and worked it back and forth, a quarter turn at a time. A bead of sweat worked its way down her cleavage. Venice Beach would no doubt be at least thirty degrees cooler. Would it have been that big a deal to pick up his kid?

She straightened and stretched. The backs of her knees ached from being locked so long in one position. Jack walked over to her and put a meaty hand on her shoulder.

"How's it going?" he asked.

"Not great." She showed him the broken bolts.

"What did that scuzball in the truck want?"

"A favor."

She knew Jack felt she was being taken advantage of by her old "lower companions" and didn't approve. In the AA questionnaire, the one with the twenty questions that determined if you too were an alcoholic, it asked if you consorted with lower companions. Ruby said that included everyone Munch used to know.

"You didn't give him any money, did you?" Jack asked.

"No, he didn't want money."

"Watch out for that guy."

She felt tears swelling behind her eyes and bent back down over the engine. "I can handle it," she said.

"You always say that. Next time one of those creeps comes around, you let me deal with them."

She shook her head, unwilling to attempt to talk through her closed throat. She'd asked Ruby once when she'd stop being so emotional. Maybe never, Ruby said. Welcome to the human race.

Munch cleared her throat. "I've got to go see my probation officer today at four."

"When are you going to be through with all that? It's already been almost a year. Can't they see how good you're doing?"

"I was lucky to get probation."

"Yeah, but three years? Jesus." Jack patted the fender of the Cadillac. "Don't worry about getting this one done. I'll call the guy and tell him we've run into some trouble. Maybe I can get you a few extra bucks for the broken bolts."

"Good luck, this guy's got the first nickel he ever made."

Jack chuckled. "You pegged him right."

"Uh, Jack?" Munch pushed back the hair from her forehead where it had worked loose from her braid. "Thanks. Thanks for everything."

"Sure, kid." He turned to go and then spotted the key on the fender. "This yours?" he asked, holding forth Sleaze's house key. "What? I say something funny?"

"No, I just remembered something about that guy who was here. He thinks he knows me so well." She took the key and slipped it in her shirt pocket.

She gathered up her tools and checked the clock. It was a little after three. Her new probation officer—the intractable Mrs. Olivia Scott—was in Santa Monica. The drive over the hill took thirty to forty-five minutes depending on the amount of traffic. Santa Monica bordered Venice, she thought as she put her tools away and locked her box. Inglewood, where Lisa lived, was only another few miles farther south. What was her big worry?

She scrubbed her hands, put on a clean T-shirt, kicked off her heavy work shoes, and slipped on a pair of Keds. The mechanics all kept lockers in the small room where the uniforms were stored. In a concession to gender, Jack had installed a latch on the door soon after he hired her. Munch always felt funny about locking the door. Perhaps it was all the time she had spent secreted in rooms, usually bathrooms, when the doors had to be locked.

A small mirror hung over the sink. She loosened her braid and ran her hands through to her scalp, ruffling her light brown hair. Usually fine and straight, now it was kinked from the day spent entwined. She liked the effect. Someday maybe she'd get someone to show her how to curl her hair on purpose.

She thought about Deb and her boy, up there in the country. She missed them both. Sleaze, as usual, had hit a nerve. She and

Deb had been best friends since they were sixteen, when Deb had first moved out from Missouri. Now she was in Oregon.

What were the fall months like there? Did the leaves on the trees all change color? And what sort of a town was Canyonville? Did it have a little general store where the locals gathered? Did the postmistress know everyone by their first name? Was there a small gas station there with a repair shop in back?

All this had been part of the big dream. Deb would get some part-time job in one of the stores so she could be home when Boogie got out of school. They would rent a small house together. They'd grow their own vegetables and have two cats in the yard, just like in the song.

The issue of Boogie's mixed blood wouldn't exist. In the country, nobody would ever say nigger.

At the end of the month, he would be turning seven. Had over six years really passed since she held out her arms to receive him after his first staggering steps? Hard to believe. When he was a newborn, Deb told Munch that she had turned his head every twenty minutes so that it wouldn't get flat on either side. Was anyone thinking of doing that for Asia?

She emerged from the back room and paused before Jack's open office door.

"I'm going over to Denny's," she said. "You want anything?"

He checked his watch before answering. She cringed in response to his unspoken disapproval at her early departure, but maybe she was reading him wrong. Maybe he didn't mean anything by the gesture, and she was just overreacting to everything.

"No, I'm good," he said.

"I finished the carb overhaul on the plumber's truck," she said. "I'll come in in the morning and adjust the choke when it's cold."

"Don't come in just for that," he said. "I'll do it."

"Are you sure?"

"Yeah, yeah."

"All right. See you Monday morning then. *Early.*"

Head still bent over his paperwork, he waved her away.

She jogged across the street without waiting for the light and was slightly winded by time she reached the coffee shop's front door.

Ruby's shift had ended, and Munch found her sitting at the counter drinking coffee and gossiping with the afternoon staff. Ruby turned when Munch pushed through the double glass doors.

"Did Jack let you off early?" she asked.

"I've gotta go see my PO," Munch explained. "She called my number." Every night, as part of the terms of her probation, Munch called a number and listened to its recorded message. After each probation officer's last name, a series of numbers was announced. Each number was in fact a person. Munch was *Scott, thirty-eight.* Thirty-eight had been included in last night's recording, which meant that she had twenty-four hours in which to report and give a urine sample. "I'd thought I'd get a cup of coffee for the you-know-what."

"How's everything going?" Ruby asked.

"Okay."

The waitress behind the counter brought Munch a large coffee in a Styrofoam cup. Munch doctored the drink with equal amounts of cream and sugar.

"Anything else?" the waitress asked.

Munch put a dollar on the counter. "No. Thanks."

"Are you coming tonight?" Ruby asked.

"I'm bringing the cookies." Munch stirred her coffee. "Maybe we could talk later."

"What is it?"

"No big deal," she said, not looking up.

Ruby stood and gave Munch a hug. "You sure?"

After all these months, Munch still had difficulty responding to Ruby's spontaneous shows of affection. Part of her wanted to answer in kind, to wrap her arms around Ruby's ample waist and bury herself in the soft warmth of her sponsor's love. But something always held her back—a moment's hesitation that always served to kill the impulse. Ruby didn't seem to notice as she finished off her hug with an extra squeeze. "We'll talk tonight," she promised.

"Yeah, I better get going," Munch said, picking up her coffee and leaving the change for the waitress who had served her.

She was on the freeway for ten minutes before she spotted the wreck closing the right lane. The accident was fairly fresh, judging from the brightness of the flares. She vaguely remembered hearing multiple sirens as she was getting ready to leave work. This must have been their destination.

Three cop cars, an ambulance, a fire truck, and a tow truck further snarled traffic. The inner lanes slowed to a crawl as each passing motorist took the look they'd paid for with the interruption of their commute. Finally it came to her turn. She almost lost control of her GTO when she recognized the blue truck with its grille flattened against a signpost. What appeared to be bullet holes punctured the driver's side of the windshield. A booted foot dangled out from beneath the open driver's door. The ambulance drivers weren't rushing to the driver's aide. One of them even lighted a cigarette. The foot didn't move. Her stomach clutched.

A cloud of tangible sorrow seemed to levitate from the wreck and land on her chest.

How could he be dead? Sleaze always landed on his feet.

Maybe it wasn't the same truck. Maybe the other guy had been driving. Where was the other guy? The only people she saw milling about the crash scene were in uniform. Both the ambulance and patrol car were empty of passengers. She strained to catch a look at the driver's face, but the doorpost obstructed her view. Blood dripped onto the asphalt.

When she didn't move ahead with the other cars, a highway patrolman waved her angrily on. She leaned across her front seat, rolled down her passenger window, and pointed to the wreckage.

"I know him. I know the driver," she said.

The cop studied her for a moment, then glanced back at the crash scene. "Pull over up there."

She nodded. She had every intention of pulling over, of going to him, but then another thought came to her. *There's nothing you can do,* the voice in her head said. *You don't need any part of this. Keep moving.*

She caught a last look at the mangled pickup, then swerved back into traffic, ignoring the people who honked and swore at her.

Goddamnit, Sleaze, now what have you done?

3

Homicide detective Jigsaw Blackstone unfolded his long legs and swung them out from beneath the steering wheel of his black, four-door sedan. Before exiting the car, he turned his rearview mirror and checked that his part was straight. He pulled a fine-toothed comb from his shirt pocket and carefully ran it through his mustache until the dark hair was arranged evenly over his upper lip.

"You're like a cat, you know that?" Alex Percz, Blackstone's partner, said.

Blackstone didn't respond.

"I'm going to check the victim," Alex said. "You just take your time."

"That's just jealousy talking."

"Did I say cat?" Alex said. "I think I meant pussy."

Blackstone smirked and returned the mirror to its previous position. He got out of the car and walked over to the highway patrolman directing traffic.

"You the first on the scene?" he asked the officer.

"Yes, sir."

"What happened?" Blackstone took a step backward and looked down at the body through the pickup truck's driver's-side window. The stiff's eyes were open; their expression seemed calm, almost bored. The skin around the head wound was scooted up; the throat shot had ripped through a carotid artery and shattered vertebrae.

"I was cruising when I came across this scene."

"So you didn't see it happen."

"No, sir."

"Paramedics get here?"

"Been and gone. Nothing they could do."

"Good. So they didn't move anything? Disturb the body?"

"No, sir."

"Anyone come forward? Any witnesses to the shooting?"

"Not exactly. A woman in a dark blue GTO slowed down while I was directing traffic and claimed to know the driver."

Blackstone looked back to where the body was positioned. "Could she see him?"

"Not from her angle; not the face anyway. Maybe the foot. I guess she recognized the vehicle."

"You let her go?"

"I instructed her to pull over. When I looked over again, she hadn't."

"Get a plate? No, of course you didn't. Was she young, old, fat?"

"Caucasian, early twenties, small build, light eyes, curly light-brown hair—collar length."

"That narrows the field."

"One other thing, sir—her hands and fingernails. They were

. . . not really dirty, more like stained. Lines of black around her cuticles and under her nails."

"All right, Officer . . ." He leaned forward to read the name tag. "Kerr. That might be something. Thanks. What was the speed of traffic?"

"Fifty to fifty-five."

"Is Cal Trans on the way?"

"Yes, sir."

Blackstone made a note in his notebook and walked back to the crash site. The tow truck driver stood at the ready, awaiting permission to haul off the wreck. Blackstone held up a hand to say not yet. He studied the accordion creases in the hood and the crushed front grille. The driver's door appeared to have sprung open on impact. If the truck had collided with the pole at fifty-five miles an hour, the signpost would have been flattened. Blackstone walked around to the passenger side, looked inside the cab, and saw the hot-wired ignition.

"Another fine, upstanding citizen," he said out loud.

The highway patrol officer looked over but said nothing.

Traffic advanced sluggishly on both sides of the freeway. Blackstone ignored the shouted questions of the motorists. People are idiots, he thought, shaking his head. But that was the job: protecting idiots from assholes. A Cal Trans truck arrived with flashing yellow arrow boards to redirect traffic. He instructed them to shut down the southbound lanes five miles before and after the crime scene.

"It's Friday rush hour," the harried Cal Trans supervisor explained. "I can give you on-ramp to on-ramp in both directions. But that's it."

"Fine," Blackstone said. "Just do it."

The coroner's wagon arrived next, escorted by another black-

and-white unit. The coroner's deputies waited until the photographers took their pictures—eight-point shots of the victim and vehicle. Blackstone made sure they captured the loose ignition wires on film. He went back to his car, opened the trunk, and retrieved his own Polaroid camera.

As he snapped his pictures, he took note of the shooter's skill. Two out of three shots had hit the driver; both had done serious damage. One shot entered through the forehead, passed through the brain, and taken with it on exit the back half of the skull. It had certainly been fatal. The other had torn out the victim's throat, another nonsurvivable wound. He was either dealing with a shooter who was a crack marksman or one with the luck of Lee Harvey Oswald. The third bullet had gone through the dash and floorboard.

Using the toe of his shoe, he opened the driver's door the rest of the way, then stepped aside while the body was loaded onto a gurney.

The coroner's deputy, wearing surgical gloves, went through the victim's pockets. Alex searched through the dense hedge of bottlebrush growing along the freeway shoulder.

Blackstone returned to the driver's side of the pickup truck, where he studied the spiderweb fractures in the broken windshield.

"Right up your alley, eh, Jigs?" Alex asked from over Blackstone's shoulder.

Blackstone let his partner's words wash over him.

"What do you think?" Alex was brushing dirt and leaves from his knees.

"The top one was first," Blackstone said, running his finger down the cracks in the glass. "See how the cracks radiating out from the bottom hole butt up against the upper web fractures?"

"I'll take your word for it."

Blackstone studied the top bullet hole and found that it was drilled neatly, with no deviation. The truck's windshield was fairly flat, he noted, but had enough of a slope that it might deflect a projectile as it passed through. The fired rounds must have entered at almost a perfect ninety-degree angle. Matching holes were torn through the upholstery of the driver's seat. He scanned the road up ahead. There were no overpasses or tall trees nearby.

"We got at least two perps," he said. "The shooter and his driver. We're looking for another truck, maybe a van or a camper, even a motor home."

"Shit," Alex said, looking down the miles of freeway, "they're long gone by now."

They looked in through the open door of the truck. The seat was soaked with blood. Bits of bone and red gelatinous brain matter clung to the vinyl and cloth. If the second kill shot was intentional, was there some sort of message implied? Nobody sings with a bullet in his throat.

Blackstone shone his flashlight into the area behind the seat and saw that the bullets had cut through the sheet metal of the cab as well.

The investigators formed an impromptu huddle out of earshot of the tow truck driver. Blackstone addressed the coroner first. "What have you got?"

"There was a wallet in the back pocket, but the ID was a forgery."

"I called in the name," CHP officer Kerr added, "but it wasn't on record with the DMV. The truck was reported stolen yesterday."

"Anything?" Blackstone asked his partner.

"Nah, he must have been alone."

"That's the way we all die, buddy."

"Thanks for the thought."

While they awaited the arrival of the firearms expert, Blackstone told Alex, "I want to find the female in the GTO. If she doesn't come forward, let's check the printing shops in the area."

"What are we looking for?"

"Female, Caucasian, early to mid-twenties, who sets type or cleans the presses."

They looked up as an orange-jacketed Cal Trans worker picked up three of their cones so that the police crime lab van could enter. Blackstone greeted Jeff Hagouchi from Firearms as he exited his vehicle.

"What have we got?" Hagouchi asked.

"One victim, shot twice, three rounds fired."

"A level shot would have taken out the back window," Hagouchi said.

"Yeah," Blackstone answered, "that's what we were thinking, but we wanted an expert's opinion."

"Then this is your lucky day."

Hagouchi brought out two long wooden dowels and pushed them carefully through the holes in the windshield until they just touched the corresponding punctures in the back seat. He had the photographers take more pictures of the windshield with the dowels inserted.

"Find any spent cartridges?" Hagouchi asked.

"Not yet," Blackstone said, pointing to the uniformed officers traversing the vacant freeway shoulder to shoulder. He took Hagouchi over to the skid marks. One of the bullets had lodged into the asphalt there. Hagouchi drew a circle around it with yellow chalk and then followed Blackstone back to the truck.

"We've got two scenarios," Hagouchi said. "I'll know more

when I examine the projectiles, of course. You got either a long-range shot with a rainbow trajectory . . . "

"Three times?"

"Or a passing tall vehicle. Find your spent cartridges and you'll have distance and angle. I'll extract the other bullets once we get the truck back to the station."

Blackstone showed Hagouchi where the bullets had punctured the steel skin of the cab behind the seat. Hagouchi whistled. "You thinking what I'm thinking?"

"Definitely not hollow points," Blackstone said, knowing that hollow points would have mushroomed on impact. "Full metal jackets?" he asked, referring to military-type bullets that were designed to take out more than one human target.

"At least," Hagouchi said. "Possibly APs."

Blackstone nodded grimly. He definitely didn't like the idea of mobile sharpshooters armed with AP rounds. He made a note to himself in his notebook, writing out the words that nobody had said out loud. There was another name for armor-piercing ammunition: cop-killers.

4

Maybe it hadn't been him, Munch thought as she turned onto the Santa Monica westbound freeway. After her initial reaction of shock and horror, a strange calm had settled around her heart. Surely if it had been Sleaze lying there dead she would feel something more. After all they'd been through together, he wouldn't depart the planet without her instinctively knowing. No, she needed more proof before she mourned him. Until that time, it wasn't real. It didn't happen.

She focused on the appointment with her probation officer.

It hadn't taken long after being assigned to Mrs. Scott for Munch to see that the woman was not looking to make any friends with her clients. Her office was plastered with plaques of appreciation from law enforcement groups. She kept a signed picture on her desk of her shaking hands with the chief of police. So much for being in the business of rehabilitation.

"Fuck 'er if she can't take a joke," Flower George would have said. But he was dead now. His ill-advised fatherly advice needed to be buried with him. All that old stinking thinking needed to go.

She was trying to stop saying the F word, too.

For now she was still caught in the system and she accepted that. The legal system—the judges, the lawyers, the cops—never expected anyone to successfully complete a three-year probation term, but she would surprise them. Probation was just a device they used to keep you on hold—their way of saying, "You can walk for now, but we got you when we want you." The random surprise testing enabled them to gather fuel for future leverage. Junkies didn't go straight. That was a well-known fact. It was the recidivism factor.

Recidivism. She'd learned the word in rehab. The statistics were that ninety-seven percent of all junkies went back to the needle.

That meant three percent didn't.

With eight months clean and sober, she was looking forward to her first sober Thanksgiving. To celebrate, she planned to go to the California Institute for Women at Corona as part of an AA panel. CIW would have been her next destination if things hadn't changed.

She'd spent the previous year's Thanksgiving holiday at the county jail, Sybil Brand Institute, awaiting trial for various and sundry drug-related charges. In her old life, everything was drug-related. If she'd been busted for jaywalking, you could bet that she was crossing the street to score some dope, get high, or turn a trick to get some money to buy dope.

Last year's incarceration had been her longest ever—over a month.

A diesel-powered black-and-white sheriff's bus spewing black smoke pulled in front of her as she took the exit for the Santa

Monica Courthouse complex. It reminded her of her many trips from jail to court, her only forays into the world during that long month. They called the bus "The Gray Goose." She didn't know why. She only knew that it was dirty inside and partitioned with steel grating. The larger rear portion of the bus—where the seats were arranged like church pews—was where they put the men. The woman sat on long bench seats lining the sides in the front. Separate, but equal.

The bus always seemed to appear next to her when her thoughts turned down dangerous paths. Another of those eerie coincidences that made her feel like God had taken a personal interest in her case. He used the hulking, black-and-white vehicles like a page mark in her life to remind her that whatever was going on, it could always be worse.

As she pulled into the parking lot, she thought about the body in the truck, the booted foot, the shattered windshield. If it was Sleaze, what would become of his kid? With Karen dead, Asia was an orphan. Maybe.

Stay in the moment, she told herself. *Park. Turn off the car. Breathe in and out.*

The lot was full of cop cars. Munch didn't lock her car. If it wasn't safe there, then the hell with it. She passed the large rusting sculpture of nautical chains on the lawn in front of the court building. The police station was on the other side of the court building. They kept the prisoners on the first floor. Milk was served with the meals, which Munch preferred to the bitter black coffee offered in Van Nuys. But unlike Van Nuys, Santa Monica had a no smoking rule. That had seemed like cruel and unusual punishment to her during her brief incarcerations here.

Never again, she thought.

She entered the court building, pushed through the door to

the probation department, and gave her name at the front desk. The woman seated there told her to go right in.

"You know the way?" the woman asked.

"Yeah," Munch said. "I've been here before." She walked the hallway in her dreams. Some nights, the hallway had no end and she was in the wrong building and running late and if she didn't find the correct cubicle soon her probation would be violated and she would be sent back to Sybil Brand. She'd wake with the sheets twisted around her legs.

Wiping her hands on her pants, she checked the clock. She was still ten minutes early, she noted, no need to panic. She headed toward her probation officer's cubicle.

Mrs. Scott glanced up as Munch entered. "I'll be right with you," she said as she reached for a rubber stamp, inked it on a pad of red ink, and brought it down sharply on the papers in front of her. Munch saw that the stamped letters read VIOLATION. The older woman put the stamp and paperwork aside, straightened the lapel of her navy blue blazer, and then opened Munch's file.

"How are you, Miranda?" she asked. Mrs. Scott was the only one who ever used that name with her.

"I'm here."

The thin orange line of the PO's lips turned down at the corners and the crease between her eyes grew deeper.

"How are you?" Munch asked.

"Let's stay on track, shall we?" Mrs. Scott said. "Are you still working?"

"I brought my pay stubs," Munch said, reaching into her shirt pocket. Of course she was still working. If any major changes occurred in her life, like changing jobs or moving, she was to notify her PO within twenty-four hours.

Mrs. Scott took the papers and handed Munch a mimeographed form. "I need you to fill out this personal financial report." Mrs. Scott went back to the file she had been stamping with her red ink. Under RECOMMENDATIONS on the last page, Mrs. Scott wrote, "30 days county time," and smiled.

Munch looked at the paperwork her probation officer handed her. The categories listed were: RENT, UTILITIES, FOOD, GAS, CLOTH-ING, and ENTERTAINMENT. On the other side of the ledger she was to put what she earned.

Munch wrote in the numbers and handed the form back. She had left the entertainment column blank.

"Aren't you saving anything?" Mrs. Scott asked.

"What do you mean?"

"You're making enough to have several hundred dollars left over at the end of the month. What happens to that money?"

"I don't know. I spend it, I guess."

"By our next appointment, I want to see some signs of fiscal responsibility."

"I pay my bills."

"And is that all you want for yourself? To just get by?"

Obviously the woman wasn't going to be satisfied unless she found something that needed correcting. "I'll work on it."

Mrs. Scott gave Munch a wary look. "I guess we'll see." She picked up a plastic cup. "Are you ready?"

"Yep." Munch stood and made for the bathroom with Mrs. Scott close behind. The hallway had a bleachy smell that always reminded Munch of cocaine. She kept the observation to herself. The clicking of Mrs. Scott's heels on the linoleum echoed off the walls.

They pushed into the women's room and Munch was relieved to see that they had the place to themselves.

She unzipped her pants and positioned the cup under herself

in such a way as not to cut off Mrs. Scott's view. Mrs. Scott believed you couldn't trust a dope fiend not to bring along someone else's sample and try to pass it off as her own. Munch didn't have to do that. Her test would be clean. She used to feel proud of the stream of drug-free urine that flowed from her body. Lately, it was beginning to feel humiliating to have Mrs. Scott there in the stall with her.

The pee overflowed the tiny container and ran down her fingers. She poured half out, carefully wiped the sides, put on the lid, and handed it to her PO.

"Anything else you want to tell me?" the woman asked before they parted in the hallway. "Any problems?"

"No, everything's fine." She blinked back the images of the blood dripping from the boot. Was he dead? Really, forever gone? She felt the weight of his key in her pocket as she walked away. Why hadn't she treated him better? Why hadn't she agreed to go see his kid? Why couldn't she at least have had lunch with him? The extra half-hour might have altered the course of events—but no, she had been too caught up in herself and her own needs.

Stop it, she thought. *You don't even know if he's really dead.* Obviously there would be no peace for her until she found out for sure.

5

She left the cluster of court buildings and headed south. As she neared the familiar streets of Venice, her mind flooded with images from her childhood—the early years when her mother was still alive. The Venice Beach she knew then had been a magical place peopled by beatniks and jazz musicians who treated her like an equal. Mama filled her young ears with promises of castles and ponies, singing her to sleep with Joni Mitchell lullabies.

Munch had believed it all—even when they "camped out" in different people's living rooms and garages and washed their hair in the Laundromat sink. She'd been such a dumb kid. She didn't wise up until she was ten, and that was almost a full year after Mama died. It had taken that long for the reality to sink in. Months and months before she finally noticed that as great and wonderful as heaven was reported to be, it was a place nobody returned from. So who really knew if it was nice at all? That's when she had learned to pay more attention to what people did than to what they said.

She lit her cigarette with the car's lighter. The smell of a match's sulphur still reminded her too much of dope, and she didn't need the sensory memory in such already dangerous territory. Venice, god. It felt weird to be there again, like she'd been away for years instead of just months. She briefly considered stopping in and seeing her old boss, Wizard, but decided that she was better off sticking to what she came for and leaving the social calls for another day.

Instead of turning left on Rose Avenue, she cut through side streets until she arrived at the alley running parallel to Hampton. The building where she had once lived with Sleaze was a horseshoe-shaped collection of single and one-bedroom apartments.

Sleaze liked Number 6 because it was a corner unit. The front door faced an overgrown hedge of oleander instead of the street. On the other side of the hedge and sharing the same alley was the abandoned Jewish Center. A morning glory vine, flush with large purple blooms, had taken over the Center's back fence and formed a web between two palm trees. She parked in the alley behind a gold Impala balanced on jack stands and stripped of its wheels, rear bumper, and differential.

Ducking between the two buildings, she picked her way over trash, following the ten-foot-tall shrubbery separating the two buildings. Halfway to the street, she crouched. The same opening—their secret route—still existed. She slipped through it, pushing aside damp white sheets that had been stretched across the bushes to dry.

When she got to Sleaze's apartment, she knocked first—softly. No one answered. She slipped the key in the lock and opened the door. The apartment was small and dark, but she didn't reach for the light switch. She stood very still. Her ears filled with the sound of her own heart. She took deep breaths to calm herself.

Now I lay me down to sleep. I pray the lord my soul to keep.

The tiny kitchen, consisting of a sink, stove, and battered

refrigerator, stood at the other end of the room. The closet-size bathroom lay to her right. She could hear the steady drip of a leaking faucet from behind the room's closed door.

She righted a baby's car seat lying on its side and picked up a rattle. The words DADDY'S GIRL were written on the pink plastic face. She stuck the toy in her pocket and stepped closer to the bathroom door.

"Sleaze?" she called in an urgent whisper, willing him to appear and aggravate her with that grin of his.

No answer.

"John?" *Please. Please be all right.*

She didn't want to open the door, but just standing there wasn't the answer, either. She put her ear to the door. The dripping was louder, maddeningly rhythmic, like Chinese water torture. She imagined all sorts of horrors: slit veins and throats; open mouths; a lifeless face staring up at her through inches of tub water.

Shaking her head, she took a deep breath and reached for the door handle.

And if I die before . . . Stupid prayer.

She put her hand on the knob. It twisted in her hand.

"Oh, fuck it," she said through clenched teeth and pushed the door inward.

No one was in there, dead or alive. She laughed out loud, relieved, embarrassed. The medicine cabinet hung open. It was empty save for a box of Band-Aids and a jar of Vaseline. A box of dried-out baby butt wipes lay open on the top of the toilet tank lid.

Inside the bathtub was a collection of infant float toys and a bottle of Johnson No More Tears baby shampoo. The drain's steel seat was eroded from the constant drip of the leaking shower faucet. She touched the side of the tub where perhaps he had leaned kneeling as he washed his baby.

But where was he now? And where was the baby? Which neighbor?

She gathered Asia's car seat and the float toys and took them out to her car. Returning to the building, she started knocking on doors. The man who answered at Number 7 was dressed only in a stained, threadbare white T-shirt and sagging briefs.

"I'm looking for a baby," she said. "Someone around here is watching her for my friend."

He scratched himself and adjusted his balls before he answered. "Huh?" He squinted, perhaps trying to remember how to speak. "I, uh . . . Whatcha doing here?"

"Never mind." She waved him back. "Sorry to disturb you."

Grumbling, the man closed his door. No one answered her knock at the next apartment over. She put her ear to the door. The unit appeared to be unoccupied. When she knocked on the third door, it rattled. She looked down and saw that the wood around the doorknob was freshly splintered. Then she heard a baby crying.

She nudged the door open with her knee and stared down the dark hallway where the crying seemed to be coming from. "Hello?" She stepped inside. "Are you all right in there?"

The baby screamed. Something about its tone alerted her on some primal level. She rushed down the hall. Another scream. The bedroom door hung half open and she knocked it out of her way.

The naked couple on the bed were definitely dead. Part of the man's skull was missing and most of the woman's nose. There was nothing to be done for either of them.

The baby was lying in the corner, hemmed in by a makeshift barrier of couch cushions and clutching an empty bottle. Munch gathered the infant in her arms and saw that she was wearing one of those baby ID bracelets on her wrist, the kind made up of tiny blocks with letters on them. They spelled out "Garillo."

Asia stopped crying and stared at Munch. Munch stared back, feeling a jolt of recognition as she gazed into the baby's clear brown eyes—Sleaze's eyes. *This could have been my baby,* she thought, reeling. Asia blinked, then gathered her breath for another howl.

"Shhh," Munch said. "You're okay." Asia smelled liked she needed changing. The front of her dress was wet with drool.

"Let's get you out of here." She glanced down at the dead couple and shook her head. This was not the time to worry about them. She picked up the empty baby bottle and jammed it into a large pink cloth bag full of other baby accessories that she found on the floor. Clutching the baby to her chest, she ran back out front, almost knocking down a Hispanic man. At first she thought he was drunk, and then she realized that he was just terribly upset.

"I call the police," he said in heavily accented English. A thin string of mucus dribbled unchecked from his nose. "I cannot believe somebody would do this thing." He buried his face in his hands and wept.

She patted his shoulder. "The cops will be here soon," she said, hearing the chorus of approaching sirens. "They'll know what to do."

He nodded and mumbled something she couldn't make out. If she stayed, the cops would want answers from her. Answers that she really didn't have. But that wasn't her main concern. She knew they would take the baby and place her in protective services. Sleaze would have a terrible time getting her back.

She left the man standing there and walked quickly around the building, out of his sight, and then back through the hedge with the baby clinging to her side. She threw the diaper bag into the back seat, strapped Asia into the car seat, and ran around to the driver's side.

When she started her car, she noticed that her hands were shaking, and that surprised her. She had been about to congratulate herself for staying so calm, but then she had always excelled during crisis. Practice, she supposed. Swallowing the hot saliva filling her mouth, she shifted the car into reverse. It kicked backward with a protesting shriek as she floored the accelerator. Asia's head jerked forward.

Munch patted her leg and said, "Sorry about that."

Asia opened her mouth and shrieked.

Three blocks later, Munch realized that Asia might be hungry. She pulled over at a liquor store and rummaged through the bag of baby stuff. Clanking around in the bottom were two cans of formula. She poked one open with her pocket knife, filled a clean bottle, and handed it to Asia.

The baby sucked fiercely.

"How long were you all by your little self?" Munch asked her, tucking a bib under the baby's chin and leaving grease smudges on the white terry-cloth.

And what was the connection between the dead couple and Sleaze? People were always getting themselves killed around Ghost Town and the Flats; maybe it was just a full moon or something. Yeah, right.

Hopefully, Lisa would be able to supply some answers.

Halfway to Inglewood, Munch's pulse had just about returned to normal. Thank God, she thought, for little favors. If her timing had been different, she might have been in the middle of a shooting or sucked into a police investigation. What good would she be to anyone dead or in jail?

A large jumbo jet passed overhead just as Munch pulled up in front of Lisa Slokum's small wooden house on 96th Street. The noise of the plane's engine drowned out Janis Joplin singing about how she once had a daddy who said he'd give her anything in sight. Munch paused before switching off the ignition, waiting for the next lines and anticipating the goose-bump-raising thrill of Janis screaming out her lyrics. When the plane's noise didn't subside, Munch closed her eyes and sang the words herself.

When she opened her eyes, Asia was staring at her.

A bare plot of earth fronted Lisa's house. The screen covering the front window was ripped and the paint was peeling on the shutters nailed permanently on either side. Two Big Wheels plastic trikes were parked to the left of the walkway. On the right, a child's wading pool overflowed with beer cans.

Munch locked her door and then went around to the passenger side and lifted Asia out. With the baby balanced on her hip, she let herself in the chain-link gate and walked up the front path. The door was open, but the screen door was shut.

There was no welcome mat.

"Hello?"

She heard a TV blasting. A door slammed inside the house.

"Lisa?"

Munch waited for a moment, then opened the screen door and called, "Hello?"

"What?"

"Can I come in?"

"It's open," Lisa yelled, sounding annoyed.

Munch stood in the doorway until her eyes adjusted to the interior darkness. She saw Lisa, finally, swaddled in blankets and lying on the couch. Behind the sofa, in the corner, was a mattress partially covered with skewed sheets. Munch pulled the screen door shut behind her.

Lisa made no move to get up or lower the volume of the television. It was a *Happy Days* rerun, Munch saw, the one where the Fonz and Mrs. C. took dance lessons, and everyone thought they were doing it.

"You can put her in the crib," Lisa said, motioning with a languid gesture towards a cradle in the corner.

"That's all right," Munch said. "I don't mind holding her." She more than didn't mind. The baby fit in the groove of her waist as if she'd been grown there. The warmth of the baby carried through the fabric of Munch's shirt and settled inside her chest.

"Shit," Lisa said, giving Munch a once-over. "I haven't seen you in a long time."

"I've been working."

"You look different."

"So I'm told."

Lisa glanced back at the TV and chuckled at Richie Cunningham's distress.

Munch perched on the arm of the couch, debating how much to tell big-mouth Lisa about what she'd found at Sleaze's apartment building.

"You heard about Karen, right?" Lisa said, nodding at the baby.

"I heard she died." Munch grabbed one of Asia's feet between her thumb and forefinger and squeezed gently. Asia flexed her foot, curling her tocs in response. Munch was seized with an impulse to put those fat little toes in her mouth. One of Asia's hands rested on Munch's cheek.

"Sleaze was the one who found her. The needle was still in the bitch's arm."

"That's cold," Munch said. The baby grabbed at the chrome tire gauge in Munch's pocket.

"He hasn't used since."

"Nothing?"

"No, he's been doing good. Just pills."

Munch nodded, remembering her old definition of staying clean. Taking absolutely nothing had been a radical concept.

"Why'd they name her Asia?" she asked.

"She looked chinky when she was born," Lisa said. "Big old fat cheeks and her eyes all squinted up."

"She's a little heartbreaker now."

"Easy to say when you're not cleaning up after her all day."

"Do you watch her much?"

"Too much. You bring any of her shit?"

Munch held up the pink bag. "Just this."

"I'm all out of clothes for her. Sleaze said you'd bring more. He, as usual, flaked out."

Munch looked past the living room doorway into the kitchen. There was a washing machine next to the sink; clothes were piled in front of it. "Do you want me to help you do some laundry?" she asked.

Lisa sighed. "This is what I'm saying. I got enough to do with two kids of my own without minding *his* little rugrat."

"Where *are* your kids?"

"They're around here somewhere."

Munch laid the baby down in the crib. "Can I use your bathroom?"

"Help yourself," Lisa said.

Munch decided that was how most things were done in this household as she walked down the darkened hallway to the bathroom. She had to skirt an industrial stainless steel sink leaning on its side against the hallway wall. "What's with the sink?" she yelled to Lisa.

"I'm going to put it in the bathroom. The one in there is cracked and the landlord won't do shit."

"You want some help with it?" Munch asked. "Maybe between the two of us we can hook it up."

"No," Lisa said. "I wasn't planning on dealing with that today."

Munch stepped over the sink into the bathroom. Mismatched towels hung haphazardly from the cracked shower door. A pair of Lisa's panties were on the floor by the toilet, looking as if she had just let them lie where they dropped. The sink was full of hair and the mirror above it had lost most of its silver backing. Munch peed without sitting down, then discovered there was no toilet paper. She ripped a page from the magazine sitting on back of the tank when she surmised from its other missing pages that this was its intended use. She then grabbed the cleanest towel she could find and dampened it with warm water from the bathtub faucet.

When she returned to the living room, she found Lisa's children standing in front of their mother demanding that she settle their dispute. The two little girls eyed Munch momentarily, then seemingly dismissed her presence.

"I thought I'd change the baby," she said to Lisa.

Another jet passed by overhead, drowning out the TV and making the walls shake. Munch found a Pampers wrapper in the bottom of the cloth bag and removed the last diaper.

Lisa's two children stood poised before their mother. The oldest of the two girls, Charlotte, was the same age as Boogie, which would make her close to seven. Munch knew that the younger girl, Jill, was four. Lisa and Munch had been pregnant at the same time. Munch often did the math.

She changed Asia's diaper, cleaning the little girl's bottom with the wet towel. The baby had a rash, but Munch couldn't find any cream or powder. She wrapped the soiled diaper in the empty Pampers wrapper and dropped the towel into the pile of clothes on the kitchen floor. The plane finally passed, and the little girls picked up where they left off.

"It was my turn," Charlotte said.

"You're a stupid," Jill countered.

"That's enough from both of you," Lisa screamed. "Why do you two always have to scream at each other? Go clean your rooms. I'm tired of always picking up after you little bitches. I could use some help around here."

Munch flinched, but said nothing.

"You want a beer?" Lisa asked.

"I don't drink anymore."

"Nothing?" Charlotte said, wide-eyed.

"Not for eight months."

Charlotte considered this for a moment. "Not even apple juice?" she asked.

Munch laughed. "I mean nothing with alcohol in it, like beer and wine and whiskey."

"Oh," she said, clearly unimpressed.

"You still smoke doobies, right?" Lisa asked, pulling out a half-smoked joint.

"No," Munch said. "Nothing. I don't use anything anymore. That includes pot."

Lisa turned to her daughter. "Honey, go get Mama her lighter." Jill ran ahead towards the bedroom with Charlotte protesting after her.

"She asked me, you little freak. Mommmmm!"

"Don't run in the house," Lisa yelled after them.

Munch moved to stand by the open door, taking the baby with her. "When is Sleaze supposed to get here?"

Lisa shrugged. "Who knows?"

43

Charlotte returned with the lighter and a roach clip. "So you don't use any drugs anymore?" she asked.

"No," Munch said.

The girl seemed to consider this information. "That's good," she said.

"Thank you."

"Does that mean we won't have to wake you up in the bathtub anymore?"

Munch stared at the child, trying to imagine what she must remember. Had she stood in the doorway while a blue-lipped Munch was repeatedly submerged in a bathtub full of ice water? The cold water was the best antidote for a heroin overdose, next to a shot of Narcan. Of course she had been there and seen. Munch had never considered the impact such a sight would have on a child. How was she supposed to make amends for that kind of shit?

"C'mere," she said. Charlotte walked over to her uncertainly. Munch knelt down and hugged her. "That's exactly what it means." She turned to Lisa. "Is there anything else you need? You got enough food and diapers?"

"I've got two dollars in food stamps that's supposed to last me to the first." Lisa carefully pinched out the joint's burning end. "I don't know how they think a person can survive on what they give you."

Munch released Charlotte and put the baby back in her crib. She reached inside her purse and pulled out her billfold. Lisa's eyes followed Munch's movements.

"Sleaze said he was going to pay me for baby-sitting," Lisa said. "I was counting on that money."

Munch extracted a twenty. "This should tide you over." She found one of the shop's business cards, wrote her home phone number on the back, and handed it to Lisa along with the money. "Call me when you hear from him."

"Yeah, and if you see the fucker," Lisa said to Munch, "tell him I'm pissed off."

"So what's new? Right?" Munch said, forcing a laugh.

"I heard that."

Munch leaned over Asia's crib and wiggled her foot. "We'll just have to see what's keeping your daddy, won't we?"

"Oh. Oh," Jill said, raising her hand and hopping on one foot. "You know who I saw the other day?"

"Who?" Lisa asked.

"Daddy. He was in a car."

"Daddy who?" Lisa asked, laughing indulgently. "Daddy Darnel or Daddy James?"

"Daddy Darnel," the little girl answered.

Munch looked back at the baby and silently promised to return.

She was already on the freeway when she realized that she hadn't left the car seat with Lisa. She fought the urge to turn around. It was hard enough to leave the kid there the first time and she had plans. She couldn't stop thinking about those liquid brown eyes staring at her, as if waiting for her to do the right thing. She'd take the car seat over tomorrow. By then, hopefully, Sleaze would have shown up and she could stop worrying.

Blinding light filled her rearview mirror and she cursed. She hated how the headlight beams of pickup trucks and vans shone right at your eye level—especially when they followed you so closely. She slowed down, giving the offending vehicle—a blue van with tinted windows—no choice but to pass her.

6

When Blackstone got back to the station, the first thing he did was open his desk drawer and sift through his file of twenty-four-hour reports. The daily bulletins were issued to all detective bureaus and listed short synopses of state and local felonies committed in the previous twenty-four hours. He found the report he was looking for and read it quickly. A little over a month ago, the National Guard Armory in Kern County had been robbed. The thieves made off with semiautomatic weapons, pyrotechnic devices, and ammunition—some of it armor-piercing.

That's got to be it, he thought. In the issued bulletin, the feds asked to be notified immediately if any state or local agencies came into possession of any of the aforementioned weaponry. The contact agent—the Special Agent in Charge—was listed as Claire Donavon. No wonder the report had stuck in his mind. He tacked the paperwork on the cork board mounted on the wall directly across from his desk.

The walls of his cubicle were plastered with evidence reports, case updates, and composite sketches. But unlike those in Alex's work space, Blackstone's were aligned symmetrically and updated periodically.

The cubicle was an innovation by the station's newest lieutenant, Mace St. John. He'd divided the homicide war room with standing partitions, and given every detective his own desk, phone, and three walls to do with as he wished. The lieutenant felt the men might work better if each was given his own space.

God, Blackstone thought, how these guys talked once they got married. You never heard a bachelor talk about breathing room.

He dialed Jeff Hagouchi's number in Firearms.

"I was just about to call you," Hagouchi said. "I got some information for you on that freeway sniping,"

"Already?"

"The bullet we dug out of the road was a 7.62 by 21 mm."

"So the weapon is going to be an M-14."

"Uh-huh. I haven't gotten to the good part. I also found a fleck of green paint in the windshield."

"Which tells us . . . ?"

"Military AP rounds are color-coded, the tips are painted green. Last month the FBI issued a memo to all the firearm crime labs. If we came across any military weaponry they asked us to let them know immediately."

"Yeah, I know. It was that Kern County armory job. Did you call the feds yet?"

"As soon as I got in. They just left."

"They came right over?" Blackstone asked, amazed at the response speed.

"Surprised me, too," Hagouchi said.

Blackstone tapped his pencil on his blotter, then drew a circle. "Was one of the agents who came by Claire Donavon?" he asked, careful to keep his tone casual.

"Do you know her?"

"We've crossed paths."

"Built like a brick—"

"Did she say if they had any leads?"

"Like they'd share them with me? You know those guys, Jigsaw. I'm just a lowly lab rat."

"Did she give you anything at all?" Blackstone asked. Was she wearing a wedding ring? he wanted to ask. Does she still wear her hair long?

"She did want to know if we'd confiscated any grenades lately."

"Like you'd call her about the ammo and not about a grenade?"

"Yeah, well, what are you going to do?"

"I'll stop by later and sign out the evidence."

"Uh, Jigsaw?"

"What?"

"She already took it."

"Damn," he said, trying to sound upset. "Looks like I'll have to talk to her myself."

"You want her number?"

"No, I've already got it." He also kept a catalogue of business cards from all the law enforcement officers he'd ever worked with. He would have held on to hers regardless. He looked down and realized that he'd unconsciously written her name inside the circle.

"I gotta go."

"Yeah," Jeff said, "me, too. Some of us work for a living."

Blackstone pushed the button to disconnect them and then dialed Claire's number.

While he waited for her to answer her phone, he toyed with the jagged skull fragment on his desk that he kept as a memento. It was one of the larger of several fragments he'd found stuck to the motor that ran the electric door of a freshly painted garage. From those few shards of bone he had built a case that went to conviction. He kept the incriminating piece of evidence as a reminder that sometimes the good guys finished first, especially when they remembered to look up.

"FBI," a woman's bored voice said.

"Claire Donavon, please," he said.

"Special Agent Donavon isn't in right now," the operator told him. "Would you like to leave a message?"

He told her he would and left his information, adding that his business was urgent. She promised him that his message would be delivered. Pushing back his chair with a sigh, he checked his watch. There were two hours left on his shift, and he didn't want to spend them sitting. His neck and shoulders ached already from bending over reports and studying crime scene photographs.

Tilting back, he studied the poster of Bobby Fischer taped above his bulletin board. The picture was taken during the match for the world championship with Boris Spassky. After winning the title of world champion, apparently Fischer had felt there was nothing left to prove and had stopped competing. In 1975, he lost his title by default. Blackstone wondered if there would ever be such a defining moment in his own life. He hoped not. He loved the work.

He entered an investigation the same way he approached a chess match. The best way to stay ahead of the game was to consider the board from the opponent's viewpoint. This meant figuring out why the guy had made his last move and what his next best possible move should be. Though in order to get into the game plan of the average criminal, Blackstone usually had to adjust himself to think stupid.

He sketched a profile of the truck and its driver as they must have been just seconds before the shots were fired. Putting himself in the driver's seat, he ran through a series of scenarios. Something wasn't adding up. He didn't believe for a moment that this had been a traffic dispute that escalated to gunfire. There was more to this one. He could smell it.

The second shot, assuming its accuracy wasn't just luck, was too deliberate. But to commit the act so openly, in broad daylight . . . And yet, no witnesses had come forward. Maybe the killers knew exactly what they were doing. The police search of the freeway hadn't turned up any spent cartridges. Quite possibly the shell casings had been picked up in the tread of another vehicle's tires and carried away. One more lucky break for the bad guys.

Sergeant Mann chose that moment to emerge from his office and walk over to Blackstone. "What you working on?" he asked.

"The freeway sniping."

"Any luck?"

"Check this out," Blackstone said. He sat up in his chair and put his hands in front of him as if he were holding a steering wheel. "I'm driving on the freeway and I see another vehicle. They cut me off and we have words." He raised his left hand in the one-fingered salute of the freeway. "The passenger of the other vehicle pulls out a rifle and aims at me." He ducked to the right.

"So what's your point?"

"It doesn't work. Our victim scooted down. Why would he scoot down?"

"What do you think?"

"I think he recognized the second vehicle before they saw him. He couldn't get off the freeway, so he slowed down and waited for them to pass. Only before they passed, they saw him and popped him."

"That's great," Philip Mann said. "All you need now is a witness, the murder weapon, and the doer to confess. Yep, sounds like you got it dicked."

"I'm just saying it wasn't random and it wasn't rage." The second thought had come to him as he spoke, but it fit. The kill shot was too right on, too precise. Rage was always so . . . messy. "I'm saying I think he recognized his assailants, that's all."

"Did the coroner ID the victim?"

"Not yet. The decedent had a phony driver's license. The truck was stolen." Blackstone opened his notebook. The events were still fresh in his mind, but he made it a habit to never make a statement to a superior officer without having his notes open in front of him. "The deputy coroner pulled a set of prints as soon as he received the body. We figure the decedent had to have a record. The print guys say they might have something by next month, sooner if the decedent had been busted locally."

"Any witnesses?"

Blackstone thought about what the traffic cop had said about the female in the GTO. "Not really. We're putting out a bulletin on the evening news. See if that shakes anything loose. The autopsy's scheduled for tomorrow."

"Why so quick?"

"Sugarman has classes on Saturday. He wanted to include the freeway Doe, said it was a textbook example of entrance and exit wounds."

"All right, keep me informed."

Blackstone noticed that he was leaving out the part about the FBI, keeping Claire Donavon to himself.

Mann ran his fingers through his hair. "Hopefully, the press release will yield some results. Other than that, sounds like we're on hold. Move on. Where's your partner?"

Blackstone looked down the hallway. "Probably in the head. He's going through this sympathy thing with his wife."

"When is she due?"

"Next month."

"What's this, his third?"

"Yeah, he's got two boys and I wish he'd stop already. He's gained ten pounds with each pregnancy." Blackstone tucked in his shirt as he spoke, admiring the feel of his own flat stomach.

"Is he hoping for a girl?"

"Don't even get him started on what he wants. He's got all his charts out. He says if Sally can just hold out until after November twenty-first then they won't have to deal with a Scorpio."

"Anything is good, as long as it's healthy, right?"

"You would think."

Blackstone watched Philip Mann return to his office and thought about the woman in the GTO. She had recognized the truck. She had to know something. Unless she was just one of those cop groupies who always wanted to get involved when they smelled a badge. If that was the case, then he knew a lot of guys who would want to find her anyway. Those citizens were usually generous with their private gifts of civic appreciation.

He started to put away the photographs with the case file he'd begun on the freeway John Doe when something in the picture of the truck's interior caught his eye. A small triangle of white against the dark blue upholstery of the seat. He scratched at the speck with his fingernail and reached for his phone. Maybe the guy at the impound yard could give it a look.

Sergeant Mann tapped on his glass wall and gestured impatiently. Blackstone acknowledged his boss with a wave, slipped the Polaroids back into the still-thin folder, and set it on the middle level of his stacking trays. He stood, put on his jacket and went to see what the sergeant had for him.

"We've got another shooting," Mann said. "You want it?" He held up the working incident report.

"Drive-by?"

"No, residential. Multiple victims."

"I'm on it," Blackstone said, reaching for the address. Halfway down the hall, he caught Alex coming out of the bathroom. "Come on," he said. "We've got another shooting. Multiple victims."

"You know your eyes glow when you say that?" Alex said, zipping up his pants.

"Why don't you finish doing that while you're still inside?" Blackstone asked. "Did you even wash your hands?"

"You know, I have a question about that. Are you supposed to wash them before or after?"

"You're a class act, Perez. Anyone ever tell you that?"

"You want me to drive, Mother?"

"No, I know right where this place is. You just finish getting dressed, all right?"

Alex straightened the strap of his suspender. He'd given up on belts. "By the way, I finally got through to that number," he said, pulling on his sports jacket, but leaving it unbuttoned out of necessity.

"The one we found in the freeway Doe's wallet?"

"Yeah. It's to a bar in Canyonville, Oregon, called the Snakepit."

"Charming. Did anyone there know our victim?"

"The guy I talked to wasn't exactly a model citizen. I called the county sheriff and he gave me the number of the resident deputy, guy named Tom Moody. Moody used to be a homicide dick with Beverly Hills PD."

"Small world."

"He said he got fed up with being told who he could and couldn't bust. Now, he says, *he's* the law. I told him I'd mail him a photograph of our freeway Doe. He said he'd ask around when he receives it."

Twenty minutes later, Blackstone and Alex arrived at the scene of the shooting. The address they sought was on Hampton Avenue, south of Rose, past a ramshackle collection of fifties stucco and wood houses, most of which sported tin-roofed, non-code additions.

The *Thomas Guide* identified the part of Los Angeles between Washington Boulevard and Rose Avenue and east of the ocean as Venice Beach, but Venice Beach had many subdivisions—demographics known to cops and locals. The single-story whitewashed stucco building in question was located smack on the border between Tortilla Flats and Ghost Town—each of which were patrolled by their own racially segregated gangs. Ghost Town was home to the all-black Shoreline Crips; Tortilla Flats hosted the Chicano V-13s. It was rumored that the wiser residents of Hampton and Electric avenues slept *under* their mattresses. At least once, often twice, a week the detectives rolled on a suspicious death call in the area.

As they pulled up to the building, there was no mistaking that something catastrophic had gone down. A crowd had gathered on the sidewalk; some had brought their own chairs. There was a

sense of festive hysteria in the air. News crews had already positioned spotlights, rendering dusk to daylight, and were conduct-
ing interviews with the yellow-taped apartment building as their
backdrop.

The cloying odor of fatty pork assaulted Blackstone's nose.
He looked across the street and located its source, a small store-
front squeezed between a coin-op Laundromat and an apartment
building. Bright white letters on the green and red awning
declared LA MEXICANA DELI. The windows were protected by
wrought-iron burglar bars. Brand names of American beers
glowed in neon letters. Behind them, cardboard boxes of canned
goods were stacked to the ceiling, doubling as added protection
against burglaries and bullets. He turned back to his crime scene.

A uniformed officer stood guard by the front door. He nodded
to Blackstone and Alex as they approached.

"Where are they?" Blackstone asked.

"Just head down the hall."

The bodies were in the back bedroom. There were two of
them, a Hispanic couple. It appeared that they had been shot as
they slept. Blackstone checked their ring fingers for wedding
bands. The girl wore a single-carat engagement ring.

He pressed a finger into her throat. The skin blanched and
remained indented. "She's been dead about six to eight hours, I'd
say."

There was a small shrine to the Virgin Mary on the dresser.
Alex crossed himself before he knelt down and examined the pile
of cushions on the floor. "What do you make of this?"

Blackstone shrugged. "Maybe some relative shared the
room."

"Yeah, that's common enough around here," Alex said.

Blackstone returned to the bodies.

"The male took the first hit," he said. "He never saw it coming." He lifted the woman's right hand and showed Alex the defense wound through her palm.

Blackstone walked outside to speak to the officer who was first on the scene. "Who found them?" he asked.

"The female victim, Cynthia Ruiz, worked at the market across the street. Her boss came looking for her when she didn't show up for work."

"What time was that?"

"Around four-fifteen. Dispatch recorded his call at four-thirty. When she didn't answer her door, he came around back and looked through the window."

"And the other victim?"

"Her fiancé, Jesus Guzman."

"Was she into drugs?"

"No, I knew them both," the cop said. "They were nice kids, no gang affiliations. I think we're looking at totally innocent victims here." He emphasized the words *totally innocent*.

Blackstone appreciated what the cop was saying. Not that anyone deserved to be murdered, but he'd seen too many cases not to admit that the victims' actions often contributed to their untimely demise. "What do you think?" he asked.

"Robbery gone bad, probably."

"Then why didn't they take her ring?" Blackstone asked.

He looked over the cop's shoulder at the door. The striker plate had been torn from the fiberboard door frame. He had the cop step aside while he took pictures of the damage. The brass 6 hung crookedly below the peephole. He moved in closer and saw an empty nail hole inches above the skewed house number. With one finger he twirled the number around and found that the nail hole in the door aligned perfectly with the drilled hole in what now appeared to be the number 9. He took a picture of this as well.

"Alex," he called.

Alex emerged from the house. "What's up?"

He showed him the house number. "Let's take a walk."

The apartment next door had no house number, but the one beyond was labeled 7. They rounded the corner. The door of the unit on the east side of the building was also unmarked. Blackstone knocked, but there was no answer.

Alex peered through one of the small dirty windows flanking the door and said, "It's too dark to see anything." He went back to their unit and returned with a flashlight.

Blackstone panned the room the best he could but saw nothing amiss. "See if you can locate the manager and find out who rents this unit," he said. "I'm going over to the market and talk to the guy."

"Hey, Jigsaw, while you're over there, pick me up some *churros*. You know, those long doughnut things. The crunchy ones."

"You're not eating those in my car."

"Yeah, yeah."

The witness repeated his story for Blackstone. How he had seen the bodies through the back bedroom window, how there was nothing to be done.

"Did anyone enter the apartment?" Blackstone asked.

"Maybe the *gavacha*."

"What white girl?"

"Aiy," he said. "The one with the baby. I should have said something before. I have been so upset. Never in my life I have seen such a terrible thing."

"Where is this woman now? Do you know her?"

"*No sé*," he said.

Blackstone took his notes, bought Alex two *churros,* and returned to the crime scene. They spent the next twenty minutes interviewing neighbors and local merchants. Typically, no one had seen or heard anything.

Through a ten-year-old interpreter—Alex's Spanish was sketchy—Blackstone learned that the building had no manager. The child explained that rent was paid to a realty office in Mar Vista. Blackstone called that office and was given the broker's home phone number. The broker in Mar Vista said she forwarded the checks on the owner. After much grumbling, she finally came up with the name and telephone number of a retired doctor living in Palm Springs. When Blackstone dialed the Riverside County exchange, he got the doctor's maid, who informed Blackstone that *Meester Doctor* would be back on Monday night late. He left his name and number, then carefully printed all this information in his notebook.

He walked back into the house for a final look-over before the coroner removed the bodies. Something cracked under his foot on the bedroom carpet—a teething ring. He picked it up and slid it into an evidence bag, being careful not to touch the surface and destroy any identifying evidence. Even babies had fingerprints.

7

Munch returned to her ground-floor apartment in Reseda. She kept the tiny one-bedroom apartment spotless, cleaning the floors on her hands and knees and polishing all the chrome fixtures until they sparkled. When she had first moved in she had regrouted and recaulked the bathroom. She had also found that when she watered the little patch of brown grass in front of her door, it came to life. Now her unit boasted a luxurious green lawn, even if it was no bigger than a three-by-five throw rug. The bush of blue hydrangea under her living room window had also responded well to a little care and encouragement.

It was a far cry from the house in Venice she had grown up in, where cockroaches scattered when she turned on the light in the kitchen. She used to hate the sight of the large bugs scurrying across the countertops, but there seemed to be no getting around it. Leaving the lights on didn't work. They would still be waiting for her when she returned, and without the sudden intrusion of 150 watts, they wouldn't even have the decency to hide.

On her way home, she had stopped at the market to pick up cookies for the meeting. She showered and changed, then waited out front for her friend Danielle to pick her up. Ruby was the one who suggested the arrangement. She said Danielle needed the responsibility and Munch needed to learn to depend on someone else.

Danielle finally pulled up at eight-fifteen. "Been waiting long?" she asked as she leaned over the seat of her Datsun to open the passenger door. Her large lips were painted a bright shade of red. "You wouldn't believe the afternoon I had."

Munch almost smiled. "We'll make it in time."

Danielle was always late and she was always sorry.

"You should let me fix this door," Munch said.

"I still owe you for all the other work you've done."

"Don't worry about it," Munch said, meaning it. She'd much rather people be in debt to her than the other way around.

When they arrived at the clubhouse, they found Ruby already inside arranging literature on the table next to the coffee urn.

"We have a little time left before the meeting starts," Ruby said, reaching for a doughnut. "If you wanted to talk."

"I saw an old friend today," Munch began, rubbing the ball of her foot into the parquet floor of the meeting hall.

"Is this someone you used with? You know how I feel about that."

"Right, end of story." The matter was an ongoing battle between the two of them. She had tried to explain to Ruby once that not all her old friends had been terrible. Deb, for instance, had always been a good influence. Deb didn't use a needle. When Munch partied with Deb, they usually only drank.

Another lower companion, Ruby had said, with a finality that got Munch's back up. Her sponsor didn't know everything about everything. Munch had even said as much. Ruby agreed that she didn't know everything, but about some things she was pretty damn sure. Munch decided not to tell her sponsor about the Snakepit.

"Why do I get the sense that this isn't the end of it?" Ruby asked.

"Well, it's not like the guy is the Antichrist. Maybe I should have tried to carry the message to him or something. Isn't that what we're supposed to be doing?"

"Honey, he's not *your* responsibility. He's in the hands of that Old Boy upstairs," Ruby said.

Munch didn't want to say anything, but there were many times when she suspected that that same old boy had gone fishing. Like try the decade of her own teen years.

"Yeah, I guess you're right," she said, stubbing out her cigarette as she exhaled the last of the smoke from her lungs. "I better go grab a seat."

"Call me."

"Sure."

"You say that and then I don't hear from you."

"I'll call you. Promise."

"Are you sure you're okay?"

Munch cracked her little lopsided grin. "There are no big deals, remember?"

Ruby pushed her shoulder. "Get out of here."

Munch feinted left and raised her fists into a pugilistic pose. She left Ruby laughing and shaking her head. As she crossed the room, she kept her eyes averted from the crowds by pretending concern over spilling her coffee. Once upon a time, she had been bold—not afraid of going head to head with anyone, anytime. Sobriety had ruined that—another of the side effects of getting well.

Danielle, as usual, was surrounded by a group of admiring men. She was wearing a hooded navy blue sweatshirt and somehow managed to look sexy in it. Perhaps it was the skin-tight jeans and four-inch heels, Munch thought. Or maybe it was the way her curly dark hair fell playfully down her back and shoulders all the way to her belt. Danielle also had a way of looking at a guy, like together they had a secret. Munch had tried to imitate that coy smile once with a tow truck driver she thought she might like to get to know better. He had asked if he had food on his nose or something.

"You want me to get us some seats?" she said.

Danielle turned at the sound of Munch's voice. "Just a sec," she said, grabbing Munch's hand and holding it as she wound up her conversation with the guy she was talking to. "Monday, then. Pick me up at seven-thirty."

The guy leaned over and kissed Danielle's cheek. She graced him with one of her secret smiles.

Munch felt her palm begin to sweat. Danielle's fingers were securely laced within hers. As much as part of her enjoyed the expression of friendship, the rest of her recoiled at holding hands with another woman. She pulled loose.

She cast a covert glance toward the group of men lounging against the back wall. "So you got a date Monday, huh?"

Danielle threw back her head and laughed. Munch watched the men watch her.

"It's an AA date. A meeting and coffee afterwards."

"Beats a blank."

"Do you want me to ask him if he's got a friend?"

"Naw, then I'd have to watch both of them ogling you all night."

Danielle laughed again. "Don't exaggerate." She looked around the room, her gaze lingering on the group of men by the coffee machine. Munch noted how the men puffed out their chests. Danielle ran her hand through her hair. Munch noted that, too.

"Anything here look good to you?" Danielle asked, as if consulting a menu.

"Every time I think a guy is cute," Munch said, "he raises his hand as a newcomer."

"Sounds like you're still attracted to the disease."

"That's what Ruby says."

"I know," Danielle admitted. "That's what she always used to tell me when I was new."

"So what's the answer?"

"Time, just give it time. C'mon," Danielle said, grabbing Munch's hand again. "The meeting's about to start."

They took their seats and the meeting began.

Munch had trouble following the discussion. She kept thinking about that boot dangling from the open truck door, and then those bodies in Venice. What were the odds that she'd be at two murder scenes in the same day? She felt as if she existed in a bubble, protected by her secrets. When that bubble finally burst, she suspected, reality would come crushing in. But until then, she planned to coast on this curious sense of detachment as long as possible.

At the coffee break, Danielle flitted from man to man. Munch envied the ease with which she made small talk. Munch sat in her folding chair and watched the large clock on the wall. She wondered if this was how she'd be spending the rest of her life, sitting on other people's furniture and waiting for time to pass.

What was the point of it all? You grow up, you go to work, you get married and have kids so they can grow up, go to work, and get married. Eventually, everybody dies. She didn't see her own involvement in the life equation. Maybe if she had her own kid, life would feel different. Relationships with men didn't seem to be happening. The few dates she had been on had all ended in disaster. Ruby had suggested that maybe Munch shouldn't reveal so much about herself, that it scared men away. Munch said she didn't want secrets in her relationships. A man took her how she was or forget him. Besides, she argued, the guy had a right to know what he was getting into. Ruby maintained that not all needed to be revealed on the first date.

The meeting started again. While the speaker droned on, Munch sat back in her chair feeling disconnected. Without really thinking about what she was doing, she grasped the biceps of her left arm with her right hand and made a fist until the veins popped up.

At last ten o'clock arrived. Munch stood by the door, holding up the wall and waiting for Danielle to say all her goodbyes.

"You about ready?" Danielle finally asked, standing next to Munch, her face flushed.

"If you are."

"God, yes. Let's get out of here."

In the car, Danielle said, "I really admire how comfortable you are within yourself."

"What are you talking about?"

"I mean, I can never sit still. I jump from person to person like a madwoman. I don't even know what I say to half of them. And then I'd look over at you sitting there so perfectly relaxed and I wished I could be calm like that."

"Any more calm, I'd be dead," Munch said. She looked out the window, then back at her friend. "Do you ever miss it?"

"Miss what?"

"The life, the excitement, the rush?"

"The jail, the shakes . . . "

"Yeah, yeah," Munch interrupted. "That's how we're conditioned to think about it now. But this is me talking to you. Don't you just sometimes wish you could be out there in the thick of it again?"

"I think that's why I go so overboard on the sex thing," Danielle said. "It's like the only thrill I have left." She turned off Sherman Way and onto Munch's street. Without looking over at Munch, she said in a softer voice, "Some people call me a slut."

"Hey, fuck 'em."

"I probably already have."

They were still laughing when Munch got out at her apartment building.

"Are we still on for tomorrow?" Danielle asked.

Munch grabbed the door handle. "Unless you've got other plans."

"We had a deal. Although I still think you sold yourself short."

"I need a lot of help." She stepped out of the car.

"It'll be fun. You'll see. I still can't believe you don't like to shop."

"There's something I need to do in the morning," Munch said, looking everywhere but at her friend, "something I need to check on."

"The stores don't open until ten."

"I'll call you in the morning."

"All right," Danielle said as she pulled away. "I'm counting on that."

When Munch entered her apartment, she realized she wasn't a bit tired. Sleep would be out of the question for at least another three or four hours. The events of the day swirled in her head. She knew they would haunt her when she closed her eyes. The committee inside her head attacked at night, when she was the most vulnerable. Tonight they would come at her from all sides, nagging her with questions that she couldn't answer.

She picked up a sponge and wiped down the clean counters, opened the refrigerator and moved a carton of milk an inch to the right.

She shouldn't have come home right after the meeting. On Friday nights, people went on from the meeting to local coffee shops, where they would talk, catching up on the latest fatalities: who had gone back out and died or gone to jail or had their ear bitten off. The survivors would sit around and drink coffee and smoke cigarettes and wonder how to fill the long hours before sleep. Tonight she hadn't been in the mood for more talk and hadn't made herself available to be asked.

Ruby was always telling her to go to the AA dances and picnics. Why all this emphasis on group activities? she had asked once. Ruby said that alcoholics and addicts were antisocial—another thing to change. Sometimes Munch wanted to clamp her hands over her ears and shield her brain from the steady bombardment of shoulds and should nots. Sometimes this being restored to sanity felt a lot like going crazy. She wished she could just take a break from it all.

The kitchen clock read a little past eleven. She sighed. The spiral notebook on her kitchen table called to her, and she eyed it guiltily.

Ruby had been after her to start writing another AA fourth-step "searching and fearless moral" inventory. When Munch pointed out that she had already done one, Ruby explained that these things worked in layers, like onions.

Munch had no idea where to begin. *The Big Book of Alcoholics Anonymous* was no help. The example it gave had a mythical inventory-taker writing about feeling resentful towards a Mr. Brown for "his attention to my wife." Maybe that kind of stuff was helpful back in 1939, when alcoholics were all men and strictly boozers. But for a modern-day dope fiend such as herself, that Mr. Brown's-attention-to-my-wife shit just didn't cut it.

Across the top of the page of college-lined paper she wrote INVENTORY. She wrote the date on the top right corner and stared at it. Boogie's birthday was at the end of the month. She hadn't seen Deb or her son in a year. Would she and Deb still be able to read each other's minds? Finish each other's sentences? And Boogie. God. What sort of memories did he carry?

She wrote *ace boon coon* across the middle of the page and beneath that *Canyonville,* then closed the book.

It was too quiet. She turned on the TV. The eleven o'clock news was on. The newscaster was saying something about a sniper attack on the freeway. She stood in front of the set and watched the footage of the blue truck being towed away on top of a flatbed. The scene cut to the Pacific Division Police Station, where a woman, who was identified as Sergeant Lopez in black subtitles, read a prepared statement.

"The LAPD is investigating a shooting that occurred on the southbound San Diego Freeway, that's the four-oh-five freeway, this afternoon at approximately three-twenty near the Santa Monica Freeway interchange. The victim is identified as a male Caucasian in his late twenties to early thirties, six feet tall, medium build. The coroner's office will release a photograph of the man sometime this week if no one comes forward to identify him. We have no information as yet on the assailants or the motive for this attack."

The scene switched to the on-scene reporter. The wind whipped the woman's hair as she stood in front of a parking lot full of police cars. She held one hand to her ear; the other held a micro-phone. She looked directly into the camera. "Police say this is the third such freeway vigilante-style shooting this year. What authorities won't say is what is being done to prevent such attacks in the future. They are asking anyone with any information about this latest incident to contact the department. If you were driving on the San Diego southbound freeway near the Santa Monica Freeway at approximately three-thirty this afternoon and might have seen something, please call the number appearing on your screen."

A telephone number flashed across the scene.

"This is Sheena Moral live from Culver City. Back to you, Jerry."

"In other news," a gray-haired anchorman cheerfully reported, "police are investigating the shooting death of a couple in Venice Beach tonight. The couple was discovered late this afternoon by a local merchant. Police say that the man and woman, identified as twenty-one-year-old Cynthia Ruiz and twenty-two-year-old Jesus Guzman, had probably been killed sometime this morning."

Munch stared at the TV. The scene switched to the apartment building. The detectives working the case were easy to spot, with their dark sportcoats and gold shields. One was a tall good-looking white guy who radiated an air of tacit superiority. He strode past the reporters and onlookers, brushing aside their questions with unsmiling curtness. She'd met his type before. The second detective was a plump Hispanic man. He looked like the kind of cop who would joke around with you. The kind who didn't feel they had to be a hardass all the time. She thought about Mace St. John, the homicide cop who had once come after her. Maybe it was time to give him a call. She turned back to the picture on her TV screen.

It was getting real, she thought, whether she was ready for it or not.

8

Munch woke the next morning and knew there was no way she could go shopping. She reached over to the nightstand beside her bed and grabbed a cigarette. Then she remembered that she wasn't going to smoke in the bedroom anymore and not first thing. She put the cigarette back in the pack.

She'd had weird dreams all night: searching for something lost, but not sure what it was that she was looking for; unable to find her voice; trying to make phone calls but not being able to dial. She had a good idea what was at the root of all those uneasy images. She needed to find out for sure if Sleaze was dead. That was all there was to it.

Surely they would just run the dead man's fingerprints through their computers. If it was Sleaze, they would find a match soon enough. She got out of bed, grabbed her smokes, and went into the kitchen to put on the coffee water. As she passed the TV, she turned it on to Saturday morning cartoons. She paused briefly to watch Wile E. Coyote fall off another cliff. Then she turned the sound down and called the Venice police department, asking for Mace St. John. The woman who answered the phone told her that the lieutenant was on his vacation and would be out for the rest of the week. So much for that ace up her sleeve.

She drank two more cups of coffee before she got out the phone book, turning to the front where county services were listed.

Under *Coroner* there were several numbers: one for regular business hours, another for emergencies, and a third for 5:00 P.M. to 8:00 A.M. on weeknights, Saturdays, Sundays, and holidays. She dialed the last number.

"L.A. County."

"Is this the morgue?"

"We are not a morgue," a man's voice informed her. "We are the Coroner's Office of Los Angeles County."

"Oh," she said, not quite sure what the big difference was. "I just wanted to check your hours. Are you open?"

"Not to the public."

Of course, she thought, they wouldn't let just anyone in there.

"I'm not exactly the public," she said, stopping short of saying that she was missing a family member. That wouldn't work. He'd want to know the name of her missing relative, how long he had been missing, and if she'd filed a missing persons report. Understandably, the coroner might also want to know why she thought her relative might be dead and at his facility.

"Are you with the CSI class that's coming here this afternoon?" he asked.

She hesitated only a second. "Yeah, when is that?" It was only a teeny lie, she decided, but one that might get her inside if it came to that.

70

"Don't you have your sheet?" he asked.

"No, uh, sorry. I don't have it."

"Great. It's today at four. I suppose you've lost your parking pass as well." She could almost see him shaking his head.

"If it was with the sheet then I don't have it," she said truthfully.

"And you want to have a career in law enforcement?"

"It's my dream," she said.

"Just get here, but you'll have to park in the public parking lot."

"I don't mind. Will we be viewing bodies?"

"Yeah, we got a full house for you guys."

"Great. I'll be there."

She hung up the phone and remembered to breathe. Then she made a third call.

When Danielle answered, Munch told her that her errand was going to keep her tied up for most of the morning and possibly the afternoon.

"Are you all right?" Danielle asked. "You sound funny."

"Yeah, I'm fine," she said and cleared her throat as if that would diminish the weight of the unsaid words there.

They said their goodbyes and hung up. Munch went to her closet and looked over her limited wardrobe. What was the well-dressed student criminalist wearing these days? She picked out a pair of camel-colored slacks and a flowered blouse and draped them over a chair in her bedroom.

She spent the rest of the morning doing busywork around her apartment. At two-thirty she put away her tools and changed her clothes.

Her hair was straight again after last evening's bath; she pulled the top half back into a ponytail, letting the rest fall softly around her ears. Danielle had had Munch buy all sorts of makeup, most of which sat in her drawer unopened. The lipstick that Danielle had picked out for her had felt too conspicuous when Munch had put it on alone in her bathroom. Without Danielle's brazenness for encouragement, she had been unable to leave her house until she wiped all of it off. Now she applied it carefully, as well as the eye shadow, blush, and blue mascara.

She found a pair of pumps that almost matched the pants. But her hands, she realized, definitely didn't go with the outfit. If she was wearing her work coveralls, they'd be fine, but now they just looked dirty. She dug out a pair of soft leather driving gloves from her dresser and slipped them on, wincing as they chafed against her numerous cuts and split cuticles. Before she left the house, she grabbed her notebook off the kitchen table, thinking that this added prop would make her look more scholarly.

The building that housed the Coroner's Office of Los Angeles County was on the eastern fringe of downtown Los Angeles. The entrance of the building was at the top of a small hill, and as Munch stood in the lobby, reading the directory by the elevator, she realized she was on the third floor.

"Can I help you?" the security guard asked.

"Oh," she said, startled. For a moment, the presence of a uniform shook her nerve. How illegal was it, she wondered, to sneak into a morgue? "I was looking for the CSI class," she said.

"You're late," he said. "They've already gone down."

"Down?"

"To the autopsy suite," he said.

"Yes, yes, of course." She pushed the button on the elevator. "I'll just catch up to them."

"It's not that easy," the rent-a-cop said. "We have security measures here."

72

Munch's stomach lurched and her resolve wavered once more. It wasn't too late to just turn around and go. What had she done so far? Just said that she was looking for the CSI class, not even a lie really. Then she got angry with herself. The whiny voice inside her head disgusted her. It was time to get off the goddamn fence.

"You need a special key to get off at that floor," he said, looking her up and down. "Kinda warm for gloves, isn't it?"

She smiled her best Danielle-smile at the guard. "You know what they say: Cold hands, but a warm heart."

The guard took a breath that puffed out his chest. "I think we can let you slide this one time."

She hoped she wasn't laying it on too thick as she ran her hand through her hair and said, "Well, aren't you just the nicest thing?" The last was a patented Deb line, some of that Southern sugar she dispensed to bend men to her will.

They rode down to the next floor in silence. She was conscious of his eyes and grateful that the majority of his attention was not directed at her face. He used his key to open the elevator door. She gave his arm a squeeze on her way out.

"Thanks again."

"Good luck," he said and pointed down the hallway, indicating where she should go. The hallway took her past several closed office doors, then opened to become what appeared to be a waiting room. Several vinyl chairs lined the wall; worn issues of *Good Housekeeping* magazine were fanned across a small coffee table.

She passed a wax mannequin covered with a plastic sheet and laid out on a steel gurney. Only the yellowish feet of the mannequin showed. She supposed the dummy was used as some sort of teaching aid, like one of those visible V-8's they had at the trade school. A man in a white smock came along and whipped off the tarp with a magician's flourish. She saw that the figure on the table was female and very detailed, right down to her pubic hair.

"Oh," she said.

"What?" asked the man.

"She's real, isn't she?"

He chuckled and made a notation on his clipboard. Munch realized the dead woman was on a scale. The corpse weighed ninety-eight pounds. She looked at the cadaver's face and asked, "How'd she die?"

The man consulted his clipboard. "Overdosed on booze and Methaqualone. See how emaciated she is? That's how these alcoholics get. They stop eating and do nothing but drink."

"Terrible," Munch agreed.

"You here with the class?" he asked.

"The guard said I'd find everybody down here," she said.

He indicated a doorway.

"Thanks."

He nodded and went back to his work.

She pushed through the thick rubber flaps and they shut automatically after her. The room in which she found herself hummed with a subdued energy. She had expected it to be colder. The smell of blood and raw meat was overpowering. She had no association to match the odor to, but she was sure she would never forget it. She made her way over to the group of men who surrounded a fixed steel table. They glanced up at her as she approached, then turned their attention back to what they had been observing.

There was a cracking noise and then she saw another man in a white smock with the words MEDICAL EXAMINER stenciled across the back manipulating the handles of a pair of large garden loppers. The clippers reminded her of the ones Jack used to trim the trees around the shop. She stepped in closer to see what he was doing. A man in a green shirt moved aside, making room for her. She discovered that the man in the white smock was snipping through the rib cage of a large black man. The skin of the dead man's torso had been cut from his throat to his pubis and pulled to the side, exposing his rib cage and stomach cavity.

"Jesus," the man in the green shirt muttered. Another man across the table began to rock on his feet. As Munch watched, the color drained from the man's face and he fell to the floor. The man in the white smock giggled.

A plastic name tag over his pocket identified him as Dr. Sugarman.

Munch looked away. She saw scales like the ones used in the market for measuring cuts of fish and meat and stainless steel ladles resting in beakers of purple fluid. The drains in the cement floor were pink with blood. She drew a deep breath and opened her notebook.

The autopsy continued for another fifteen minutes. Dr. Sugarman explained why it was important to gather the heart blood, feel the texture of the liver, and study stomach contents. Munch learned what the ladles and scales were for. After Sugarman finished with the organs, he went to work on the head. She watched as the skin of the corpse's scalp was cut across the back from ear to ear and then pulled inside out over the man's face.

"And this," Dr. Sugarman said, "is where the expression 'To pull the wool over one's eyes' comes from."

A few of the other students laughed weakly; the man in green swallowed audibly and looked away. Sugarman used a Stryker vibrating saw to cut through the skull. At two different points he cut V-shaped notches into the bone.

"Why am I doing this?" he asked Munch.

"So you know how it fits back together," she said.

"Ahh, very good. Are you considering a career in pathology?"

"I've just always been good at taking things apart and putting them back together again," she said.

He popped off the skullcap and removed the brain. Despite herself, Munch found the whole thing fascinating. You just needed to take a step out of yourself, she decided, and not think of the body as a somebody.

The man she had met in the hallway weighing the dead woman escorted two men dressed in dark suits into the autopsy suite. She immediately recognized them as the same two cops she had seen on the news.

"Welcome, detectives," Sugarman said. "I hope you don't mind an audience, but this will be an excellent opportunity for these people to study entrance and exit wounds." He turned to the man she had met in the hall. "Class, meet our deputy coroner, Donald Moss. Donald, if you will."

Donald snapped four x-ray films onto a display box mounted on the far wall and then pushed a small black button located to the side. The fluorescent light stuttered for a second, then shone brightly behind the images of partial skeletons. The first two films were of skulls: frontal and profile shots.

Sugarman addressed the cluster of students. "The detectives are here to view the autopsy of a homicide victim. We'll finish this one later," he said, patting the arm of the deceased black man.

He had the class assemble before the x-ray view box. Using a long, thin wooden dowel, he showed them the various points of interest.

"And here," he said, his pointer touching the top half of a

frontal shot of the skull, "is where the bullet entered." He pointed to the next film. "Here is the same skull in profile. The damage from a high-velocity bullet is considerable. As the bullet passes through solid matter, it creates a vacuum—a small tornado surrounds its path. You'll remember your laws of physics. When vacuums are created, matter rushes in to fill the voids."

"What are those bits of white?" a student asked.

"Good question. Fragments of lead that sheared off the bullet." Sugarman moved his pointer to the base of the skull. "As you can clearly see, the throat shot severed the brain stem. Either one of these wounds would have been fatal, but the detectives assure me that the head shot was fired first, so this is what we will record as the cause of death."

Sugarman moved down the line to the film of the lower torso. "We took these x-rays with the subject fully clothed. You see these dime-shaped spots over the pubis? Any guesses?"

When nobody volunteered, Sugarman said, "The subject is wearing button-fly jeans."

Munch breathed through her mouth deeply and slowly. She felt the pulse in her throat throb. Sleaze always wore button-fly jeans.

Sugarman nodded to Donald.

Donald walked across the room and opened up the doors to what Munch realized, as she felt the blast of frigid air, was a cold storage room. He wheeled out a body on a gurney. The corpse was covered with a plastic sheet.

Sugarman pulled back the sheet. "Gentlemen and lady," he said with an acknowledging nod to Munch, "meet John Doe three-oh-five."

Munch took a deep breath and then looked into the clouded brown eyes of her old friend and sometime lover. Her mouth dried up and her ears rang. She missed the next few things Sugarman said. All she could think was: "He's got a name. He's got a name."

"The first thing we must do," Sugarman said, standing over the body, "is observe. Since this is a homicide, we must document every step of our examination. Donald doubles as our photographer."

Blackstone and Alex pulled on surgical gloves while Sugarman lectured. Blackstone leaned into Alex's ear and whispered, "Ten bucks says the big guy loses it."

"Which guy?"

"The one in the green shirt, standing next to the broad with the binder."

"You're on."

Donald stepped forward and snapped pictures, paying special attention to the wound areas. He took shots from the front and side.

"Let's get some of the exit wounds," Blackstone said. He and Alex rolled the body over so Donald could take pictures of what was left of the back of the head and neck.

Sugarman removed a thin chain from around John Doe's neck and said, "One necklace, gold-plate."

Donald put down the camera and made a notation on his clipboard. He left the room and returned with a large cardboard box, which he placed beside the corpse.

Blackstone noticed that the one woman among them had been forced to stand outside the circle. He watched her rub at her eye with a gloved fingertip and swallow hard. She was also looking a little pale. Maybe she wanted to be outside. He leaned over to his partner and said, "Double or nothing the broad loses it, too."

Alex looked over the woman, who was scribbling notes in her binder. "You're on," he said, then turned his attention back to their homicide victim.

John Doe 305 was still fully clothed. Over his long-sleeved thermal, he wore a black T-shirt with the Grateful Dead skull and roses logo emblazoned across the front. His Levi's were worn but clean. The pockets were empty, having been gone through at the crime scene by the coroner. That search had not yielded much: some loose change, a Zippo lighter, and a nearly empty wallet. All those had been tagged and stored on Friday.

Sugarman explained the effects of rigor mortis and how it was caused by the collection of lactic acid in the muscles. "Because our homicide here is a shooting victim, special care must be taken in the removal of his clothes. Every tear and burn mark must be catalogued. We can't just cut off the shirt."

"This is going to be good," Blackstone whispered.

"By working the muscles," Sugarman said, grasping the stiff arm of his John Doe, "we should be able to restore some pliability to the arms." He massaged the shoulder and biceps, then pulled the arm straight back. The shoulder socket made a sickening crack as it was manipulated.

The color completely left the face of the student in the green shirt. His eyes rolled back in his head. As his big body hit the floor, he tipped over an empty gurney and a tray of medical tools. Sugarman grinned from ear to ear. The small woman in the flowered blouse left the room. Alex pulled out a twenty from his wallet and handed it to Blackstone.

It wasn't until the student had been revived, the gurney righted, and the strewn equipment collected that the autopsy could continue. The woman never returned.

The corpse was naked now. The discarded clothes had been

carefully stored in the cardboard box. Each article of clothing was put in its own bag to prevent contamination. Later the serologists would study each item, testing that all the blood was from the same source, and looking for stray samples of hair and fibers. But for now, all attention was directed to the body, which the ME examined closely for scars and tattoos.

"The left arm shows scarring from intravenous drug use," Sugarman announced. The students pressed in to see actual needle marks up close.

"What's this on his fingertips?" one of the students asked.

"Fingerprint ink," Sugarman explained and went on to lecture that the coroner's responsibilities included the identification of the deceased, protection of their property, and notification of the relatives. He then explained that the coning of the skull bone puncture wound informed him as to the path of the bullet and had each of the students take a close look at the throat before he began cutting.

Blackstone wandered over to the box of clothes. He noticed a piece of binder paper lying on the floor and bent over to pick it up. Scrawled across the paper were the words: "His name is John Garillo."

"Shit," Blackstone said. "Alex, come on. We got to catch that girl."

They ran out to the hallway. The elevator door was shut. Blackstone stabbed furiously at the button.

"What's up?" Alex asked.

Blackstone showed him the note, holding it carefully from one corner.

"You think that was the broad from the freeway?"

"Has to be."

The elevator opened. They got in and pushed the 3 button.

"Come on, come on," Blackstone said, tapping his foot and willing the lift to move faster. The door opened to the empty lobby. Alex rushed to speak to the guard on duty while Blackstone ran to the exit. Standing on the sidewalk, he knew that it was hopeless.

Alex joined him. "What do you think?" he asked.

"You go observe the rest of the autopsy," Blackstone said. "I'm going to take this over to the lab and see if they can lift some prints. Run the name John Garillo through NCIC and see what comes up. I'll meet you back at the station."

"All right," Alex said. "I'll catch a lift with a blue."

"You do that," Blackstone said. He realized that he felt a strange sort of exaltation. That surprised him. If anyone had asked him how he thought he might have felt losing a key witness by seconds, he would have guessed angry. He never would have imagined feeling charged by it. Hell, he realized, he was grinning.

9

Munch left the parking structure in a state of high anxiety. Not even caring where it took her, she jumped on the nearest on-ramp and got into the fast lane. Her ears were still buzzing, making it difficult to form coherent thoughts. She turned on her air conditioning, aiming the blast of cold air directly at her face.

It was stupid to leave his name like that. She could have just as easily called it in anonymously. The cops would run his name through their computers and maybe come up with the address in Venice. She tried to remember if she had touched anything there.

She kept repeating the words to herself, *He's dead. He's dead. He's dead.* Tears streamed from her eyes and she welcomed their relief.

An eighteen-wheeler to her right sounded his air horn. She realized she had encroached on his lane and swerved out of his way. In her haste, she overcorrected. The GTO rattled as its tires ran over ruts in the center divider shoulder.

"Easy does it," she said out loud, and forced herself to slow down. She took several deep breaths and checked her mirrors for cops.

A mountain range she didn't recognize loomed to her right. Mature evergreens marked palatial homes. Her gas gauge hovered between a quarter of a tank and empty. Spotting an Arco sign, she got off the freeway. After filling up and checking the station's map, she discovered she was in some place called La Crescenta. She said the name out loud, liking the safe solid sound of it. With her finger, she traced the chain of freeways that would take her home to the Valley.

In Burbank, she hit a snarl that slowed traffic to a standstill. She used the time to check her face in the mirror. Her mascara had run, staining her cheeks with dark blue rivulets.

For a brief instant, she saw her mother's face looking back at her. It was only lately that she had begun recognizing her mother's features in her own. The shape of their chins and mouths was similar. Her eyes weren't brown, but they were large like her mother's. People always used to say how pretty her mom was. And besides, it could be much worse, she thought, touching the mirror. What if she awoke one morning to see Flower George in her reflection? Just the thought of it sent an involuntary shudder down her spine.

She shut off the air conditioning, feeling calmer. The steady hum of the road beneath her, coupled with the anonymity of being just one more traveler on a road of many, soothed her overwrought nerves.

Sleaze was dead.

What would Ruby say about all this? Probably something about how death was often the inevitable result of using. Munch didn't think she could bear hearing any glib AA clichés. Trite truisms didn't make a friend's death any more palatable. She could think of only one person who would truly understand: Deb.

She hit the steering wheel with her palm. Goddamn him to die and leave her all this shit. Now what was she supposed to do? And what about Asia? If Lisa was her only relative, would she be automatically placed there? More like sentenced, if that were the case. The kid deserved better. Sleaze would have wanted more for his little girl.

It was almost seven by the time she got back to her apartment.

She parked in the alley and came in through the back door. The back door was a big selling point when she rented her apartment. Having another way out was an advantage she wouldn't have felt comfortable without. She knew what it meant to live without options.

Dropping her notebook on the kitchen table, she kicked off her shoes and sank heavily into a chair. The card Sleaze had written Deb's number on was propped up against the salt shaker, its invitation clear. She reached for the phone and dialed the combination of digits that would connect her with her old life. The phone rang six times before it was picked up, and even then, it was a few more moments before anyone spoke. She heard the familiar sounds of glasses clinking, jukebox music, and boisterous voices yelling over the music. Finally a man's gruff voice spoke into the phone.

"Snakepit."

"Hi, is Deb there?"

"Hold on," he said in an annoyed growl. "Deborah!" Munch heard him yell.

She waited; her stomach growled, and she remembered she hadn't eaten.

"Nah," the man said, returning to the phone. "She ain't been in tonight."

"Can I leave a message?" she asked.

"No," the man said. "This ain't her goddamned answering service." He hung up.

She stared at the telephone. The buzz of the dial tone had never sounded so rude. She didn't realize how badly she missed Deb until just then. The ache for the familiar sound of her friend's voice filled her chest. She loved Deb like a sister, more than a sister. The things they had been through together bonded them for life.

Deb had been there for her at one of the worst times of her life. It was the morning after she had been released from the hospital, leaving behind the little blob that would later turn out to be the only baby she could ever have had. Nobody had warned her how attached you could become to a two-month-old lump of tissue, neither boy or girl. She hadn't even been showing yet. The grief she felt afterward caught her totally off-guard, leaving her as bereft as if she'd known the kid for years.

Deb didn't comment on the one-hundred-proof Southern Comfort Munch had been guzzling the day before and how that might have brought on the miscarriage. When Munch arrived at her door, Deb simply led her inside. She was cooking French toast for Boogie. Munch sat on the counter and watched, too numb to do anything else.

"Want some?" Deb had asked.

Munch had devoured plateful after plateful, surprised at her need. But then, she had never tasted love before.

And now Deb and Boogie were living in the country, happily ever after and without her.

After she hung up the phone, she said a quick prayer that

wherever Deb was, she was safe and happy. While she had the celestial line open, she added, "You made Sleaze, so do the right thing by him, too. Please."

She often called her Higher Power "You," figuring any other-worldly force who could read her thoughts was also perfectly capable of sorting out when It was being addressed.

When Blackstone left the coroner's, he drove straight to the Sheriff's Department crime lab. The facility was the best in the city—every bit as good as the Department of Justice's—and only a few blocks away. He signed in at the front anteroom and was buzzed through the heavy door that led to a corridor decorated with past triumphs of forensic investigation. The first picture he passed was of a severed thumb on the floor of some room. Some miscreant's attempt, he knew, to conceal his identity.

Further down the hall there was another photograph of a bag of Chee-tos with a pack of matches taped to the cellophane wrapper—a poor man's incineration device.

The rogues' gallery continued. His favorite was of the reported suicide victim lying on the floor beside her own murder weapon. The gun was positioned close to her hand, but alert investigators had noted the blood on her palm. And how would the blood be there, the serologist had testified in court, if that hand had been wrapped around the butt of a pistol? Her husband's conviction date was noted in the caption.

There were also several photographs of Sheriff's Investigators standing on a wooden porch, shotguns resting in the crooks of their arms, the windows behind them shot out and yellow tape strung across the front door. It was taken right after the bust of a cop murderer who left two highway patrolmen's bodies dumped along the freeway. The caption listed the suspect as DOA.

Still holding the piece of binder paper by the corner, Blackstone entered the first door on his right. FINGERPRINTS was painted in black on the top glass half of the door. He was pleased to see that the technician on duty was Mike Kellman.

"I need some prints lifted," he said.

Kellman took the paper from Blackstone and set it on a rack in a glass aquarium.

"Is this for a homicide?" he asked.

"It's a long story. Can I wait for them?"

"Sure," Kellman said. "It'll take a little while. We'll need a set of your prints for elimination."

"Just my thumb and forefinger," Blackstone said, inking and rolling his fingers on a fingerprint card.

"Give me all ten just to be safe," Kellman said.

"You're the doctor."

Kellman dusted both sides of the sheet of paper with carbon powder, using long tweezers to flip the paper over. He made little clicking noises in the back of his throat as he worked. Occasionally, he said, "Hmm," and pressed his lips together.

Blackstone waited a half hour before he asked, "Anything?"

"Just yours," the tech said, setting aside his magnifying glass. "But you got some indented writing here." He held the paper with tweezers over the bright light on his workbench. "Take it on up to Questioned Documents and see what they can do."

"Thanks." Blackstone vaulted the short flight of stairs two at a time to the second floor. When he entered the room marked QUESTIONED DOCUMENTS, he found the pair of techs who worked there hunched over a microscope arguing over the markings on a twenty-dollar bill. They were a real Mutt and Jeff team: one was tall, the other short and stubby. Blackstone could never keep their names straight. Both had pale waxy complexions, dandruff, and were in need of manicures. He'd learned from past experience that prolonged greetings weren't necessary or welcomed.

"You guys got a minute?"

They looked up at him with glazed eyes. The short one leaned over and reached for the tweezers gripping the binder paper. Blackstone caught a strong whiff of scalp oil.

"What you got here?" the taller one asked. "Blackmail? Extortion attempt?"

"Possible accessory to murder," Blackstone said, embellishing a little. "Kellman thought there was some indented writing you might be able to lift."

"If it's there, we'll get it," the shorter one said, breathing hard through his nose.

"You guys really ought to try to get out more," Blackstone said, watching as they carefully suspended the paper over an ALS light.

The taller one pulled the door shut and dimmed the lab's light. "Check it out," he said.

"Here it comes," Chubby echoed.

Blackstone looked over their shoulders and saw four groups of faint lines and squiggles. Seconds later those characters solidified into recognizable letters and numbers. Mutt and Jeff played with the angle of the light until each word could be read. On the top of the paper INVENTORY appeared. Below that, *Canyonville,* and next to that the words *ace boon coon.*

"What's that in the upper corner?" Blackstone asked. "Those numbers?"

"It's a date. Yesterday."

"Thanks, boys," Blackstone said, slipping the binder paper into an evidence envelope. "Looks like the pieces are starting to fall in place."

But who was she, he wondered as he left the building, his mystery woman? She obviously knew the deceased and cared about him enough to identify him. What was her connection to Canyonville? Did *Inventory* refer to some sort of contraband? Weapons? Dope? Stolen goods? What would her next move be? And what the hell did *ace boon coon* mean? Was it some sort of code? Did the first letters of the words, *a b c,* stand for something else?

He pulled out his notebook and listed each question separately to be dwelt over later. He underlined the words: *Who is she?*

When he returned to the station, he learned that Alex had already run the name John Garillo through CLETS, the California Law Enforcement Teletype System, and had gotten an instant hit. Jonathan Garillo had last been arrested in Venice on August 2nd. The charge was a 647F, public drunk. Alex had just pulled the hard copy of the arrest report when Blackstone caught up to him. The attached photograph certainly looked like their Doe; the fingerprint card would of course cinch the decedent's identity.

According to the arresting officer's narrative of the incident, the suspect had been apprehended on Lincoln Boulevard after the officers observed him walking erratically. Garillo claimed to be just visiting friends in the area and failed the field sobriety test.

After a four-hour detainment, Jonathan Garillo had been released to a woman who identified herself as Lisa Slokum, his sister. The report also listed all calls the suspect had made while in custody. There had been only only two, but both were to the same number. Alex called the number and listened to a disconnect recording. He contacted the phone company and back-tracked the listing. It belonged to Lisa Slokum and the billing address was in Inglewood.

Blackstone phoned Sugarman and brought the coroner up to speed.

"You think the sister might have been our uninvited guest?"

"The thought occurred to me."

"Are you going to try to find her tonight?" Sugarman asked. "I'll need her to come down and make an official visual identification. There's also the matter of funeral arrangements."

Blackstone checked his watch. "I could run out to Inglewood and be downtown by, say, seven." One of the women from the secretarial pool delivered a picture of Lisa Slokum—it was a booking photograph. Obviously, she and her brother were cut from the same cloth. He also realized—looking at her sullen, chubby face—that the sister wasn't the woman he sought.

"It can wait till tomorrow, if you want," Sugarman said. "Wait a minute, you're off tomorrow, aren't you?"

"Yes." Blackstone dragged out the word, dangling an unsaid *but* on the end of it. He hated to delegate any part of his investigations, but he'd also been promising himself to get a life outside of job and he did have a chess tournament at mid-morning. "I suppose I can have two guys from the morning crew run out there and see if they can locate the sister." As he spoke, he wrote out a memo detailing the situation to Tiger Cassiletti and Bumper Morris, the two dicks who worked Sunday morning.

After they hung up, Blackstone made a copy of the arrest report and the sister's picture, adding them both to the steadily growing file of the homicide investigation. He made more circles on his blotter. In each he wrote names and brief titles. The top circle was given over to *Jonathan Garillo—Victim*. He drew a line connecting it to the second circle, *Lisa Slokum—Victim's next of kin*. With all these lowlifes involved, something was bound to break soon.

10

As she cleaned her small apartment Sunday morning, Munch couldn't stop reliving sneaking into the coroner's office: the delicious thrill of being in a forbidden place before the shock of seeing Sleaze. Wasn't it just like God to pair those two things? Just as she was enjoying a taboo-breaking rush . . . Bam. Old friend dead, killed in action, a stark reminder of the inherent risks of her old life.

But still, it was hard to shake that feeling of excitement when the cops entered the room. She had even brushed by one of them, touched his sleeve on the way out the door like an Indian warrior counting coup. Even now the memory of that moment sent a thrill through her stomach. She chuckled out loud, envisioning the students who keeled over at the sight of blood.

She was shutting off the vacuum cleaner when she saw her answering machine blink red as it answered a call. She picked up the receiver and silenced the outgoing message.

"Were you asleep?" Danielle asked.

"No, I had the vacuum on. What's up?"

"Just calling to see how you were."

"Oh, just lovely. How are you?"

"I went out with Derek last night."

"How was it?"

"I don't know. Okay, I guess. Sometimes these guys on the program seem like such wimps."

"I know what you're saying. It's like show some spine. I don't want to hear about your childhood."

"Exactly."

Munch looked out the window.

"What are you doing today?" Danielle asked.

She almost said waiting, but then Danielle would ask waiting for what. "I'm just going to hang around here. I've got a lot of stuff to catch up on."

"All right," Danielle said. "Maybe I'll catch you later."

"Sounds good."

Lisa's call came at twelve-thirty.

"I didn't know who else to call," she said, her tone flat.

"Lisa? What's wrong?" Munch asked, hating the necessity of her playacting.

"He's been dead since Friday. John is dead."

"How?"

"He was shot."

She heard the baby crying in the background. "You want me to come over?"

"I'm not too proud to ask," Lisa said.

Munch set down the phone, realizing too late that she should have asked Lisa if the cops were going to be there. That was all she needed, to be over at Lisa's house when the detectives arrived with their questions.

At one o'clock, just before she left, Munch called the Snakepit again. This time a woman answered. Munch asked if Deb was there and the woman said to hold on. Munch took in a deep breath and noticed she had crossed her fingers.

"Hello?"

"Deb?"

"Munch?" They both laughed with excitement. "Oh . . . my . . . lord," Deb said, her Southern drawl as pronounced as ever. "Where are you, woman?"

"L.A."

"How the hell are you?" Deb asked.

"I'm good. Wow, it's good to hear your voice. How's my little Boogieman?"

"He's growing like crazy," Deb said. "He asks about you. Shit, I thought we'd lost you forever. Nobody ever sees you anymore. What's taking you so long to get back to us?"

Munch felt a twist in her stomach and wondered if it was possible to be homesick for a place she'd never been. "You say Boogie's gotten big, huh?"

"Why don't you come see for yourself? Get your ass out of L.A. and come visit. Hell, come stay. You know there's always room for you here."

"Doesn't he have a birthday coming up?"

"That's right. You haven't missed one yet. The Medford airport is about a hundred miles from here. You could be there in three hours."

"I've got a job," Munch said.

"Just tell Wizard you need some family time."

"I don't work for Wizard anymore. A lot of things have changed."

"I've got a lot to tell you, too."

"Deb, I have some bad news. It's Sleaze. He's dead."

Her words were met with silence.

"I know," Munch said. "I still can't believe it."

"It's worse than that," Deb said.

Munch wondered what could be worse than being dead.

"He was a snitch," Deb said.

"Where did you hear that?" Munch asked, feeling a prickly sensation up the back of her neck. Did Deb feel that his murder was justified? Deserved? She was talking about Sleaze, not some stranger. Besides, Sleaze would never rat. "No way. Who told you that?"

"Oh, you can believe it all right. When's the last time you saw him?"

Surely, she meant alive. "He came by my work a couple of days ago."

"You know about Karen?"

"Yeah, I heard all about it. Lisa said Sleaze found her with the needle still stuck in her arm."

"He changed a lot after that—weirded out on us."

"I met his kid," Munch said.

"I bet she's a cutie."

"She is. It's gonna be rough for her, being an orphan and all."

"Karen's people will take her, I guess, or Sleaze's. She's too young to know any different." Deb paused to cough. "How about you? You been good?"

"You wouldn't believe how good," Munch said, wrapping the phone cord around her fingers.

"Roxanne's been staying with me. C'mon, just hop on a plane and we'll pick you up. I've got my ol' man's truck."

"Sleaze said you had an ol' man."

"Forget about Sleaze. Here, Roxanne's right here. She wants to say hi."

Munch heard more shouting and laughing while the phone changed hands. She could almost smell the beer, picture the hazy veil of smoke hovering over the pool tables. "Hey," Roxanne said.

"How's it going?"

"You're coming up?"

"I'm thinking about it."

"Don't—" Roxanne was cut off as Deb grabbed the phone back.

"This will be great, the three of us together again. We'll cause some fun."

"What about your ol' man? What's his name, anyhow?"

"Tux. He's out of town right now, but he should be back by the weekend. He's a long-haul trucker." Deb laughed suggestively.

"Sounds good. How is he with Boogie?"

"Real fine," Deb said. "He takes him with him sometimes on overnight runs."

"Really?" Maybe he wasn't an asshole. "That sounds great. Do they ever get down my way?"

"He goes all over. I know what you're thinking."

"I just—"

"Forget it, he's mine."

"I've missed you, Deb."

"Hey, Munch?"

"Yeah?"

"Call me Deborah now."

"Sure," Munch said, happy to see that Deb was obviously growing. "I'll see about coming to visit and call you back."

"I can't wait."

"Me either."

On her way to Inglewood, Munch stopped at the market and loaded up on supplies. She didn't get to Lisa's until after two. Juggling the groceries to one arm, she knocked on the frame of the screen door.

Lisa's eyes were red and her face puffy and blotched when she appeared in the doorway. She nodded once to Munch, unlocked the door, then turned around.

"This is terrible. How did you hear about it?" Munch asked, following her into the dark living room.

"Two pigs came over this morning with pictures. They pulled my name from his rap sheet." Lisa showed Munch the policemen's business cards and then threw them in the trash. "They wanted me to come down and look at the body," she said.

"I'm sorry," Munch said. "That had to be the worst."

"I didn't go."

"Why not?"

"What was I supposed to do with the kids? Take 'em with me?"

Munch could see her point. "I brought some stuff." She pushed a bag of groceries into Lisa's hands. "Where are the kids?"

"The girls are in their room. The baby's sleeping."

Lisa took the bag of groceries into the kitchen. Munch sank down to the floor and began sorting the laundry piled there.

Lisa popped open a beer and watched without interest. "They said I needed to make arrangements. You know, like the funeral shit."

Munch stuffed a load of whites into the machine, sprinkled it with the detergent she had brought, and started the cycle, turning the controls to HOT.

"When is the funeral? I'd like to go."

"I don't have money for a funeral. That shit costs thousands."

"So what happens now?"

"They said the coroner had a release form for me to sign and then he'd take care of it."

"Are you going to sign it?"

"What difference does it make? He's dead, right? Buying some big expensive coffin ain't gonna bring him back."

"Will they let you know where they bury him? I'd like to put some flowers on his grave."

"Cheaper to burn him."

"Yeah, you're probably right about that." Munch moved on to the sink and began washing the dishes stacked there. She turned the water on hot—as hot as she could stand it—and held her grease-stained cuticles under the rush. "I'd rather you didn't say anything to the cops about me going over to his place," she said.

"I don't tell the pigs nothing," Lisa said.

"Do you know something?"

"Like what?"

Munch scraped at something hard and yellow stuck to the inside of a coffee mug whose handle was broken off. "When Sleaze stopped by my work, he told me that he was fixing to split."

"He was always going somewhere."

Munch handed her a dish towel and a wet plate. "Yeah, you got that right. How long was he in Oregon?"

Lisa looked at her before answering. Munch detected a note of hostility before Lisa said, "Long enough to piss some people off."

"I talked to Deb," Munch said. "She said Sleaze was a snitch."

Lisa flinched. "She told you that? What a cunt."

Munch handed Lisa another plate. Lisa apparently still held a grudge for the time Deb slept with Lisa's ol' man. Not that either woman was still with the guy, so who cared anymore? Besides, shouldn't she be pissed at the guy?

"I told her no way, Sleaze wouldn't talk to the cops."

Lisa spun around and faced her. "You know, you're really something. You don't come around forever, then you show up talking long shit about who would do what." She threw down the dish towel, discovered her beer was empty, and opened another one. "Don't fuck with what you don't understand."

"What does that mean?"

"It means some things are better just left alone."

Munch held up a baby bottle. "Where does this go?"

Lisa took it from her and jammed it into a cabinet over the sink.

Munch dried her hands on the dish towel. "I didn't come here to fight with you. I'm just trying to help."

"Yeah? Well, who died and made you Glenda the fucking good witch?"

"Hey, I'm hurting, too."

Lisa concentrated for a moment on getting the cabinet shut before all the assorted plastic containers and plates fell out, leaving that calamity for the next person. "Fucking Deb really thinks she's some kind of hot shit," she said, "her and that little nigger kid of hers."

"Watch it," Munch said, feeling her muscles tense. There was talking trash and there was crossing the line. Lisa treaded on dangerous ground when she put Boogie down.

"Sorry," Lisa mumbled. She walked out to the front room and grabbed a cigarette from the open pack on the coffee table.

Munch turned to the stovetop. Dirty pots and pans were stacked two deep above the burners. "There was a guy with him on Friday," she said as she poured rancid grease from a heavy cast-iron skillet into a can she dug out of the trash. "Long black hair, had a jail tattoo on his neck—one of those Aryan Brotherhood lightning bolts. Any idea who he was?"

"No," Lisa said.

"You sure?" She lifted the lid on a saucepan and saw that it was filled with hard cold rice.

"What? You writing a book?" Lisa asked. "Just drop it. It's over now."

"What are you talking about?" Munch dumped the rice in the trash and put the pot in the sink to soak. "How can it be over? Doesn't it bother you that the killer is still out there?"

"And they'll always be out there," Lisa said.

"What's that supposed to mean?"

"It means the world is full of assholes and all we can do is all we can do." She lit her smoke, slipping the spent match into an empty beer can. "Speaking of which, I'm calling my social worker tomorrow."

"About?"

"My niece." She exhaled in the direction of the baby. "Karen had her at home and never registered the birth, which was pretty stupid, you know? How you gonna get welfare if you can't prove you had the kid?"

The sound of something heavy falling in the bedroom carried to them, followed by a child crying. Lisa made no move to investigate.

"So there's no record of her birth anywhere?" Munch asked.

"No."

"Do me a favor, Lisa. Don't sign her away, too. I'll help you out with diapers and food. Just give me a little time to see what I can work out." She walked into the front room and stood over Asia's crib. The baby smiled in her sleep. Munch stroked her cheek. It was soft and warm. How hard could it be to raise a kid? Her apartment was plenty big enough to accommodate a crib, a playpen. She'd need to find a good babysitter for during the day, while she worked. "You gonna be here tomorrow evening?"

"Sure. Where am I going to go?"

"I thought I'd stop over after work."

"Suit yourself."

Apparently Lisa was too proud to say thank you.

Asia sighed in her sleep and smacked her lips. Munch touched her back lightly, hoping to transmit reassurances that all would be well. *Don't worry, I won't leave you too.*

She shut the door gently on her way out.

After Munch left, two men entered Lisa's house from the back door.

"What did she want?" the taller one asked.

Lisa spoke to the second man, the one with the tattoo on his neck. "She was asking about you."

"By name?"

"Nah. She just said some dude was with Sleaze on Friday with long black hair. She described your tattoo, but she didn't know who you were."

"Is this bitch going to be a problem?" the other man asked, his large body filling the door frame.

Almost against her will, Lisa glanced at the revolver jammed in the waistband of his leather pants. "I don't think so, Tux."

He stepped forward, gathering her hair in his big hand and jerking her head back. "You better hope not, bitch. 'Cuz I don't give a fuck what happens. I'll chain you both up and use you for target practice. You know that, don't you."

"You've got nothing to worry about from me," she said.

11

Alex Perez arrived at work at ten o'clock on Monday morning looking more rumpled than usual.

Blackstone threw the car keys to his partner. "We need to take a ride out to Inglewood," he said, "and pick up Garillo's sister. Sugarman needs a visual identification from a family member."

"Why didn't somebody go out there yesterday?" Alex asked, yawning.

"Cassiletti said she had a bunch of kids and no car. He also said she was pretty hostile."

"In other words, he didn't want to fuck with her."

"I guess not," Blackstone said.

Alex scratched his head and rubbed his eyes. "Let me grab a cup of coffee before we go," he said. "Number two son kept us up all night. You want a cup?"

"No," he answered, checking his watch. He wanted to get out

to Inglewood and back as quickly as possible. "I've got a call in to Special Agent Claire."

"Is she the one you worked with on that serial rapist case?"

"She's the one."

"Well, at least we got an in."

"Let's see if she returns my call."

While Alex fetched his coffee, Blackstone leaned back in his chair, stroking the ends of his mustache and taking a moment to recall the last time he had worked with Claire Donavon. It was two years ago, when he was still investigating sex crimes. The case they had worked together had been one of those frustrating situations where the perpetrator was known to them, but impossible to build a case against. The rapist chose his victims well. He used a condom and remembered to take it with him afterward. Even when caught with circumstantial evidence, he was too smart to incriminate himself. Stalemate.

The FBI took an interest when one of the victims turned out to be the niece of the L.A. bureau director. There had been a lot of heat on the case. Special Agent Claire Donavon was known for her ability to connect with the subjects she interviewed and was brought in as the interrogator.

He had found himself strongly attracted to her, an attraction that ran deeper than his unconscious male response to her superb physical attributes—it took more than that to pique his interest. He'd always had his pick of women. His married friends were constantly fixing him up with some cousin or friend of their wife's. The first thing they usually told him was how pretty the woman was—as if that meant so much.

Claire Donavon, for instance, had so much more going on behind those green eyes of hers. He'd witnessed firsthand her unwavering tenacity, sharp reasoning skills, and powers of observation. She hid the steel edges under an earth mother facade of curves and dimples. Maybe that softness wasn't a facade, perhaps distraction was a better word. In this new age of women's lib, she'd found a way to make her femininity work for her. Smart.

The break in their case had come when she'd finessed a confession from the perp. Somehow she'd dug up the fact that he'd been fired unfairly from a managerial position at Kmart. His boss had been a woman. Claire had even interviewed the perp's mom and had a detailed history of the guy's bedwetting. She understood, she said, how difficult to please mothers could be. She had convinced the perp—and everyone listening to the interview—that she really understood where he was coming from. Ten minutes with the guy and she had had him bawling on her shoulder, giving up everything.

Later, she brushed off everyone's compliments, said all the answers had been in the guy's file. There was no denying that she was good, damn good. But when all was said and done, she was still a federal agent first, which meant that she took more than she gave.

The last time he'd seen her was in court. Following their combined testimony, the rapist had been sentenced to thirty years. She and Blackstone had gone out afterward for drinks, but she had had to leave to meet her boyfriend. Not a husband, he remembered.

"She'll call," Alex said, returning with a mug of coffee and a donut and seemingly reading his partner's thoughts.

"Are you ready?" Blackstone asked, coming to his feet and slipping into his sports coat.

"Would you mind driving?" Alex asked.

"Your moon in Uranus again?" Blackstone asked.

"I'm just tired, that's all." He affected a hurt expression. "You know, you don't do yourself any favors closing yourself off to what you don't understand."

"Are you saying I don't keep an open mind?"

"You're an Aries. You can't help yourself."

"Just give me the keys."

It took over half an hour to reach Lisa Slokum's address in Inglewood. They parked across the street and studied the neighborhood. Most of the houses sported burglar bars and pictures of Dobermans wired to their chain-link fences. The shriek of jet engines drowned out the static and chatter of their police radio. They had left the volume up loud. In this neighborhood, they didn't want to be mistaken for potential robbery victims. The two detectives walked to the door together. When the chubby woman in the bathrobe came to the door, they showed her their badges.

"What do you want?" she asked. A baby cried behind her.

"Are you Lisa Slokum?"

"Yeah."

"We need you to come to the coroner's office and make a positive identification of your brother's body," Blackstone explained.

"Why do I have to go?" she asked.

"Are there other relatives you'd like us to contact?" Alex asked.

"No," she said. "There's nobody else."

"Then you're it," Blackstone said.

"The other two cops showed me his picture. I already told them that it was him. All you guys think you're such big heroes, but you always want someone else to do your job for you. Catch the fuckers who killed him if you want to do something."

Blackstone looked up and mentally counted to five. "Do you know anyone who wanted your brother dead?" he asked.

She shrugged.

"Did he have any woman friends who worked at a printing press? Anything like that?"

She pressed her lips together and shook her head no.

"Where did he live?"

She sighed impatiently and scowled. "He moved around a lot."

"Did he have a girlfriend? A wife? Any children?"

"I don't know shit," she said. "All right? You want me to look at his body, you're going to have to give me cab fare. I ain't taking the fucking bus."

"Why don't you get dressed," Alex said, "and we'll take you down there now."

"What about the baby?" she asked.

"Bring the baby, too," Alex said. "We like kids. Right, Jigsaw?"

"Where are your other children?" Blackstone asked, spotting the toys littering the front yard and remembering what Cassiletti had said in his report of yesterday's contact.

"They're in school," she said, rolling her eyes. "What do you think?"

He checked his watch again. "We'll wait out here while you get ready."

All the way downtown, Lisa Slokum kept up a running tirade about cops and their ineptness. When they got to the coroner's viewing room, Lisa wailed loudly when confronted with her brother's remains, which got the baby going. Blackstone noticed that the baby was the only one actually producing tears.

On the ride back to Inglewood, Alex fed the woman and her baby M & M's from a bag he produced out of his coat pocket. He put the baby on his ample lap and kept her entertained with faces and a variety of sound effects. She tugged on his lips, earlobes, and nose and laughed when he said, "Oww!" At one point she almost broke the thin gold chain that held his crucifix.

Lisa Slokum also calmed down, limiting her histrionics to audible sniffles. The detectives dropped her off at her Inglewood address and gave her their business cards. Neither man held much hope of receiving any help from her.

"Cute kid," Alex said as they drove away.

Blackstone reached under his seat for the box of pre-moistened towelettes he kept there and shoved them at his partner. "Fifteen years and she'll be a carbon copy of the mother," he said

"You're probably right," Alex said, sighing. "Shame." He wiped off his hands and stuck the used towelette in his pocket.

After returning to the station, the two detectives contacted print shops for the remainder of the afternoon, working from the Yellow Pages. It was tedious work, involving much repetition, language barriers, and unanswered calls that would have to be noted and tried again. Three hours later, they had found only twelve shops that had female typesetters, but none of those women matched the physical description of the woman they sought.

Blackstone looked up from his desk when he heard a contralto voice asking for him. He stood, straightening his slacks, and ducked his head out his doorway. "Claire?" When they first worked together, she had insisted that they all address each other on a first-name basis. Her lack of pretension had been refreshing.

She walked towards him with arms extended. To his surprise, she hugged him. "How are you, Jigsaw?"

"Let me get you a chair," he said, borrowing one from another cubicle and dusting off its seat.

"I understand our investigations have crossed," she said, taking the offered chair and setting her purse on his desk.

Blackstone smiled. She was direct. He liked that. "What do you have for me?" he asked.

She laughed easily. He liked the way the three small moles on her left cheek formed a crescent when she smiled. "That's not the way it works, I'm afraid. I understand you identified the victim of last Friday's freeway homicide."

"Are you here to return my evidence, Claire?"

"When you need a ballistics match, you'll have the Bureau's full support."

"All right. Then what *do* we owe the honor of this visit to?"

"I have a favor to ask of you," she said. "This case has certain delicacies. I understand you plan to release a photograph of the deceased to the press."

"Now that he's identified," he said, shrugging, "there's really no need to circulate his picture."

"I'd like you to go ahead and do so anyway," she said.

"In exchange for?"

"I'm asking as a professional courtesy."

Alex Perez chose that minute to stick his head in the doorway. "What's up?" he asked.

Blackstone made introductions.

"Jigsaw treating you all right?" Alex asked her.

"Oh yes." She crossed her legs and glanced up at the Bobby Fischer poster on Blackstone's wall. "Ah, the master himself." She turned to Alex. "Are you a fan of Bobby's as well?"

"Sure," he said. "I mean, he beat the Russkies, am I right?"

"Do you play?" Blackstone asked Claire, feeling a strong need to have her attention directed back on him.

"It's not always easy to find a good game," she said. "I submitted a membership application with the Santa Monica Bay Chess Club."

"I competed there yesterday," he told her. "I'll put in a word for you."

107

"And did you win your match?" she asked.

"Yeah, how'd it go, Jigsaw?" Alex asked.

"My opponent conceded after the thirty-ninth move," Blackstone said. "He didn't have enough material left to mate."

"I didn't know chess was so sexual," Alex said. "Maybe I should take it up."

"It's more a matter of mental intercourse," Blackstone said, looking straight at Claire. "How about it?"

She blinked, caught off-guard. "You mean you and me?"

"A real opponent is so much more interesting than solitaire."

"How do you play solitaire chess?" Alex asked.

Blackstone realized that he'd forgotten that his partner was still in the room; maybe it was just wishful thinking. "The chess magazine I get publishes games played by the masters. You try to figure out their next moves, then you check your move against theirs. Don't you have some calls to make?"

Alex grinned. "Yeah. I better go back to that."

"Thank you, Detective," Blackstone said and then turned back to Claire. "They've been using a lot of Fischer's games lately. It's been quite a journey, trying to get into his head."

"Any success?" she asked.

"Sometimes. Are you interested?"

"I can't . . . tonight," she said.

"Tomorrow's good with me," he told her.

"I'll be downtown tomorrow afternoon."

"Swing by when you're through. I should be home by six," he said. "You know that smokestack you see off the Five freeway that has BREW 102 written on it?"

"Yes."

"That's me. I'll leave the gate open."

"I'll bring Chinese," she said. "In case the game runs longer than we expect."

"That's what I like about you, Claire. Always thinking ahead."

"And the photograph of your victim?" she asked.

"Page three, how's that?"

"Thank you."

"Whoa," he said. "I'm not letting you off the hook that easy. Who was this guy to you? Give me something."

"I would if I could, honestly."

He smiled at her qualifier. *Honestly* had to be the singularly most abused word. He turned when he heard the door to Sergeant Mann's office open. A thin blond man exited. Judging from his air of self-importance, Blackstone made him as another fed. The partner, no doubt. "All right, Claire," he said when the second agent was in hearing range, "I'll see you tomorrow night."

The thin man glanced at Claire sharply, but she didn't meet his eye. What was going on there? Blackstone wondered. Did the two of them have anything going? Or did he just disapprove of her mingling with the local talent?

The blond man reached out a hand to Blackstone. "Jared Vanowen," he said. "FBI."

Blackstone swallowed a smile. Pompous idiot. "Jigsaw Blackstone, LAPD." The two men gripped hands. Vanowen wore a gold fraternity ring set with a blue stone on his right hand. Blackstone squeezed the man's fingers and was gratified to see the fed wince. Claire crossed her arms over her chest, and Blackstone suddenly felt foolish and juvenile. Alex emerged from his cubicle, sucking a piece of beef jerky and easing the moment's tension.

"This is Alex Perez," Blackstone said, releasing Vanowen's

hand and nodding toward his partner. Alex and Vanowen exchanged nods.

After the two agents left, Alex sat on the edge of Blackstone's desk.

"I think the print shops are a dead end," he said.

"That's why I'm cultivating a second source."

"You think she'll tell you anything?" Alex asked.

Blackstone reached for his phone. "Let's put the word out on the street that we're interested in some military-issue weaponry that might have started surfacing last month. See what we can turn up."

"Give ourselves a little something to barter with, eh?"

"You've got to be in the game to play the game."

"Should we keep trying print shops?"

"No," he said. "You're right. That lead is going nowhere."

After his partner returned to his cubicle, Jigsaw swiveled in his chair until he faced his typewriter. Early on he had been cautioned on the importance of maintaining copious notes. The cop who had tutored him assured him that the truth would always protect him. Document everything, he had been taught. Cover your ass.

So when he typed up the evening report, he mentioned the visit to Lisa Slokum and the FBI's involvement. He also made note of the lack of success that they had had in tracking down the woman from the freeway, who, his gut told him, was the same woman who had appeared at the coroner's office. Turning back to his blotter, he drew another balloon in pencil and started to write *Jane Doe*, but then erased the *oe* in Doe and wrote *Jane Dirty Nails* instead. Using a straight edge, he connected her to John Garillo with a solid pencil line and carefully printed the two times she'd been spotted.

12

Jack called Munch into his office at mid-morning on Monday.

"You got a call," he said. "Maybe you better take it in here. She sounds pretty upset."

"Who is it?" Munch asked. Jack just shrugged his shoulders on his way out the door. She picked up the receiver.

"Hello?"

"They made me go look at his body," Lisa said. "I hate those motherfuckers."

"Who?"

"The pigs."

What about the murderers? she thought but said, "The cops are just doing their job."

"Yeah," Lisa said, sniffling. "Everybody's just doing their job."

Munch looked out the office window and saw Jack talking to a customer in a Pontiac Le Mans station wagon. His body blocked the face of the customer, but the car was familiar. It had been in last week, and she had replaced the brakes front and back. Jack stood, saw her looking, and motioned for her to join them.

She held up a finger. "Did the cops say if they had any suspects?"

"Their investigation is going to be bullshit, I'll tell you that right now."

"Why do you say bullshit?" she asked.

"You think they really care who killed him?" Lisa said. "You know what they asked me? They wanted to know if he had any female friends that worked for a printer. What kind of fucked-up question is that?"

Munch felt something drop inside her intestines and instinctively drew her hands into fists. Were they looking for her? "Did they say when they'd be back?" she asked.

"They won't be back," Lisa said. "You still coming over tonight?"

"Yeah, after work. Stay cool." She hung up and went outside. "Problem?" she asked, addressing both Jack and the scowling man behind the wheel.

"For two hundred dollars," the man said, "my wife's brakes should feel like new."

"Are they pulling?" she asked.

"No," he said.

"Squeaking?"

"No, but look how far I have to press down the pedal."

She looked in the window and watched as the man demonstrated.

"My wife didn't know enough to complain." He gave Jack one of those you-know-how-women-are-with-cars looks. Jack's expression was noncommittal.

"You've got power assist on these brakes," she explained.

"They always feel like that standing still. What's important is how they stop the car when it's moving." *What's important,* she was really thinking, *is that your wife isn't dead. Nobody you knew was shot over the weekend. Probably nobody you ever knew was ever shot. That's what's important.*

"Tell you what, Bob," Jack said, reaching in his pocket for a dollar. "You go across the street and get yourself a cup of coffee, and we'll adjust the brakes."

After the customer had left, Jack turned to her. "Watch the phone, I'm going to take this around the block."

"You want me to put it on the rack first?"

"No, I want to check it out before we do anything. Get started on that VW clutch cable."

He pulled back into the shop's driveway ten minutes later. She chewed her lip, awaiting his verdict.

"Are they okay?" she asked.

"Yeah, when that guy gets back, you let me handle him."

"Here he comes now," she said, seeing him emerge from Denny's.

Jack waved and then waited for the customer to cross the street. "Let's go for a ride, Bob," he said, patting the man's back. "You drive."

They returned in another ten minutes. Both men were smiling. Jack got out at the curb, and Bob went on his way.

"He looked happy," she said, joining her boss as he looked after the retreating vehicle.

"Jerk," Jack said, without letting the word disturb the smile on his face.

"Well, at least he's a satisfied jerk. What did you do?"

"The brakes were perfect. I just moved the seat up."

"Good one."

"What was wrong with the girl on the phone?" he asked. "Or is it personal?"

"Her brother got killed."

"Oh, I'm sorry."

"You didn't like him. It was that guy who came by last Friday."

"I didn't wish him dead," he said, shocked. "What happened? How'd he die?"

"She said he was shot."

"Geez, I knew that guy was trouble, but shot? You better stay away from those people."

"I promised her I'd stop by there after work tonight."

"You sure that's safe?"

"I already said I would."

"You want to leave early? Me and Lou can handle things."

"No, I'll work all day." She wasn't about to leave early again. She already had enough things to feel guilty about. Visiting Lisa again tonight meant she would miss the meeting she regularly attended on Monday nights at Tarzana Hospital. Ruby would be concerned if she knew that Munch hadn't been to a meeting since Friday. Good habits were the easiest ones to break, Ruby always said. Munch decided that what her sponsor didn't know wouldn't bother her.

13

By the time five o'clock rolled around, Munch was exhausted. She plunked down wearily in the seat of her GTO, pressed down the accelerator twice before turning the key, and then settled back to let the Pontiac's engine warm up. Rolling her head to one side, she spotted Asia's car seat. The sight of it brought a smile to her lips. How satisfying it would be to be working this hard for somebody else.

She'd never realized before that a baby could have such a personality. She'd always thought them just crying, sleeping blobs until they were old enough to talk and say something interesting. But she had been wrong. She'd really connected with that little baby of Sleaze's.

Just thinking about the little rugrat made her want to be holding her again. She patted the empty cushion of Asia's car seat. It crinkled as if lined with plastic. It wasn't very cushiony, either. What had they used to stuff it? Plastic bags and old newspaper or something? She pulled the seat closer to her and studied it, finding the places where the cushion attached to the plastic frame and unsnapping it. She located a zipper in the back. Restuffing the cushion would be a simple matter.

She unzipped the zipper. A rectangular, shrink-wrapped package of papers fell out. Beneath that was a second plastic bag filled with yellowish-white crystalline powder: meth.

Oh, shit.

She jammed the dope back into the cushion with shaking hands.

Sleaze, you jerk.

She recalled his words: "I just need you to take the baby over to my sister's and pick up a few things at the apartment."

I'm an idiot, she thought.

Her car still revved on fast idle. She tapped the accelerator, and the engine settled down.

The first packet slipped to the floorboard between her feet. She bent down and retrieved it. Using the small screwdriver that she always carried clipped in her front pocket, she slit open the hermetically sealed plastic bag. An assortment of documents spilled into her lap: photographs, maps, hand-lettered lists of names and dates.

She looked at the pictures first. They were a series of photos of two men speaking. The first guy she recognized as the dude riding shotgun with Sleaze the day he came in. The second man in the picture—the one in the suit and dark glasses—was definitely some kind of cop. The two men were exchanging envelopes and sneaking furtive glances. She singled out one picture that clearly showed the long-haired guy's face as well as his tattoo and stuck it in her visor.

Underneath the pictures she found a floor plan of a building—some sort of warehouse, it looked like—and a schedule of names and times. The names were all preceded by ranks and the times were all written militaristically: 1100 hours, 2300 hours.

Beneath the floor plan and timetable, she found hand-lettered lists of dates, dollar amounts, and number/letter annotations: M14 (1 case), HC #35 (6 cases), 7.62 X 22mm AP (200), M16 (3 cases). They appeared to be records of payoffs and monies collected for weaponry. Tux's name was mentioned often. That had to be Deb's Tux. The dates, all of them late August and early September, had been circled. Curiouser and curiouser. What had Sleaze stumbled into? He hated guns. Was this what he had snitched about? Then what was the other guy in the picture doing?

And what about the dope?

She snuck a look at the car seat with its terrible cargo. The best thing to do would be to just get rid of it. Flush it quick before she had a chance to think. But then again . . . That much shit was worth thousands of dollars. Was it smart to just throw it away? Was it smart to do anything else?

She could use that money to pay for Sleaze's funeral. Surely that was only justice. What was left could help defer the cost of a babysitter while she was at work. The beauty of dope money was that it would be cash. Cash that wouldn't be figured into the financial report for her probation officer. Maybe this was God's way of helping. He did have a pretty weird sense of humor sometimes.

She stacked all the paperwork back together, stuffed it back into the plastic as best she could, and stuck it under her seat.

She drove home carefully, stopping twice as long as necessary at four-way stop signs. When she got home, she lifted the car seat out of her car using only her fingertips, handling the thing like it might turn around and bite her. Her phone was ringing when she got to her front door. She answered it out of breath, holding the car seat at arm's length.

"Yeah?" She noticed her voice had taken on a suspicious tone.

"Will you accept a collect call from Lisa?" the operator asked.

"Sure, why not?" She set the carrier on the floor.

"Hey," Lisa said. "You coming over tonight?"

"Yeah, I wanted to clean up first."

"I was thinking," Lisa said, "when you were over at Sleaze's place, did you see Asia's car seat?"

"I did."

"Do you have it? 'Cuz I was thinking we should have it here, in case we need it."

Munch closed her eyes and shook her head. Lisa knew a lot more than she was saying.

"Yeah, I'll bring it over tonight," Munch said. She heard traffic noises. "Where are you calling from?"

"The liquor store."

"Who's watching the kids?"

"They're okay by themselves for a little while."

Munch wondered how she'd arrived at that conclusion. Lisa obviously believed in the hasn't-killed-them-yet parenting method. "I won't keep you, then. You go on home and I'll see you in about an hour."

After they hung up, Munch ran her bath. All she could think about were the drugs in her house, singing their siren promises.

Was she happily sober?

Jesus, where had that thought come from? Where was her gratitude? *Thank you, God, for not making it heroin that Sleaze was smuggling,* was the only prayer she could come up with.

She rushed through her bath and dressed quickly. Still barefoot, she grabbed the car seat cushion and took it into the kitchen. Until she could decide the best way to handle this situation, she needed to hide the dope. Too bad she couldn't figure out a way to hide it from herself while she was at it. She picked up the flour canister and then set it back down. Too obvious. She opened the refrigerator and considered pouring the milk out of the carton, but nixed that idea as well. You could always tell when they had been opened.

A message kept flashing in her brain: Should she sample the merchandise?

Maybe she could hide it in the trash cans out in the alley. Pickup wasn't until Monday. No, that wasn't good, either. What if someone went through the trash? Kids, even, looking for recyclables. She rummaged through her kitchen drawer until she located a ball of twine. Unwinding six feet of it, she fashioned a noose with a slip knot. She unzipped the car seat, lassoed the bag, and pulled the twine tight around the center of it. The last thing she did was wipe the bag clean of any possible fingerprints.

She walked outside to the storm drain, lowered the dope down the gutter, and tied the other end of the string to the grating. If the string broke, there were going to be some busy rats tonight.

On her way to Inglewood, billboards along the freeway invited her to fly to Hawaii. She thought about the thousands of dollars that would be hers for the taking—just a few phone calls to the right people. The battle raging between her ears gave her a headache.

At Culver Boulevard, four bikers on Harleys thundered past her single file, filling the car with the roar of their engines. They pulled in front, and she saw that they were wearing Hell's Angels colors. Why did the sight of them still thrill her? For the briefest instant, she wished she had Harley-Davidson wings on her back window instead of her rainbow-colored EASY DOES IT.

She got off at La Tijera and caught the red light at the top of the off-ramp. While she idled there, the sheriff's bus groaned to a stop next to her. She stared so hard that the driver waved to her. Smiling weakly at the private joke between her and her maker, she waved back.

Point taken, God.

She stopped for gas at an independent station that still sold 98 octane. While she waited for her tank to fill, she stashed the packet of paperwork under the spare tire in her trunk and stuck the picture of the tattooed man in her shirt pocket.

When she got to Lisa's house, she brought the now-emptied car seat in with her. Lisa's eyes widened slightly at the sight of it.

"Where are the kids?" Munch asked. The question already felt part of her routine. Funny how quickly new habits developed.

"In their room." Lisa said her line of script over the sound of the TV.

Munch walked over to the kids' room and opened the door. Jill and Charlotte were drawing on each other with Magic Markers. Asia, naked save for the indelible star now scrawled on her chest in black ink, reposed on the floor next to them sucking on a pen. It made a soft plopping noise when Munch pried it gently away from her.

"Where's her diaper?" Munch asked.

"Mommy said to let her air out for a while," Charlotte reported.

Munch lifted Asia onto her hip and stepped back into the main room. Lisa had her hand up the back of the car seat cushion. She jumped guiltily when she saw Munch.

"Something wrong?" Munch asked.

"No. I, uh—"

Munch cut her off before she had a chance to come up with any bullshit. Lisa had already answered the question Munch wanted answered. "Have you guys eaten?" she asked.

"I was going to fix the girls some cereal," Lisa said.

Munch reached for her wallet. "Why don't we get a pizza?"

"Yeah!" the two girls shouted in unison from their room.

"I'll go pick it up," Lisa said. "I've been in this house all day watching the baby. I could use a break."

"That's fine," Munch said. "You go, I'll watch the kids."

Lisa took off on her bicycle. Munch put a fresh diaper on Asia, dressed her in a bright pink romper, and held her until she grew limp with sleep. After settling the baby in her crib, Munch went into the kitchen. She spotted the homicide cops' business cards on top of the trash and retrieved them. After brushing them off, she stuck them in her pocket and then rejoined the girls in their room.

Miscellaneous game pieces ground underfoot as she stepped across the stained carpet of the girls' room. A naked, ink-stained doll sat propped against the bed frame. Wrinkled and soiled clothing lay everywhere.

Jill, the younger one, was eager to show Munch her treasures. She kicked aside a damp coat balled in the corner and retrieved a rock with sparkling bits of quartz in it. Munch acted suitably impressed, turning the rock in her hand so that it caught the light.

It gratified her that the two girls had warmed to her. They had regarded her with some suspicion on her first visit, but now seemed willing enough to include her in their world. She didn't kid herself, the promised pizza didn't hurt.

"I tell you what," Munch said, "Let's surprise your mommy and clean your room."

"Okay," Jill said.

"Everything is just how Mommy wants it," Charlotte protested.

"She won't mind if we hang up some of your clothes, will she?" Munch asked, picking up a set of overalls and shaking them out.

"Those go in the closet," Charlotte said sullenly.

Munch opened the closet and found it filled to overflowing.

"What is all this stuff?" she asked, pulling out a cardboard box full of high-heeled shoes, brightly colored scarves, and wigs. The ladies' footwear had been carelessly stowed. Most of the pointed tips curled up and the patent leather showed deep cracks.

"Those are for when we play dress-up," Charlotte said, trying to stuff the box back in the closet. But whatever had been behind the box had shifted and the box no longer fit. She let out a wail. "Now you ruined everything."

"We can make it all fit again," Munch said. "We just need to organize things a little better. Let's check out your dresser." She opened the top drawer of a large chest of drawers in the corner. "If we fold your shirts, they'll stay nicer."

"That's not how Mommy wants it," Charlotte insisted, her voice rising in pitch.

"Do mine," Jill said.

"All right, which ones are yours?"

She pointed a chubby finger. "This ones."

Munch wrestled the lowest drawer open and found it stuffed with socks. She dumped the drawer out at their feet, and began to sort. "It's good to be orderly, isn't it?"

"Yes," Jill said, snuggling into her lap. "Very good."

Charlotte sat on the edge of the bed and watched them. She sniffled loudly, plainly perturbed at no longer being an object of attention. "We're moving to the country," she said abruptly.

"You are?" Munch asked, surprised. Lisa had said nothing about moving.

"My mom said we're going to get a house and, if I promise to take care of it, she said I could have a horse."

The seven-year-old's declaration took Munch back to her own mother and all the promises, especially when old mom had a buzz on. Munch's early years had yo-yoed between feast and famine. Nothing for breakfast, then Mama would spend fifty bucks on a pair of patent leather shoes that Munch outgrew in a month.

You're my little princess, Mama would say, her eyes ringed black with too much eyeliner. Munch could still see the unearthly glow of her mother's brown eyes, feel the flutter of her hands, and hear the lull of her voice as she mumbled her crazy, unrealistic promises.

Those promises were pipe dreams, Munch knew now, born of opiates and good intentions.

"Daddy James said he'd come, too," Charlotte said.

"That's nice. Where's your *real* dad living now, Charlotte?" Munch asked. "Your Daddy Patrick?"

"Oh, he's dead," Jill explained with a four-year-old's pragmatism.

"Like Uncle John," Charlotte said.

Munch nodded awkwardly, fighting back sudden tears. "And what about *your* real dad?" she asked Jill.

Both girls wrinkled their noses. "Daddy Darnel talks too much and he gets all sweaty," Charlotte said. "Yucko."

"Yeah," Jill joined in, giggling. "Yucko, bucko."

"We don't like him anymore," Charlotte said. "He's a zombie pig."

"Yeah, he's a loser," Jill added, making an L with her thumb and forefinger.

Munch swallowed back a smile.

"Daddy James takes me lots of places," Jill said.

"Yeah, he's nice," Charlotte said. "Mommy says that we'll all live together."

"In your country house?" Munch asked.

"Well, maybe by the beach. We haven't decided."

Munch almost laughed. The kid might as well plan to move to the moon.

"That sounds great," Munch said. "Maybe I'll come visit you there." She didn't see the point of spoiling this kid's delusions. Let her believe what she could as long as she could. It only got worse.

"You know, when I was your age I used to like playing let's pretend. I wanted to live in the Old West when I grew up."

One day, maybe not today, the girls would need to sort out what was real and what was not. "I know," Munch said, "let's make a pact—just the three of us."

"What's a pact?" Jill asked.

"A secret promise of something we'll do one day. You want to?"

"Okay," Charlotte said, speaking for both of them.

"Hold out your right hands," Munch said, helping Jill. She dropped her voice to a whisper and the girls leaned in close. "Ten years from this day, when you're both grown up, we'll all meet again on this very spot."

"That's it?" Charlotte asked.

"You have to cross your hearts and swear," Munch added.

The girls solemnly complied.

She pictured herself explaining to Charlotte and Jill at that future date how their mother had been a flake and that all her promises, though possibly made in good faith, had been bullshit. She would tell the two girls that they were born into the family they were born into and that was their fate. She would explain to them both that they had only themselves to take care of themselves—that they could count on no one. Well, maybe God, but even He had His own agenda.

And if they asked her, "Wasn't there anything you could have done for us then?"

What would she say to them? That it wasn't her business? That she'd been too caught up in her own problems?

Speaking of which . . .

She pulled out the picture in her pocket and showed it to the girls. Charlotte took the photo and studied it for only a moment before she asked, "Who's this?" Munch saw she was pointing at the man in the suit.

"I don't know. How about the other guy?" Munch asked, pointing to the long-hair. "Do you know him?"

"Sure, that's Daddy James."

Jill popped up, reaching for the picture. "I want to see. I want to see."

Munch obliged her.

"Uh-huh," Jill agreed. "Daddy James."

Munch felt a coldness fill her heart. Lisa said she didn't recognize the description of the guy in the truck with Sleaze. How deeply was she involved? Munch's reverie was cut short by the sounds of Lisa wheeling her bike in through the doorway.

"You two stay in here. I need to talk to your mommy for a second."

Munch walked out to the front room and held up the photograph to Lisa. "Anything you want to tell me?"

Lisa grabbed for the picture, but Munch pulled it back.

"Where'd you get that?" Lisa asked.

"You know this guy?" Munch asked.

Lisa's gaze strayed to the bedroom where the kids played. Munch saw the calculations going on behind her eyes. "Yeah, I know him." She put the pizza down.

"This is the guy I saw with Sleaze, the one I was asking about with the lightning bolt tattoo."

Lisa lit a cigarette, taking a long time to take a drag, watching Munch through the smoke with her little pig eyes. "So what about it?" she finally asked.

"You know where he is now?"

"What's it to you?"

"He might know something about who shot Sleaze."

She turned weary eyes to Munch and said, "Listen, I know your heart's in the right place. But believe me, you don't want to get involved. These people don't give a shit who gets hurt, understand?"

Munch remembered the bodies in Venice.

"The best thing you can do," Lisa said, "is to freeze. Pretend you don't know anything."

Well, that was almost true, Munch thought.

The girls came running into the kitchen. Lisa cleared the table and Munch pulled up four chairs. Asia woke up crying. Munch lifted the baby out of her crib and gave her a bottle. The little girls chattered as they picked toppings of the pizza, making up a game with the rings of pepperoni. With Asia sitting on her lap, Munch ate a slice of pizza. She never felt the food hit her stomach. She couldn't stop thinking about what Deb had said about Tux taking Boogie on the road with him. It didn't take much to put that whole scenario together. The guy was just using Boogie as a cover, a diversion. The idea sickened her. The first time a man had treated the boy decently and it was in the commission of a felony. When she said her good nights, Munch gave all the children an extra-long squeeze. She could barely bring herself to look Lisa in the face.

Lisa watched Munch's car drive away and then flicked her porch light three times. An eighteen-wheeler parked down the road fired up its diesel engine. Lisa waited as it pulled away from the curb and stopped in the street outside her gate.

She glanced nervously up and down the street, wondering what other eyes were on them. Her palms beaded with sweat when the door to the semi swung open and the large, leather-clad driver stepped down.

"Did she bring it?" Tux asked.

"Yeah, but the shit was gone already."

"Fuck. You saying that bitch ripped me off?"

"No, she's all AA'd back. She don't use or drink or anything." Lisa scratched at a piece of dried food on her shirt. "Maybe the dope was gone from before."

Without warning, Tux's hand shot out, delivering a back-handed slap to Lisa's face and knocking her off her feet. She didn't try to get back up, just held an open palm out as if to ward him off.

"Don't fuck with me, you stupid cunt," he said. "There wasn't time. Give me her address. I think it's time I pay this bitch a little visit."

"I don't know where she lives," Lisa said.

Tux took a step forward, grabbing her wrist and pulling his fist back.

"Wait," Lisa said, trying to protect her face with her free hand. "She only gave me her phone number, but I know where she works."

"Yeah," Tux said. "So do I. What does she keep coming over here for if she's so holy roller?"

"She wants the baby, Sleaze's little girl."

"For what?"

"She wants to like adopt her."

"If she keeps fucking with our business, she can kiss those plans goodbye. You tell her that. Better yet, let me see that kid. I'll deliver the message myself."

Munch pushed the speed limit all the way home. Before she took the next step, she needed to take care of a few loose ends.

She parked in the alley behind her apartment and grabbed the pocket knife from her glove compartment. Looking both ways to make sure no one was watching, she slipped the knife open and crouched down to the sewer grate. She groped for and found the twine. It severed easily. She let go of the string and was rewarded with the sound of the dope splashing as it hit waste water. Shit to shit. It felt good, but she didn't spend any time congratulating herself. Not for something she should have done in the first place.

She went back to her car and retrieved the packet of documents from under her spare tire. Inside, after locking her deadbolts, she fanned the contents of the packet across her bed.

It wasn't until she got to the bottom of the pile that she found the things that disturbed her the most. It was an interoffice memo on FBI stationery recommending that the raid on the Canyonville compound be "delayed until the end of October when the marijuana crop will be gathered and baled."

It was almost ten when she called the Snakepit. The bartender summoned Deb to the phone.

"Hey," Munch said, "it's me."

"You coming up?"

"How about if I pay for you all to come see me?"

"I can't leave just now. It's a harvest moon, if you know what I'm saying."

"I really need to see you guys," Munch said. Did the feds have the Snakepit's phone tapped?

"Well, get your ass up here, woman."

"No, that won't work. I'm kinda in the middle of a few things myself right now. I'll catch you later."

She hung up the phone, went back out to her car, and stuffed the packet of paperwork back under her spare tire. When she came back inside, she emptied the contents of her pockets on the dresser. She fingered the business cards for a moment, reading the names. She thought about the two cops she had seen on TV and at the coroner's office. Detective Alex Perez had to be the friendly-looking one.

14

Blackstone checked his messages upon arriving at work Tuesday morning and learned that Bernie had called. When he dialed the Vice extension, Bernie answered on the first ring.

"What's up?" Blackstone asked.

"You were interested in military weaponry, right?"

"You got something?"

"You're going to owe me a drink."

"All right, all right. What did you hear?"

"Why don't you meet me in Santa Monica and you can hear for yourself."

"When?"

"Eleven good for you?"

"Where?"

"Chez Jays."

"That little joint across from the pier?"

"I'll see you there."

* * *

Chez Jays would have been easy to miss. The low wooden build-ing dissolved easily into the surrounding backdrop of hotels and office buildings, just as the unremarkable blue letters on the faded sign over the saloon-style doors did nothing to call attention to the place. But that, Bernie said, was part of its charm. Blackstone knew that the proximity of motel rooms with their special hourly rates also added to the restaurant's allure.

The tiny bar and grill did a phenomenal amount of business. The owner was a character actor with many ties to the Hollywood crowd. He'd managed to hit a vein with his small establishment—finding just the right measures of exclusiveness, location, and visi-bility. The drinks were strong and the scampi fresh. But if you didn't know someone connected to the film industry, you would be hard-pressed to get a reservation for dinner.

The lunch crowd, Bernie assured Blackstone, was different.

Blackstone waved off the valet. The lot held only maybe twenty cars, and it was less than a quarter full. He chose a spot on the end away from the other vehicles. Even if someone parked next to him, they would have to pull in on his left, which meant that their driver's door wouldn't be opening into him. He would have preferred a spot sheltered on either side from inconsiderate drivers who thought nothing of nicking paint jobs, but was forced to make do. Hopefully, Bernie's information would be worth his while.

He stepped into the darkened restaurant and took a second to get his bearings, resting a hand on the chest-high ship's wheel anchored to the floor. The smell of beer and whiskey assaulted his nostrils, and he blinked several times to make the transition from bright daylight to the smoky twilight atmosphere. Red-and-white-checked tablecloths covered the vacant tables in the center of the room. The majority of the midday clientele sat at the J-shaped bar, waiting, no doubt, for the sun to go down. They were served by a burly bartender who called each of them by their first name.

"Be right with you," he said when he noticed Blackstone standing there. He had to raise his voice to be heard above the TV that was mounted high in one corner and tuned to a game that no one was watching.

"That's all right," Blackstone told him. "I'm meeting some-one."

The bartender had already turned away, busy loading his cash register with soggy one-dollar bills.

Blackstone spotted Bernie at one of the red Naugahyde-covered booths near the back. He wasn't alone. The gaunt Caucasian woman with him had a used look about her. Her hair was pulled back in a ponytail, and she wore one of those T-shirts they sold on the boardwalk with lace around the collar and the sleeves.

Bernie's hand rested on the back of the booth, almost touching her neck. He saw Blackstone out of the corner of his eye and held up his fingers, motioning Blackstone to hang back.

Blackstone pawed at the sawdust on the floor and studied the signed movie posters taped to the walls. The phone rang and the bartender answered it, listened a moment, and then said, "He's still not here." The patrons laughed. Bernie motioned for Blackstone to join them.

As Blackstone slid in the booth opposite the pair, he overheard the woman saying: "I kept telling him not the fashe, you know?"

Her voice was garbled. Bernie murmured something, patted her hand, and then acknowledged Blackstone.

"Jigsaw, this is Angie."

She turned sad eyes to greet him. The blood vessels were broken in the left eye; her upper lip was split and swollen. "How do you do?" she said between clenched teeth. Her lips curled back far enough when she spoke so that he could see the wires that held her jaws together.

He guessed she was in her twenties and then quickly calculated the rest of her pedigree: doper, hooker, petty thief. "What happened to you?" he asked.

"Shun of a bitch went off on me," she said.

"Angie got ahold of a real freak," Bernie cut in.

"Put me out of bishness," she lisped as saliva leaked down her chin. She mopped the drool with a cocktail napkin.

"Tell him what you told me, Angie."

"Champion shaid to make shure you promish," she said. For Blackstone's benefit she added, "Champion ish my man."

"You tell him if the information is good," Bernie said, "I'll lose some paperwork. You check it out on the street, my word is good."

"I know it is," she said. They exchanged private looks and she continued. "Thish guy was amped to the max."

"What guy?" Blackstone asked.

"I should of jusht shined him, you know?"

Jigsaw looked over at Bernie. Bernie nodded for him to be patient.

"He shaid either I blow him or he'd blow me up."

"Blow you up?" Blackstone asked.

"He shtuck a grenade between my legs and told me to make a wish."

"A grenade, like a hand grenade?" Blackstone asked.

"Yeah, like what elshe would I mean?"

"What did this guy look like? Did you get a name?"

"I got all that already, Jigsaw," Bernie cut in. "White guy, mustache, reddish hair. They didn't exchange names, but she described two tattoos that the guy had on his forearms. On the right, he had crossed pistons and the words *Ride to Live, Live to Ride,* surrounded with a ring of red and black swastikas. And you're going to love this. On the left forearm he had a four-inch-diameter blue target with the words *One Shot, One Kill* written above and below."

"That's a Marine tattoo, isn't it?" Blackstone asked.

Bernie nodded. "Force recon, sniper corps."

Blackstone whistled. "What about the car?"

"It was a Hertz rental with Oregon plates. We're checking on it."

"And a car sheet," she said.

"What's a car sheet?" he asked.

"You know, like to put a baby in?"

"You mean a car seat?"

"Yesh."

"You done good, Angie," Bernie said. "Now Jigsaw here is going to buy us both a drink."

Blackstone left after paying for their Long Island iced teas. The trip had been well worth it. The Oregon plates on the rented vehicle cinched his suspicions that the FBI's case involving the stolen National Guard weaponry also involved a smuggling operation across the Oregon/California border. Smugglers often used rented cars that they paid for with cash. When Bernie described the target tattoo, Blackstone's scalp had tingled. The guy was an expert sniper, if you believed the skin advertisement. The crossed piston tattoo was also familiar as a favorite of bikers, and bikers loved their speed. It was all starting to fit.

He shuddered at the image of a group of meth-fueled neo-Nazis armed with automatic weapons and explosives. If they didn't get a handle on this one fast, the streets were going to run with blood. It had already started.

When he got back to the station, he gave Deputy Tom Moody a call.

"I just got the picture of your John Doe," Moody said after Blackstone identified himself.

"I've got a name to go with the picture," Blackstone said. "Jonathan Garillo."

"How'd you ID him so fast? Get lucky with the prints?"

"No, some woman came to the coroner's office while we were doing the autopsy. She wrote his name on a piece of paper before she fled the scene."

"Who was she?"

"We're still working on that. We were able to lift some words off the paper she left us. One of them was *Canyonville.*"

Blackstone heard Moody suck and inhale. He pictured the sheriff holding a pipe and staring thoughtfully out his window. "What else?" Moody asked

"*Inventory* and the words *ace boon coon.* Ring any bells?"

"Nah, that's a new one on me. Inventory could be something interesting."

"That's what I thought. This Jonathan Garillo might have hung with bikers."

"Yeah, we got some of those assholes up here," Moody said. "Gypsy Jokers, Hessians, all your Bay Area rejects."

"I think this all ties into a bigger investigation," Blackstone said. "Last month the Kern County National Guard Armory was burglarized. The thieves made off with explosives and weapons."

"Yeah," Moody said, "I know all about it. M-14s started showing up here three weeks ago. I notified the feds."

"So you're working together?" Blackstone asked.

Moody's laugh was bitter. "They told me to stay out of their way. In other words, fuck you very much."

"Well, maybe we can help each other," Blackstone said.

"Sounds good to me," Moody said. "Goddamn feds are dragging their heels."

Blackstone promised to stay in touch and hung up.

Alex stuck his head in the doorway. "I got through to that doctor in Palm Springs," he said, "the one that owns the apartment building on Hampton. He told me that unit number six was rented to a guy named John Garillo."

"So maybe we got a case of mistaken identity," Blackstone said, "and Garillo was the target all along."

"I called Jeff," Alex said, "and told him to compare the bullets from the Garillo case with the double in Venice. He says he'll do the best he can. Too bad the feds kept the other bullets."

"We'll just have to work around that." Blackstone drew another circle, one large enough to accommodate both victims' names: Ruiz/Guzman. He drew a line connecting the victims, then backtracked through his notes. The Ruiz woman's boss, the bakery owner, had mentioned a white woman at the scene with him—a woman with a baby. He made a note to show the man the mug shot of Lisa Slokum. Then he tapped his pencil point on Jane Dirty Nails's circle. Or could it be her?

15

Claire Donavon thought that the file room of the Federal Building on Wilshire Boulevard in Westwood was one of the most comprehensive in the nation as well as the most orderly. Referred to as the catacombs, it was located in the basement, three floors underground. Bright fluorescent lights kept the labyrinth of hallways lined with filing cabinets in a state of perpetual brightness.

The personnel files were arranged alphabetically and cross-referenced by profession. They included quarterly evaluations, original applications, and psychological reviews, and were full of interesting asides that often proved invaluable. Today, she was interested in city employees. Her operatives watching the house in Inglewood had made note of the license plate of Lisa Slokum's visitor. From there it had been an easy matter to come up with a name. Not surprisingly, Lisa Slokum's caller—the woman who had already caused them problems—had a record and was on probation. Useful.

The file the FBI agent thumbed through now caused her to smile. Before becoming a probation officer, Mrs. Olivia Scott had applied to six different law enforcement agencies—another wannabe. The woman would be no problem at all. Before she left, Claire Donavon looked up one more file and then headed for Santa Monica.

It took less than three minutes from the time Claire entered the Santa Monica Courthouse building to when she was seated across the desk from the probation officer.

"FBI?" Mrs. Scott said, fingering the embossed business card. "You know, when I was your age they didn't allow women to be field agents in the FBI."

"That's a shame," Claire said. "The agency cheated itself out of many wonderful applicants." Mrs. Scott had applied in '68, but Claire didn't disclose that she knew this. She never tipped her hand when it wasn't necessary.

"I'll help any way I can. Anything you need"—Olivia Scott leaned closer and lowered her voice—"any way you need it handled. You'll find me most cooperative."

Claire smiled. "I appreciate that. A case I'm working on involves one of your clients."

"I don't believe in coddling these people," Olivia Scott said. "Half of them—and I'm being generous with that statistic— should never have been allowed back on the streets. They're animals. Who is it that you're interested in?"

"Miranda Mancini."

"Really?"

"You sound surprised."

"I shouldn't," she said. "Nothing in this business should surprise me. I just thought . . . never mind. What has she done?"

"I wish I could disclose that to you."

"I understand," the probation officer said, disappointment showing clearly on her face. "Just tell me what you need."

"Let's start with her file and the terms of her probation."

"Certainly." Mrs. Scott turned to her filing cabinet. "Our clients," she said the word as if it tasted foul, "have no rights in regards to search and seizure. I can draw up a warrant and have it at her work in forty minutes. I don't believe in coddling these people."

"Yes," Claire said. "You mentioned that."

At mid-morning, Munch lifted the Dodge Dart's rear tire off its studs. Her mind wasn't on her work. She balanced the tire on her knee for a second and then set it on the floor. She took a deep breath, held it, and then wrestled off the brake drum. Asbestos dust swirled around her head. At one point, she had taken to wearing a surgical mask when she worked on brakes. Then one day she caught herself lifting the mask to take a drag from her cigarette and realized she was being ridiculous.

"Does he need them?" Jack yelled from the office.

She leaned forward and studied the lining of the brake shoes. "Yeah, he's almost to the rivets."

"I'll call him," Jack said.

A moment later he reemerged. "You got it," he said. "I ordered your parts."

"Uh, Jack?" she asked.

"Yeah?"

"What would you think about me bringing a baby to work?"

"Are you pregnant?"

"No," she said quickly. "It's my, uh, goddaughter."

"You got a goddaughter?" he asked.

"Yeah, it's a recent development. Anyway, I was wondering if she could like tag along while I was working."

"How old is she?"

"Six months. If I set up her crib in the—"

"Stop right there," he said, holding up his hand. "A garage is no place for a baby. What were you thinking?"

She was thinking there were worse places, but said nothing. His expression told her that nothing she could say would affect his decision. She recognized stubborn. It had been a stupid idea anyway. Why hadn't she realized that when she rehearsed the pitch earlier? Time for plan two.

"I need to take a few days off," she said.

"When?" he asked.

"I was hoping the rest of the week."

"Is anything wrong?"

"I just have some things I need to take care of."

"Check with Lou," he said.

She looked across the lot and saw the other mechanic, Lou, shaking hands with a teenage boy. He flashed her a grin and walked over to her.

"I'm thinking of taking some vacation time," she said when he joined her.

"What did Jack say?"

"He said I should check with you."

"I'm taking a week in December," he said. "When did you want to go?"

"Now."

"Kind of sudden, isn't it?"

"Just tell me yes or no."

"Geez, so go. I was just asking. You don't need to bite my head off." He fanned a fistful of twenties at her. "I sold the Impala," he said. They had bought the car together last month when the owner couldn't afford to repair it. Lou had bought a used transmission, and she had installed it. After some minor cosmetic improvements, they painted "$600" on the windshield in white shoe polish and parked the Chevy on the corner, taking care to wash off the grime that settled on the paint job every couple days.

"You get our price?" she asked.

"And he paid cash."

"That's my favorite kind of money." She held out her hand, and he counted out her cut—fifteen twenty-dollar bills.

"So what are you going to do?" he asked.

"Do?"

"On your vacation. Are you going anywhere special?"

"I have some stuff I need to take care of," she said.

"Well, have fun."

"Oh, yeah. Nothing but."

Just before lunch, as she was washing up, Jack knocked on the door to the back room. "Are you decent?" he asked.

She dried her hands. "It's open."

He came in and sat on a case of coolant bottles. He watched her for a moment and then asked, "So you'll be back Monday?"

"Yeah."

"You aren't in any kind of trouble, are you?"

She crossed her arms over her chest. "Can't I just take a little time off without everyone giving me the third degree?"

"Relax. I'm just concerned," he said. "I know you've had some shake-ups lately. I told Lou—"

She sighed. Anyone who said women gossiped obviously hadn't spent time around a bunch of men. "No offense, Jack, but I really wish you'd keep out of my personal life."

He stood without saying another word and left. She watched him go, saw the slump of his shoulders and the shake of his head. She almost called after him to tell him never mind, that it was all right, but she didn't. She had a right to her privacy, after all, and not to be the subject of their speculations. There was caring and there was interfering. Jack needed to learn those limits.

When she stepped out of the back room, she saw Mrs. Scott pulling into the shop's driveway. Another woman followed in a separate car. Both women parked in the adjoining lot, side by side. Neither smiled or reacted when an eighteen-wheeler behind them applied its air brakes. Munch felt a momentary weakness flash through her legs and then straightened her back. What was the worse they could do, kill her and eat her? Screw 'em.

The two women exited their cars. Mrs. Scott beckoned Munch to her with an imperious finger. Munch dusted herself off and approached slowly.

"What's up?"

Mrs. Scott smiled thinly. "Special Agent Donavon has some questions for you."

Special Agent? Munch set her face in a blank expression, neither bored nor worried, and waited.

The FBI agent turned to Mrs. Scott. "I hope you don't mind, but I need to speak to Ms. Mancini alone."

Mrs. Scott minded very much, Munch saw as the probation officer walked stiffly back to her car. It probably killed her to be so close to the action and shut out. Munch would trade places with her in a heartbeat. She turned to Special Agent Donavon. "Will this take long? I'm pretty busy."

The agent looked around before speaking. "You like working here?"

Was there some sort of implied threat in her tone? "I guess. Pays well, the people are nice." What did she want?

"What was your relationship with Jonathan Garillo?"

Munch forced her face not to twitch. "He's someone I used to know."

"Did he visit you before he died?"

"Yes. He came to see me the day he was killed." She figured she wasn't telling this woman anything she didn't already know.

"What did he say to you?"

The shadow from the semi hadn't moved. There was no parking on Sepulveda Boulevard and the light should have changed by now. Movement out the passenger-side window caught her attention. A man's arm, clothed in a black leather motorcycle jacket, reached out. The hand adjusted the side mirror, which jiggled in time to the diesel rig's idle. She saw the passenger's garbled reflection and realized that he was watching her. She couldn't make out his face, only that he had reddish hair and wore mirrored sunglasses.

"Ms. Mancini?"

"Hmm?"

"I asked you what the two of you spoke about."

Munch looked back at the agent. "Not much. He wanted me to come hang out with him. I told him I didn't associate with his kind anymore. That I was on probation."

"Did he give you anything?"

"Just a hard time," Munch said. The woman didn't smile.

The hand retreated from the window and then returned. This time it waved something. A pink flag. No, not a flag. She saw the sleeves, the feet at the bottom of the pant legs. It was a baby's romper. Asia's romper. The one she had been wearing the night before.

"You've never done federal time, have you? Mrs. Scott is fully prepared to assist me in any way I choose. For instance, if someone were in my way, interfering with a investigation, and she could put that person away for thirty days . . . "

Munch knew this power game only too well. This was the part where she was supposed to roll over and show her soft underbelly. She cast her eyes down and let her shoulders slump. "Please don't do that. I haven't done anything wrong." She gave the agent a hopeful, tentative smile back, hoping she'd buy the act.

"I don't want to hurt you," Claire Donavon said. "I want to feel that you're doing everything you can to be a good citizen." She put a hand on Munch's shoulder. Anyone observing their exchange would think they were getting along just fine. "But if I find out you've been fucking with me," the FBI agent continued, smiling with only her mouth, "I'll nail your little ass to the wall."

"You will, huh?" Munch blinked once, feeling the anger rush up her neck, making her fist clench. She shrugged off the agent's hand, hoping the guy in the eighteen-wheeler was watching. "Why don't you take your best shot, bitch, and spare me the bullshit."

Claire Donavon studied Munch for a long minute and then beckoned to Mrs. Scott. "Your client has just told me that she's been associating with known felons. I believe that violates the terms of her probation."

Mrs. Scott produced a pair of handcuffs. Munch glanced at the semi, heard the thunk of gears shifting. The truck groaned as its brakes released. She didn't look over in her co-workers' direction. She didn't want a last image of the expressions in their eyes as she was manacled and placed in the back seat of Mrs. Scott's car.

The drive to jail seemed to take no time at all.

16

That evening, when Blackstone got home, he studied his living quarters from Claire Donavon's eyes. Would she appreciate his strategic location? Or would she wrinkle her nose at the proximity of the freight trains and the looming profile of the downtown office buildings?

His mail was mostly junk. He put it to use lighting a fire in what had formerly been used as an incinerator but now served as his fireplace. The high ceiling and open floor plan of the converted brewery made it difficult to heat, but he wanted Claire to be comfortable. This was a calculated sacrifice to his own comfort. And later, if his loft got too warm, he could always crack open the skylight transom directly over his bed.

Again, he surveyed the room through the eyes of his visitor. Everyone's first impression was always how unobstructed his space was. It was the cathedral ceilings and the absence of inner walls, he knew. The color scheme also enhanced the room's natural simplicity. What walls weren't brick or steel, he'd painted white. The arched ceiling was blond pine and a masterpiece of engineering that eliminated the need for center beams. Instead, the roof was supported by an intricate network of collar braces and crown supports that ran the length of the building and resembled the skeleton of an overturned ship. She would like it, he decided.

While the room heated, he retired to the small but efficient kitchen in the corner space beneath his bedroom loft to make ready for his guest. Sink, stove, and refrigerator were all within easy reach of each other. A butcher-block counter sat atop a storage area. Filling a teakettle with water, he set it on a medium flame. Then he laid out the tea bags, sugar, and two cups. They would eat at the counter, he decided, and set two places. Arranging the plates, napkins, and silverware just right seemed to take him an extraordinarily long time. He checked his watch. He hadn't even showered and changed. He should have told her to come later.

He rushed through his shower, barely taking the time to dry himself. His chinos stuck to his legs as he tried to pull them over his still-damp skin, and the first two shirts he put on were all wrong. Without even realizing it, he had strapped on his gun belt over his pants. Six-fifteen found him standing before his open armoire, undecided what to do with his weapon. He usually kept the two-inch Smith & Wesson Chief Special in the holster at the base of his spine or beside his bed next to the phone. Surely, this evening would not be one of those occasions that required deadly force. He slid off his belt, putting the gun in the pocket of his coat, then refolded a shirt he'd disturbed and pulled a sweater on.

Twenty minutes later, he heard the dogs. His only neighbor was a dog kennel and the boarders there always let him know when a car approached his gate. Their chorus of frantic yelping now told him that his guest had arrived

"I'm sorry I'm late," Claire said when he opened the door.

"Did you get lost?" he asked, taking the bag of Chinese take-out from her arms.

She held up dirty hands. "Flat tire," she explained. "Do you have somewhere I can wash up?"

He directed her to the bathroom and then laid out their dinner. Minutes later she emerged from the bathroom. He noted that she had applied a fresh coat of lipstick.

When they finished eating, he suggested they take their tea into the main room and get comfortable. She surprised him when she ignored the obvious choice of the couch and instead remained standing in front of the fireplace.

"Are you cold?" he asked.

"No, it just feels good to stand. I've just been sitting all day, doing paperwork." She pointed to the lone picture on the mantel. "Your mother?" she asked.

"The grand dame herself."

"She looks—"

"Prosperous?" Blackstone asked.

"I was going to say elegant. I like the coat. Is it sable?"

"You have a good eye," he said.

"The frame is Cartier, isn't it?"

"I'm doubly impressed. It's somewhat ornate for my tastes, but it was a birthday gift from Evelyn last year, so what could I do?"

"And Evelyn is?"

"My mother."

"And your father?" she asked.

"Two husbands ago. We don't hear from him much. Are you always this inquisitive?"

"Comes with the job, I guess. Does it bother you?"

"For you I'm an open book. In the spirit of interoffice cooperation and all that."

Her fingers grazed the Lalique crystal frog next to the framed picture. "You don't seem to be hurting," she said.

"It doesn't cost that much more to go first-class," he said. "Not if you focus on the things that really interest you." Her hands fluttered nervously to the top button of her blouse. A trace of black grease was still visible on her knuckles. She had also chipped a nail.

As they talked he opened the bottom drawer of the chessboard table and removed a heavy box wrapped in a soft white towel. Balancing the box in his lap, he folded the towel twice and used it to wipe off the table's clear lacquer surface, taking a moment to admire the alternating squares of burgundy Italian elm burl and blond maple that lay beneath the protective coating. If only life were laid out in such an orderly fashion, with each space denoted geometrically and all players a known quantity.

"How about you?" he asked. "Do you have family near?"

"They're in Arizona," she said. "Tempe."

"That's a college town, isn't it?"

"Yes. Both my parents are professors."

"What did they think about you joining the FBI?"

"They were disappointed. My father thought I could be anything I wanted."

He grunted a small laugh. "Sounds like something Evelyn would say."

When he was satisfied that the cloth had not found any stray dust, he lifted the lid off the rosewood box on his lap. The chess pieces were individually wrapped. They were made by Jaqué, the prestigious London firm. The set had cost him over a thousand dollars, but it was well worth the expense. Each piece was hand-carved and -weighted. The black pieces were ebony, the white, Indian boxwood; circles of leather had been glued to the bottoms.

The chessmen weren't overly ornate. The knight was the classic horse head, not some armor-clad crusader aboard a rearing steed. Serious players cared more for the weight and feel of the pieces. He'd seen some sets where it was impossible to distinguish bishops from pawns, kings from queens, and had refused to play with them.

Working from the magazine notes, he arranged the pieces of the Fischer-Najdorf game played in 1962. The game had gotten interesting after the thirteenth move. Fischer had begun his favorite way—moving out his king's pawn to free diagonal files for his queen and bishop. Najdorf had responded with the classic Sicilian defense. They had exchanged material, a knight and two pawns each. Fischer castled, Najdorf did not—devoting his energies instead to forming a strong center position.

It was at this point that Blackstone invited Claire to sit.

"I'll take white," he said.

"That makes me Najdorf, I suppose," she said.

"Do you mind?"

"Not at all. Where's your chess clock?"

He pulled out the dual-faced timer. "What should I set it for?" he asked.

"Let's try five-minute intervals."

"Speed chess?" he asked.

"It's a good exercise for making yourself rely more on your intuition," she said. "Is it your move?"

He answered by placing his queen on A4. "Check," he said.

"You picked an interesting place to begin," she said and brought her knight over to protect her king.

"Good move," he said.

"It was the obvious choice," she said.

His heart beat faster. Now the game was going to heat up. He considered the board and said, "I know about the Canyonville connection."

She looked at him, but said nothing.

He captured her bishop with his rook. She lifted an eyebrow. His rook was vulnerable to a center pawn. Hardly an even trade of material. She took the bait.

"So you understand our involvement," she said, capturing his rook.

"Was John Garillo an informant?" he asked.

"I'll check with the head office."

He moved his knight towards the center of the board. "To see if he was or to see if you can tell me?"

"Either or both," she said, her eyes never leaving the board. The ticking of the clock seemed to fill the room. She brought her kingside bishop out, clearing the rank of squares between her king and rook. She was looking to castle, a good protective move. It had just come too late.

He moved his knight again. "Check."

Her only out was to move her king, which meant she couldn't castle later. It was against the rules for her to castle out of check. Obviously, she was a stickler for rules. She moved her king a square toward him. She had only two choices.

Again he brought his knight around. "Check."

"Why do I feel this sense of unrelenting pressure?" she asked. She moved her king out of check.

His next move would involve some finesse. He moved his bishop, removed his hand, and then quickly tried to slide the piece back to its original position.

She stopped him. "You took your hand off."

"I meant to—"

"Sorry," she said, "but that's the rule."

"I don't think you're sorry at all," he said, smiling ruefully. He watched her assess the board. Her eyes darted from space to space as she played out the consequences of her next action. He knew what she was thinking. She was asking herself how she could capitalize on his mistake. Moving his bishop there had left it vulnerable to her bishop. But if she captured him with her bishop, he could retaliate with the pawn in front of his king. Then she could bring out her queen and threaten his king, perhaps shift the momentum of the game.

She captured his bishop. He groaned for her benefit, then captured hers. She obviously didn't understand the principal of positional sacrifices, either.

"Would you like some more tea?" he asked, his hand hovering over the stop button on the time clock.

"Stalling for time?" she asked.

"It's your move," he reminded her, stopping the clock. "This is a friendly game, Claire. Or did you want to make it more interesting?"

"What did you have in mind? A wager?"

"That would work," he said. "What shall we put at stake?"

"How about a no-lose proposition?" she asked, her eyes locking on his. They were very clear, he noticed.

He put his hand on hers, caressing the flesh of her wrist with his thumb. "How this evening ends," he said, his voice suddenly throaty, "what happens between you and me, won't be decided by anything but mutual consent. I think we have that already. Don't we, Claire?"

He had her full attention. He could see it in the way her eyes watched his lips move as he spoke.

"What *do* you want?" she asked in a husky voice. She didn't pull her hand away.

"If I win, I get to ask you a question that you must answer. If you win, I'll owe you an answer."

"How do I know that you have any answers that I'm interested in?"

"Nothing's more dangerous than a biker on speed with a live grenade, don't you think?" he said.

She looked at him, then back at the board. "Am I being hustled here?"

"Do you want to concede?" he asked.

Instead of answering him, she brought her queen out. The pawn he had used to capture her bishop was all that stood between her queen and his king. He slid his kingside rook to the center of the board. She responded by moving her queenside rook a square forward—out of its corner. She restarted the clock.

"When will you be done with my evidence?" he asked.

"Is that your question?"

"No. It's premature for me to collect on our bet. I haven't won yet."

"That's right," she said.

He moved his rook across the board, threatening her queen. If she captured his rook with her queen, then his knight would take her queen and put her in check.

"Rat," she said.

"Tell you what," he said. "I'm going to take us off the timer." He turned the clock off; she didn't object.

She pondered her next move for fifteen minutes. Then a smile spread over her face as she moved her queen back to stand beside her king. It was a good move, but not good enough to save her.

He moved his queen one square diagonally. His play was what is known in chess as a quiet move. Quiet moves are played during an attacking sequence and, although they pose no immediate threat, will clear the board for a much more aggressive move later. Often quiet moves are the deadliest of all.

She brought her queen out again, biting her lower lip. He could see that she was feeling desperate to bring out material, to give herself offensive options. She closed her mouth again and he found himself studying the moisture that remained on her lips.

Noticing his delay, she looked up from the board. For a moment their eyes locked, then he captured the pawn next to her king.

"Check."

She couldn't take his bishop without moving into check from his queen. She moved her king out of harm's way. He moved his bishop.

"Do you want a notepad?" he asked. She nodded yes.

While she plotted her options, he studied her face. The line between her eyes deepened and her nostrils flared slightly. She wasn't in check. Yet. But he had rendered her helpless. He was watching her eyes the moment that realization dawned on her. He also realized that he had an erection.

"So what's your question?" she finally asked.

"I'm not ready to ask it yet."

"What happens now?"

He stood and took her hand. "Come on," he said, pulling her to her feet. "I want to show you the rest of the house."

Later, hours later, her head nestled in the crook of his arm. As she ran a lazy finger up his breastbone, she said, "That was a nice touch earlier."

He smoothed back her hair. "Which?"

"You know," she said, "when you pretended to make a mistake. I'll have to remember that."

"If you want to stop by tomorrow," he said, "I'll give you what I have on that biker with the grenade."

"Sounds like a very bad man," she said, teasing his nipple with her teeth.

Blackstone let out an involuntary groan. "Yeah," he said, rolling toward her, "he beat up a hooker, but she came forward."

"Umm," she said, grinding into him, "that was good of her."

He burrowed his face into her neck and she said something that he missed. She pushed him away and asked again. "Did she ID the car he was driving?"

He had to take a second to compose himself; he was having trouble concentrating. His blood, it seemed, was busy elsewhere. "Rental, Oregon plates. Mercury Comet, she said."

She put a hand to his mouth. "No more shoptalk, okay? Tomorrow will take care of itself." Then she pulled him on top of her. This time he was the one to stop.

"My turn," he said. "Was John Garillo working for you? Was he a snitch?"

"I think you wasted your question. It sounds like you figured that one out for yourself."

"Does that mean yes?" he asked. But she didn't answer, she was too busy doing incredible things with her lower anatomy. He wondered briefly if she was into yoga or some other exotic discipline. All talk of the job was soon forgotten.

They made love until they were both spent. Afterward, Claire fell immediately into a deep sleep.

Blackstone listened to her rhythmic breathing. Somewhere outside, a freight train lumbered down the tracks. Southbound, he decided, with a full load. He knew all the sounds the trains made: the whoosh as two passed each other, the screech of their brakes. Even at a distance of miles he could tell whether they were approaching or departing. He stared at the stars and catalogued the day's events, including this most pleasant of endings. He had no regrets, and judging from her contented smile as she slumbered, neither did she. Yet something nagged at the edge of his consciousness, something he'd seen or something he'd heard, but he was too tired to chase the elusive thread of reasoning. If it was important, he decided, yawning, whatever it was would come to him tomorrow.

He shut his eyes and a last image of the room formed in that netherworld of consciousness between dreams and reality. The lamp by his bed became a queen. His last muddled thought as he drifted off to sleep was that she had him in check and he'd better do something about that.

17

Munch woke up Wednesday morning to the sound of a phone ringing. It obviously wasn't for her. She rolled over in her cot and stared at the graffiti-covered walls, surprised that she had slept so well. Throwing off the thin wool blanket, she stood and walked over to the door of her cell.

"Can I make a phone call?" she asked the guard.

The guard, a red-headed black woman, looked up from her newspaper. "Maybe later." The guard went back to her paper and then looked up again, taking in the sight of Munch in her grease-stained overalls. "You work at a gas station or something?"

"A garage in the Valley." *At least I did until yesterday,* she thought. Who knew what was going to happen now.

"What kind of stuff you do? Change oil?"

"Tune-ups, brake work, clutches, electrical. You name it."

"You ever work on Chevys?"

"Chevys are my favorites," Munch said, moving closer to the bars that separated them. "What kind you got?"

The guard put down her newspaper. "A '67 Camaro."

"Rally Sport?"

"Super Sport."

"Great car."

"When it's working," she said.

"Have you been having problems?" Munch asked.

"Yeah, when it gets hot—"

"It won't start," Munch finished her sentence for her.

The guard scooted her chair over to Munch's cell. "I put in another battery, ignition switch, a starter—"

"That's not the problem," Munch said. "It doesn't even click when you turn the key, right?"

"That's right."

"But then you wait twenty minutes and it starts right up."

"Yeah, yeah. That's exactly right."

Munch read the woman's nameplate. "I've fixed that before, Officer Reese," Munch said. "You sure I can't get to a phone any sooner?"

The guard looked both ways. "I don't know what you did, honey. But I've got orders to isolate you."

"I guess a cigarette is out of the question."

"Sorry," she said. "How did you fix those other cars?"

"I wired in a second auxiliary solenoid. Bring me a piece of paper and a pencil," Munch said. "It's easier to explain if I draw you a schematic. You can take it to your mechanic and have him fix it."

The guard fetched Munch a yellow legal pad and a ballpoint pen. She watched as Munch drew a rectangle with two small posts, which she labeled with plus and minus symbols.

"This is your battery," Munch explained. "It puts out twelve volts."

The guard nodded.

"All right," Munch continued. "Your starter solenoid"—she

drew a cylindrical object at the bottom of the page—"is mounted on top of your starter and requires eight to ten volts to engage your starter. A solenoid is basically a gatekeeper. When it gets the message from the ignition switch, it opens the flow of current between the battery and the starter. You still with me?"

The woman nodded again, clearly intrigued.

"Is your car an automatic?"

"Yes."

"All right." Munch drew several more squares and circles, explaining how each component worked. "The wiring insulation in the older Chevys tends to break down and leak current, especially when it gets hot. The starter solenoid requires an electrical signal of at least eight volts to operate, but by the time the current gets there it's only six or seven volts."

"Until it cools off," the guard said, excited at the revelation.

"Exactly," Munch said. "What I do is wire a Chrysler solenoid, which only requires five volts to operate, in series to deliver the needed eight volts to the GM solenoid." She quickly sketched the second solenoid into her schematic. "Think your mechanic can handle that?"

"Shoot, I'd rather take it to you, honey."

"If I ever get out of here," Munch said.

The guard reached in her purse and grabbed a cigarette case. Then she unlocked the door to Munch's cell. "C'mon," she said. "You can smoke that in the bathroom."

Munch smiled gratefully. "Any chance we'll pass a phone on the way?"

The guard looked both ways before answering. "I don't think so," she said.

"Hey, you've got a job to do," Munch said. "I can dig it."

The woman looked down the hall again, toward the phone. Munch knew she was weakening.

18

When Blackstone got to work Wednesday morning, he was in a rare good mood. The air was crisp and blown clean by the Santa Anas. Traffic had moved quickly on his way into the station. The coffee in the lounge was fresh and hot. By 9:15 he was seated comfortably at his desk, completely caught up on his paperwork and ready for the day.

Alex arrived at 9:45, a record-breaking fifteen minutes early. He got himself a cup of coffee and then joined Blackstone in his cubicle to go over the day's agenda.

"You got anything crunchy?" Alex asked.

"Don't you eat at home?"

"Yeah, I just got a taste for something salty." Alex reached into his pocket, but only found two toothpicks and a pack of matches. "So how'd it go last night?" was his next question.

"What do you mean?" Blackstone said.

"You and the G-babe. The two of you got together last night, right?"

"Yeah," Blackstone said.

"What happened?"

"We played chess."

"Who won?"

"We both did." Before Alex could respond to that, he added, "We played more than one game."

"Did she tell you anything?"

"I think we can pretty much bank on the assumption that Jonathan Garillo was a federal informant. Claire didn't deny the Oregon connection or that this involved the weapons stolen from the National Guard Armory. I told her about the guy with the grenade."

Alex eyed him askance. "You gave her that?"

"Yeah, sure. Why not? I think Claire is the type who remembers favors." He didn't add that she was a different kind of agent than they were used to or how he came about that knowledge.

"By the way," Alex said. "The guy from the bakery came down last night and looked at mug books."

"And?"

"The broad he saw with the baby wasn't Lisa Slokum."

"Let's hook him up with a sketch artist," Blackstone said.

The phone rang and they both looked at it. Blackstone picked up on the second ring and identified himself.

"Thish is Angie," a woman's voice lisped. "Remember me?"

"What is it?" he asked.

"I seen the guy," she said.

"The one that assaulted you?"

"Yesh. He's in Venish. I tried calling Bernie, but he's off today."

"You got an address?" Blackstone asked. "We'll take a ride over there."

"No, I jusht shaw him on the shtreet in front of Numero Uno's. I could show him to you."

"Would you be willing to press charges? Testify in court?"

"Yesh, just bust the guy."

"Give me your number, Angie. I'll call you right back."

Alex Perez had stopped drinking his coffee and was listening intently to Blackstone's half of the conversation. After Blackstone hung up, Alex stared ahead—strangely quiet.

"What?" Blackstone asked.

"Nothing, what's going on?"

"That hooker that Bernie knows, Angela Shaw, says she saw the guy that did her. She wants to roll over on him."

"Does it have to be today?" Alex asked.

"Is that a problem?"

"No, I guess not."

"What did it say?" Blackstone asked, suddenly realizing the source of Alex's uneasiness.

"What?"

"Your horoscope."

"I know you think it's stupid," Alex said. "But I'm telling you, nine times out of ten . . ."

"What did it say?" Blackstone asked again.

"I got it right here," Alex said, retrieving a scrap of newspaper from his pocket. "Avoid unnecessary risks at work. Update insurance coverage or licenses that are about to expire. A Capricorn may have an unpleasant surprise for you." He finished reading and looked at Blackstone expectantly.

"Sounds like an insurance agent wrote that," Blackstone said.

"Yeah, well, before I left for work this morning I checked my premium notices."

"And?"

"My life insurance note is due."

"Alex, I've told you a thousand times. You can't take all that mumbo-jumbo to heart. It'll just mess up your head."

"All right, Jigsaw," Alex said, putting the scrap of paper in his wallet. "Let's go bust this creep."

Blackstone dialed Claire's number, and then called Angie back and told her to meet them at the Shell station on Venice and Pacific. As an extra precaution, the detectives donned Kevlar vests. The plan was straightforward. Alex and Blackstone would cruise the vicinity with the woman in the back seat. Two other units would be nearby waiting for radio contact.

"What did Claire say?" Alex asked.

"She wasn't at her desk when I called," Blackstone said. "I left her a message."

When they got to the Shell station, Angie was there already, standing by the pay phone and glancing nervously up the street.

"Should I ask her if she's a Capricorn?" Blackstone asked Alex before they exited the car.

"I already checked her rap sheet," Alex admitted. "She's a Virgo."

"Isn't that the virgin?"

"Yeah."

"Enough said."

Blackstone beckoned to Angie and she sidled over to them, giving Alex the once-over. "Who's thish?" she asked.

"My partner, Detective Perez. Get in." She did. "So you say

you saw this guy outside the pizzeria on Washington?" he asked, watching her in the rearview mirror. She nodded an affirmative, her eyes shifting from side to side.

"Let's go," she said, wiping perspiration from her upper lip.

Blackstone and Alex exchanged quick looks.

"I shaw the dude hours ago. Where have you guys been?"

"Not so fast," Blackstone said. "We've got some ground rules to cover." He waited until he established eye contact with her in his rearview mirror. "Are you listening?"

"What kind of rules?" she asked.

"First of all, you see the guy, you just tell us. You don't point and you don't shout. You got that?" He didn't want the suspect alerted, especially if he were some hopped-up biker freak loaded with heavy artillery.

She started to say something, but Blackstone quieted her with a look and held up a second finger. "Two. If we spot him, you stay the hell out of the way. You clear about that? I don't want you leaving the car." And he didn't want any distractions if things got heavy.

"I'm the victim here," she said sullenly.

"I'm serious, Angie."

"All right."

"So run it back to me," Blackstone said.

"I make the guy," she said, "and then I duck."

"All right. We're good to go." Blackstone merged into the traffic headed southbound toward Washington. They pulled up across the street from a small market three doors down from the Numero Uno pizzeria. A steady flow of foot traffic streamed in and out the store's doors. Angie studied the people, but said nothing.

"Let's cruise the canals," Blackstone said after twenty minutes. "Maybe he's staying at one of the houses in there." He turned to his partner. "Keep a look out for modified Harleys, too. Those bikers tend to hang in packs."

They cruised a narrow one-way street that took them across an arched bridge. Angie straightened suddenly.

"There!" she shouted. "That's the shun of a bitch."

"Be quiet," Blackstone hissed, slowing the car to a crawl. The man she pointed to seemed unaware of them. Blackstone wanted to keep it that way for as long as possible. "The guy in the blue T-shirt?"

"Yesh."

Alex picked up the microphone, requested backup, and gave their location and a description of the suspect—whom he also described as possibly armed and dangerous.

"He's going back into the house," Blackstone observed. "Looks like Three-oh-Nine over the front door. Single-story dwelling, attached garage."

Alex relayed this new piece of information on the airwaves while Blackstone studied the lay of the land. The only car parked on the road was three houses up. Its tires were low on air and judging from the weed growth, it hadn't moved in at least a month. The house that the suspect entered was on a canal, which meant that his only route of quick escape was the narrow road running in front of it. When the other unit radioed to confirm that they were in place on Venice Boulevard, then he and Alex would approach the house.

A red Cadillac Sedan de Ville pulled up behind the detectives' car. Blackstone waved the car to pass them. Instead, the driver of the Cadillac parked and got out.

"What the . . . ?" Blackstone said. "Who the fuck is this?"

"Champion," she said.

They watched the pimp—a white guy wearing a long duster,

snakeskin boots, and velvet pants—exit his vehicle and limp towards them. Blackstone saw that Champion's left leg was inches shorter than his right. He used a cane with a silver handle that thumped as he approached. Each time he stepped with his left foot, his right hip shot out at a sharp angle. On his head he sported a floppy velvet hat worn low over his left eye, which only added to his slanted bearing.

"What's he doing here?" Blackstone asked.

She didn't have time to answer before Champion's hand was on the rear door handle.

"That be him?" he was asking, pointing at the same guy in the blue shirt who was now aware of the commotion fifty yards away. Champion whipped off his hat to reveal an Art Garfunkel blond Afro. The suspect ran into the house.

Both detectives got out of the car. Their bust was quickly going to hell.

"I kill the motherfucker," Champion said, making a fist. A large gold Super Bowl IX ring shone on his right index finger. "Mess with my bitch."

Blackstone decided he particularly disliked this guy. And what was with the black speak? He didn't hate white bad guys any more than black bad guys, but this phony crossover shit annoyed him deeply.

"You," Blackstone said, pushing a finger into Champion's chest, "will stay exactly where you are. One more step, one more word, and I'm running both of you in for obstruction. Angie, get back in the car." He looked over at Alex and saw that his partner had drawn his gun.

"What do you think, Jigsaw?" Alex asked, eyes shining with fear and excitement.

"He's not going anywhere. We'll wait for backup." The words

were no sooner out of Blackstone's mouth when they heard a loud cracking of wood and angry squeal of spinning tires. The garage door of the house burst outward as a Mercury Comet with Oregon plates and a Hertz bumper sticker barreled through it. The car was still in reverse when it reached the street. The driver hit his brakes, sending him skidding into a turn and raising a black cloud of burnt rubber. The car paused briefly with the passenger side facing the detectives. They could see the driver frantically working the gearshift.

"He's running," Alex yelled, aiming his gun. "Halt," he shouted at the man in the car. "Police."

The driver responded by pointing the business end of an M-14 at the detective and shooting out his own passenger window. Alex ducked back to the shelter of his car and returned fire. The popping of his .38 sounded woefully inadequate. He fired off six rounds. One shot punctured the Comet's front tire. The other five peppered the side of the car, just denting the metalwork.

Blackstone also had his weapon out and shot at the moving vehicle. He ceased fire when he saw the backup unit approach from the north. The suspect was trapped. Both ends of the street were covered and the back door opened to the canal. Blackstone took cover behind a row of trash cans.

The Comet abruptly shifted into reverse and hurled back inside the garage. The driver jumped from his still-moving vehicle, leaving his door open, and bolted back into the house.

"Are you all right?" Blackstone called to Alex across their unit's open doors.

"Yeah, yeah," Alex answered, his forehead beaded with sweat.

"He's got nowhere to go," Blackstone yelled, crouched behind the trash can enclosure. "We'll set up a perimeter. Call for SWAT."

Alex climbed back into the car and grabbed the microphone. Blackstone heard his partner describing the situation to Dispatch. Alex peeked over the dashboard as he relayed his information. Blackstone heard the sharp whine of a bullet. There wasn't time to move or warn. The action beside him unfolded in slow motion. He saw the blossoming of fracture lines on the windshield and Alex's head whip back. He heard his own voice shouting, but it was too late.

The microphone fell from Alex's hand. His head lay back against the seat, mouth slightly ajar, eyes half-closed, blood welling from the wound above his ear. Angie screamed.

Blackstone sprinted the short distance back to his car and pulled Alex down across the front seat. Another mistake, he knew, to leave his own cover. Fuck it. He pushed his palm over the now-gushing crease wound in his partner's head. With his other hand he picked up the fallen microphone and uttered the most dreaded code in the police department. "Nine, nine, nine." *Officer down.*

Blood from Alex's wound leaked out between Blackstone's fingers. "You're going to be okay," Blackstone kept repeating. Alex made no response. Blackstone saw that the bullet had penetrated the seat.

"Angie," he yelled. "Are you shot?"

"No," came her muffled reply.

He told her to stay down. She offered no argument. He started the car. A spray of bullets pierced the windshield in a line above the top of the dash. The back window blew out.

"Down," he repeated. He cocked the steering wheel all the way to the left and put his car in drive. The car rolled forward as he attempted to make a blind U-turn on the narrow roadway. The passenger windows exploded, showering them with chunks of tempered glass. Blackstone put the car into reverse and backed up into their previous position. The side of the car was no match against the sniper's firepower. They were trapped.

Within minutes the air filled with the sound of sirens and screeching tires. Police cordoned off the neighborhood and announced to the populace to stay in their homes. Blackstone heard a voice, amplified through a bullhorn and directed at the shooter inside the house, say, "Let's be smart about this."

The radio reported that the fire engine was on its way. It would be at least twenty minutes before the SWAT team arrived. Blackstone didn't think Alex had that kind of time.

"Do the right thing," the negotiator said. "You've got nowhere to go. Don't make us use tear gas."

Blackstone heard a door open and snuck a peek over the dashboard. He watched as the suspect came out the front door, hands held high above his head. When the shooting started again, Blackstone was only a little surprised. The suspect's head jerked back as a round caught him between the eyes, plastering skull fragments to the door behind him. Many other shots followed, but they were superfluous. There would be hell to pay later. Too many witnesses would say that the suspect had been unarmed and that the police had gunned him down in cold blood.

Too fucking bad, he thought.

If his hands hadn't already been occupied trying to keep Alex's lifeblood within his body, Blackstone might have been the first one to pull the trigger and save the taxpayers all that money. Someday, he decided, he would meet the guy who had drilled the asshole. He would thank the guy personally. But for now, he concentrated on keeping Alex alive.

Angie poked her head over the back seat. "Is he going to be okay?" she asked.

"I've got to get him to the hospital." He took her hand and pressed it over Alex's wound. "Keep pressure on it." He slammed the car into gear and shouted, "You're doing good, buddy. Hang in there."

Champion's Cadillac blocked part of the road. Blackstone rammed it out of his way.

Champion shouted, "Hey!" but Blackstone ignored him. He'd deal with that asshole later. Flooring the accelerator, he calculated the quickest route to Marina Mercy Hospital. The trip there was going to be the longest mile of his life. On Washington Boulevard, he hung a left that sent them skidding, but maintained control.

Angie still held on to Alex. The skin around Alex's mouth had a gray cast to it. Blackstone jammed on the gas, and the car shifted hard.

Dispatch reported unit after unit responding to the 999 call. Blackstone's unmarked unit had no siren. He flicked the switch that caused the headlights to flash left to right. As he turned south on Lincoln, he picked up a motorcycle escort.

The emergency room team was out in front with a gurney when he pulled in the driveway of Marina Mercy. Able hands jerked open the passenger door and lifted Alex's inert body onto a stretcher.

Blackstone came around to follow them inside. He was the first to notice when Alex's skin began to twitch and jerk. Within seconds, everywhere he looked on his partner's arms and face he saw hundreds of tiny muscle spasms.

"What's happening?" he asked the attending physician.

"Seizure," the doctor said. "One thousand milligrams of Dilantin, stat," he yelled, pushing Blackstone aside.

The team of medical personnel and their patient disappeared

behind the curtains of the treatment room. Blackstone had never felt so helpless in his life. How was he going to tell Sally?

He walked back outside to his car just as Champion's red Cadillac turned in off Mindanao. There was a screeching moan as the dented right front fender rubbed against the tire. Angie was still seated in the back of his unit, blood on her hands, eyeing him fearfully.

He had a sudden fantasy of pulling out his gun and shooting her in the head, then he'd go after the pimp. In his mind's eye, he saw both their heads lolling against the leather headrests of the red Cadillac.

"Are you hit?" a voice asked.

He looked up and saw that the speaker was Sergeant Mann. "No," he answered. "It's not my blood."

"How's your partner?"

"They're working on him now. I don't know."

"What happened here?" Mann asked. "What were you doing at that house?"

"Assault complaint," he said, pointing at Angie. "Victim ID."

"Does this involve a homicide investigation?"

"Yes, sir." Blackstone pulled out his notebook and flipped back a few pages. "There's a connection to last Friday's sniper attack. As I'm sure you recall, the ammunition recovered was military and tied to last month's National Guard armory burglary in Kern County."

"Right," Mann said. "And you liaised with Special Agent Claire Donavon, the one with all the moles."

"Beauty marks, sir. Yes, that's the one."

"Anything come of that?"

"In the works. She asked me to release a photo of Garillo, the sniper victim, to the press."

"Why did she want that?"

"She didn't say."

"You still haven't explained why you and your partner were here today."

"I put the word out on the street that I was interested in any military weaponry that might have surfaced in the last month."

"Go on," Mann said, head bent and listening carefully.

"Yes, sir. The female"— he pointed to where she cowered in his back seat—"Angela Shaw, aka Angie, reported an assault by a man with a grenade."

"Who's the yo-yo in the red Caddy?" Mann asked.

"Her pimp. He calls himself Champion." He didn't mention the agreement to drop charges on Champion in exchange for Angie's information. Technically, the deal Blackstone and Bernie had made with Champion was illegal, even though it went on all the time. He didn't trust the sergeant well enough to risk getting Bernie's ass in a sling. Besides, it really didn't make a difference.

"I think I'm getting the picture," Mann said. "You went with Angela Shaw, the victim of an assault, to apprehend her attacker—" he flipped open his own notebook—"Darnel Willis."

"Was that the shithead's name?" Blackstone asked.

"According to his driver's license," Mann said. "Did Ms. Shaw identify Darnel Willis as her assailant?"

"Yes, sir."

"Then what happened?"

"The pimp showed up unexpectedly. Willis caught wind of us, barricaded himself in the house, and started shooting."

"And that's when Detective Perez was hit," Mann said. "All that is pretty clear. But we're going to have a problem with the officer-involved shooting. Darnel Willis was DOA. Did you notice where the first shot that struck him came from?"

"No, sir. There was a lot of activity at the time and I was occupied with my partner."

"I saw the head wound on Willis," Mann said. "The exit wound blew out the back of the guy's skull. We've confiscated all the officers' weapons who discharged shots. I'm going to need yours also."

Blackstone retrieved his revolver from its holster and handed it to the sergeant butt-first.

"The guy's head was putty. There's no way a police .38 could have done that kind of damage," Mann said.

Blackstone nodded. The police-issued .38 was notoriously underpowered. The thinking was that a police weapon should only have the force necessary to stop a criminal, but no more. The powers that be reasoned that anything more powerful might put the innocent public at risk.

"You know what they're going to say downtown, don't you?" Mann said.

"Sir?"

"They're going to say an officer had an unauthorized weapon."

"They'll have to prove it, won't they?"

"Meanwhile, the press will crucify us. They're already describing Darnel Willis as a motorist. Can you believe that shit?"

Blackstone didn't know what to believe anymore. An officer is shot in the line of duty and what was downtown worried about? If a cop used a non-issue weapon. It was crazy, totally crazy. Like his worst fucking nightmare come to life. The seconds leading up to the shooting played over and over in his mind: Alex picking up the mike; Alex bleeding and unconscious; his own voice screaming to Alex that he would be okay.

"I told him to get on the radio," he said.

"You followed procedure, right?" Mann asked.

"By the book."

Mann looked at him for a long time before asking, "Anything else you have to say about all this?"

"No, sir," Blackstone said. What could he say? That he'd like to find the shooter so he could shake his hand? "What should we do about these two?" he asked, indicating Angie and Champion.

Mann sighed. "Kick 'em loose, for now. I'll check with the DA and see if he's willing to file."

"All right."

"What are you going to do now?" Mann asked.

"I'm going to sit with Alex for a while. Sally's probably on her way."

Mann nodded, then put a hand on Blackstone's shoulder. "I'm going to need a full written report on my desk tomorrow morning. Were you ever able to get the feds to tell you anything about their case as it related to your homicide?"

"Agent Donavon hinted to me that Garillo had been supplying her office with information."

"Then that really doesn't figure," Mann said. "If this Garillo guy was an informant and hit because of it, then why would the feds want to advertise that?"

The sergeant's question left him with a sick sense of foreboding. Who was using who here?

19

Officer Reese told Munch to call her Sissy. She was pretty good people once you got to know her, and Munch was doing her damnedest to make a new best friend. It was apparently a slow day for criminals in Santa Monica, as Munch had the entire holding cell to herself. At midmorning, Sissy turned on the television and turned it so Munch could watch, too.

A *Beverly Hillbillies* rerun was interrupted by a news flash. There had been a shootout in Venice involving fatalities.

"Motherfucker," Sissy said, staring at the mug shot superimposed over footage of a body being wheeled into the coroner's wagon.

"What?" Munch asked.

"That boy shot a cop."

Munch recognized the picture of the shooter. It was Darnel, Lisa's Darnel, red hair and all. Son of a bitch.

Another picture appeared in the lower right-hand corner of

the screen. The newscaster said something about Detective Alex Perez fighting for his life after the late-morning shootout in the canal section of Venice Beach. Munch said, "Oh," surprised at how sad she felt. "I wonder if he has kids."

"I think so," Sissy said.

"I need to get a message to his partner," Munch said.

"Say what?"

"You won't get in trouble for letting me call a cop."

"They told me no phone calls."

"All right, how about if you get a message to him?"

"What's his name?"

"Blackstone, he's a homicide detective with the Venice PD."

"What do you want me to tell him?"

"Tell him I don't work at a printing press, but I need to talk to him." She could only hope that he would come alone.

20

Other officers joined Blackstone at the hospital as their shifts ended.

At one-hour intervals, the nurses allowed him five-minute visits in the ICU. Standing over his partner's hospital bed, he stared at thick layers of surgical gauze encasing Alex's skull. White tape, crisscrossed under his nose and over his chin, held the breathing tube inserted into his trachea still. His eyelids glistened with Vaseline. The eyeballs underneath were absolutely still. That couldn't be good.

A nurse came in and checked Alex's vital signs.

"How's he doing?" Blackstone asked.

"Check with the doctor."

Blackstone elicited her promise that he would be apprised of any change, and then went back out into the waiting room and tried to pray.

He called the office from the hospital lobby. Claire had left him a message that she would be out of town for the next few days. If he needed to get in touch with her, he could leave word at the Bureau.

When he returned to the waiting room, a fictionalized court-room drama played out on the TV overhead. The show was interrupted by an afternoon news break. Some liberal movie actress was calling for a widespread investigation into the police force's use of unauthorized weapons. Blackstone watched the interview in numb disbelief. He'd like to take that bitch down to South Central and drop her off. He'd come back in an hour, after she'd had a little taste of life in a war zone, and see if she'd changed her tune.

He threw down his magazine and left the room. He didn't know where he was headed, he just knew that he needed to be alone to deal with his emotions. Walking quickly, he took several turns and then wound up behind the kitchen. Crates of wilted produce were stacked against the wall. Steam rose from vents. An open Dumpster emitted putrid odors.

Staring out to nowhere, fists balled in his pockets, he thought of Alex not wanting to go on the call. Had he taken his investigation too far? Was he too gung-ho, too fucking John Wayne?

No, he decided. This was the job. For the most part tedious and boring, then life-and-death with no warning. They'd been following a logical succession of leads. His reports would reflect this. Would Sally understand? Would her children?

He replayed the crucial minutes of the shooting in his mind. What should they have done differently? He had never dreamed the suspect would open fire on them like that. There was no reason for it. Expect the unexpected. Alex shouldn't have broken cover. He had been careless and they had been hopelessly outgunned.

Blackstone kicked an empty can of whole tomatoes and watched it wobble away. A man in a white kitchen staff uniform stuck his head out the door and started to yell something. Blackstone turned and faced him. Whatever the man saw in Blackstone's expression caused him to shut the door quickly and without protest.

Grease. The thought came to Blackstone suddenly. When Claire had come to his house, her hands had been lined with black grime from changing her tire. What if the woman on the freeway worked with cars or some sort of greasy parts? He pulled out his notebook and made a notation.

He stood there for another ten minutes, then returned to the parking lot where he'd left his car.

"Jigsaw?" a voice said from behind him.

He spun around and confronted the haggard countenance of Sergeant Mann. The sergeant looked even worse than Blackstone felt. Deep lines creased the senior officer's face; dark bags hung under his eyes. "Sarge?"

"I'm still waiting for your report," Mann said. "I know how rough it is, to have your partner wounded, but the job goes on."

"Yes, sir. I was planning to return to the station and type up my notes right after I leave here. How's the investigation going?"

"I've been on the phone all morning. The mayor's on my ass, demanding answers. Heads are going to roll on this one."

"Have you found the kill bullet?"

"I don't know. I haven't been able to get back to the house. From what I understand, the structure was pretty shot up. Speaking of bullets, I need you to turn in your vehicle so we can collect the evidence inside it." Mann's expression softened. "Why don't you take the rest of the day off after you finish your report? Get some rest. There's nothing more you can do here."

"Thank you, sir," Blackstone said. "You're right, there's nothing more I can do here."

Blackstone returned to his car and discovered that he had locked his door. Pretty funny considering that the rear and side windows were all shot out. He shook his head at the force of habit and brushed chunks of tempered glass off the seat.

He didn't drive back to work. The report would have to wait.

Twenty minutes later, he was standing where he'd been when he told his partner to radio in for tear gas. He faced the house. There was a puddle of dried blood where Darnel Willis had died. The front door where Willis's blood and brains had sprayed had been removed from its hinges and taken away. He made a note to follow up on that.

Sawhorses strung together with yellow tape marked the crime scene perimeter. A patrol car manned by two officers guarded the house and kept the curious at bay. While he watched, a woman who appeared to be in her twenties, wearing a long gypsy skirt and granny glasses, threw a bouquet of flowers towards the house.

He shook his head in disgust. She was honoring that asshole. Making him into some kind of a martyr. That rapist, woman-beating cop shooter.

A man wearing a blue parka emerged from the doorless entryway. Blackstone called to him.

"This is a federal investigation," the man said, holding up a hand to indicate that Blackstone should stay back.

Blackstone showed the fed his shield. "It was my partner that got shot."

"I'm sorry about that," the agent said. "But I can't let you in here."

Blackstone started to say something, something involving the man's mother, and then realized it would do him no good. He returned to his ruined car and drove to the impound lot so the boys in Firearms could do their thing. After being admitted through the front gate, he was told to park wherever he could find a space.

The stolen blue pickup from the Garillo case was still there. He walked over to the truck and looked inside. The back of the bench seat had been removed and the windshield had collapsed in on itself. He opened the door and ran his hand along the back of the seat cushion. Nothing.

Something brushed against the back of his head. A business card had snagged on the roll of sheet metal where the roof of the cab met the door frame. He plucked it loose, brushed off dried blood, and was able to read the lettering: Happy Jack's Auto Repair. How long had that been there? He put the card in his pocket and walked across the street to the crime lab building.

He found Jeff Hagouchi perched over his microscope.

"I brought in my unit."

"How's Alex?" Jeff asked.

"Still under," Blackstone said. "If he remains stable, they'll slowly wean him off the anti-seizure drugs."

"He's a fighter," Jeff said.

"Sergeant Mann said the bullet that took out Darnel Willis was more powerful than a thirty-eight. Did you get a chance to check it out?"

"No. I never got to see it," Jeff said. "The feds got there first. They were there all morning."

"Doing what?" Blackstone asked.

"They took the door, for one thing," Jeff said. "That's where the bullet that killed Darnel Willis ended up."

"Why are they handling the investigation?" Blackstone asked. "IAD has their own investigators. Something's going on."

"It's worse than that, buddy," Jeff said. "The feds took the weapons that they found in the house and issued warrants to confiscate all related material in this case—including the bullet that wounded Alex. How are we supposed to prove that Willis shot Alex? It's all fucked up. Now they're saying that Willis's civil rights may have been violated. I hope you covered your ass."

Blackstone stared at Jeff, but he wasn't really seeing him. He felt like he had been a step behind for days and he didn't like it. Opportunities always existed. You just needed to remember to stop and look for them. When you're on the defensive, scrambling backward, sometimes you forget that.

"What about that double homicide in Venice? We received information that it ties in to the Garillo case. Did you get a chance to ID those bullets?"

Jeff reached for a file and thumbed through it. "Yeah, you're going to love it." He took out a document and handed it to Blackstone. "They were 7.62 by 21 millimeters, but not armor-piercing."

"Did you tell the feds?"

"You know, in all this excitement, I might have forgotten."

Blackstone read over the report, nodding his head. It had taken him long enough, but he was starting to smell the setup. "I play correspondent chess games," he said, looking at a spot somewhere over Jeff's left shoulder. "I play against opponents from all over the world. People I never see—only their moves."

"What's that—" Jeff started to ask.

"There's this one guy named Wang. He's a grand master. Lives in Hong Kong. I thought I had him in a game we played last year. I had his queen and both of his bishops. His king was backed into a corner. The next postcard he sent me had a Chinese pictograph on the back cover and then his move on the front. I didn't know what the writing meant, of course, so I ignored it. I didn't spend more than five minutes figuring what I was going to play next. I had him and I knew it."

"Maybe you should go home, Jigs. Get some rest."

"The thing is, two moves later he put me in checkmate. Later, I had the pictograph translated. The guy I took it to explained to me that the pictograph was actually two symbols superimposed: danger and opportunity. He said it was the Chinese concept of crisis."

"That's really interesting, Blackstone. But what the fuck does it mean?"

"It means that it's time to go on the offensive. Give me your car keys." He handed Jeff his own. "You never saw any federal warrant."

"How long do you think I can pull that off?"

"Hopefully long enough to dig the bullet out of the seat of my vehicle and get a look at it under your microscope."

"What am I looking for?"

"Compare it to the bullets from the double homicide, for starters. Just be sure you document everything."

"Anything else?" Jeff asked.

"Get ahold of Sergeant Mann and tell him what the feds are doing."

"What are you going to do?"

"I'm going to call in a marker," Blackstone said. "All right if I use the phone in your office?"

"Help yourself, Jigsaw."

Claire Donavon had given him the number that rang directly to her desk. She answered after the first ring.

"I've just been back to the house," he said.

"You just caught me," she said.

He liked how she didn't play it cute by asking which house. "Did your people retrieve the bullet that killed Darnel Willis?"

"It's a little soon to know anything, honey. I'll be happy to call you in a few days when I get back into town. I really am literally walking out the door."

"Claire, I need your help. My partner is in the hospital. The department is under fire. We might have a riot brewing. I need some answers."

"You're going to have to trust me," she said. "You remember how I told you that this case had certain delicacies? That still applies. Lives depend on our maintaining a strict need-to-know policy on this investigation."

"Lives or careers, Claire? Forget need-to-know," he said. "I think I've earned a right to know. Give me that much."

"I'm sorry," she said. "Honestly. But your involvement right now is far too personal. I promise you that when we get our lab results back, we'll share them with you. Until then, there's nothing more to say."

He hung up on her. Childish, he knew, but it had felt good. That feeling faded when he realized that he'd forgotten to ask her why she wanted him to publish the picture of John Garillo. He tried to call her back; after twenty rings a recording came on and told him to stop trying.

The next number he called was the one he found on the bloodstained business card. A man answered, "Happy Jack's, Jack speaking."

"Hi, Jack," Blackstone said in the cheeriest voice he could muster. "Do you have a woman who works there?"

"Munch? She's not here," he said.

Blackstone's stomach muscles tightened. Bingo. "Will she be back soon? It's very urgent that I reach her."

182

"She's . . . off for a few days. You'll have to try again on Monday."

"This is Detective Blackstone. I'm with the Homicide Division of the Venice PD. It's imperative that I speak to her. Do you have her home phone number?"

"Don't you guys talk among yourselves? What's all of this about? Does this have something to do with that friend of hers that was shot last Friday?"

"You know about that?"

"Not a whole hell of a lot. The guy was in here a few hours earlier. Wanted her to do him some kind of favor, but she don't mess with his kind anymore."

"Since when?"

"Hey, I know where you're going with this," Jack said. "And you're wrong. I'd vouch for Munch Mancini any day of the week. She shows up for work every day, sober as a judge."

Blackstone wrote down the name and then looked at the business card again. The shop was in Sherman Oaks. Judging from the address, it was close to both the 405 and the Ventura freeways.

"What time did Ms. Mancini leave work last Friday?" Blackstone asked.

"I don't know how much I should be saying about all this. Maybe we should get a lawyer involved."

"You're the one who said she had nothing to hide, sir."

"How do I know if you're even really a cop?"

"If it'll make you feel better, you can call me right back. I'm at the crime lab now." He gave Jack the number and the extension, then hung up and waited for the man to call him back. When the phone rang two minutes later, he picked it up before it had completed its first ring.

"She left at three-fifteen," Jack said. "I remember because she had a four o'clock appointment with her probation officer in Santa Monica."

"Do you have a phone number and address for Ms. Mancini?"

"Why do you need that?"

"I'd like to talk to her, sir."

"Just a minute," Jack said. Blackstone heard what sounded like a filing cabinet opening. Jack read off an address and phone number in Reseda. "Does this mean she isn't in jail?"

"Why would she be in jail?"

"That's what I don't understand either, but they took her away yesterday and she hasn't called. I tried to find out what was going on, but I just got the runaround."

Blackstone thanked Jack for his help and then hung up. The next number he dialed was Munch Mancini's home number. When her machine answered, he hung up. He sat back and thought a moment, then called the station. The operator had over twenty messages for him.

"Everybody sends Alex their prayers," she said.

"Anything else?" he asked.

"Some woman in custody in Santa Monica wants to speak to you. She said she needs to talk to you and that she never worked at a print shop."

"What's the name?" he asked, knowing the answer before the operator spoke.

"Munch Mancini."

"What's she in custody for?"

"I don't know. You want me to call over there and find out?"

"No. I'll handle it. Thanks."

21

Blackstone waited in the small visiting room for Munch Mancini. She arrived accompanied by a guard and uncuffed. She didn't refuse the hand he offered. They both sat in scarred wooden chairs.

"How's your partner doing?" she asked.

"What do you know about that?"

"Just what I saw on TV. Is he going to be all right?"

"We're not sure yet."

"I'm sorry. He looked like a nice guy."

"He still is."

"Right."

"What's your involvement with all this?" Blackstone asked.

"It's a long story," she said.

Blackstone folded his hands in front of him. "Why don't you start at the beginning?"

Where did this story begin? she wondered. Would he be interested in hearing about her convoluted relationships? Or did the story begin eight months ago when she was reborn sober and thrown wide-eyed into a new world with a whole new set of rules? No, she decided, none of that would matter to him. He was a cop. She took a deep breath and began. "Last Friday, my friend John Garillo came to visit me at work. Hours later, he was dead."

"Why didn't you come forth earlier?"

"I didn't have anything to offer," she said.

"But now that you're in custody, you've suddenly remembered something that will help with the investigation."

"It's not like that." She walked to the window. "I've always wanted Sleaze's killer to be caught."

"Sleaze?" Blackstone asked. He pulled out his notebook.

"That's what we called him. Sleaze John." She looked out the window, wishing she was dealing with the other cop, the one who was shot.

"And you contacted me because . . . ?"

"You need my help," she said.

"And what do you need?" he asked.

"Let's just say I've buried enough friends for one week."

"I'm listening."

"The way I see it," she said, "a lot of people have gotten hurt lately—your partner for one." The last two days had given her a lot of time to think. She was pretty sure she had reconstructed the events that led to Sleaze's murder—not to mention the killings in Venice, which also had to tie in somehow. She had reached one inescapable conclusion. The FBI knew where the guns were and had delayed their arrests. They were as much to blame as anyone else, and they were supposed to be the good guys. She took a breath for courage and then laid it out for Blackstone. "According to some information that I fell into, these shootings could have been avoided."

"What kind of information?"

"Pictures, an interoffice memo."

"Whose interoffice memo?"

"The FBI. Get me out of here and I'll show them to you. Then we'll figure out how we'll handle it from there."

"Let's take this one step at a time."

"Fine," she said. "Get me out of here."

In the hallway outside of Courtroom 212, Blackstone caught up with Chris Hoag. Chris had been a DA for as long as Blackstone had been on the force.

"Hey, Jigsaw," Hoag said. "You testifying today?"

"No, I'm working on a case and I need a favor."

"Search warrant?"

"Court order to release a witness from custody. She's upstairs."

"How soon you need it?"

"How soon can you do it?"

Hoag grabbed his arm and led him toward the elevator. "What's she in custody for?"

"Probation violation, but it's bullshit."

"Who's her PO?"

"Olivia Scott," Blackstone said.

Hoag shook his head. "That bitch is going to get the city sued one day, you mark my words."

Hoag's secretary typed up the court order. Hoag walked it past the judge and collected the necessary signatures and stamps. The custody sergeant had Munch sign for her property. It took him a while to locate the manila folder holding her keys, wallet, and money. By four o'clock, Munch was a free woman.

"Where to now?" Blackstone asked.

"Inglewood. We need to have a little chat with Lisa Slokum."

Traffic was congested on the Coast Highway and, according to the traffic report on the radio, was bumper to bumper all the way to the airport. Blackstone requisitioned an unmarked unit that was equipped with a magnet-mounted red strobe and siren. He used both to part the traffic.

Munch clutched the handholds mounted on the dash as they swerved in and out of the busy lanes.

She told him how Claire Donavon had questioned her and then jailed her.

"What I'm not sure of," Munch said as they got off the freeway in Inglewood, "is how she knew who I was."

"What do you think?" Blackstone asked.

"I think someone with a big mouth has got a lot at stake and doesn't care who gets hurt."

When they got to Lisa Slokum's house, the front door was open, as was the gate. A white Buick Riviera was parked in front.

Munch and Blackstone got out of his car and walked up the front path together.

A thin, well-dressed white man who looked to be in his sixties exited the house. He stood on the front porch shaking his head. As Munch and Blackstone approached, the man regarded them with interest.

"I'm not quite ready to show the place yet," he said. "My last tenant left it in quite a mess."

"She moved?" Munch asked. "Where?"

"Even if I knew, I couldn't tell you," he said.

Blackstone flashed his badge. The landlord wasn't impressed.

"She gave me notice two weeks ago," he said. "I didn't ask any questions. It's weird, though. She left all her furniture, most of their clothes, too, it looks like."

"Can I look?" Munch asked.

The man shrugged. "Suit yourself."

She went to the little girls' room first. It was hard to tell because of the overall disorder, but it did seem as if some things were missing. She looked for Jill's special rock, but it was gone. She opened the closet. Clothes she remembered washing no longer hung there. The box of dress-up accessories had also been removed.

They were all gone.

She walked back into the front room. Her thoughts scrambled and raced, making it difficult to concentrate. She rubbed at her chest, trying to ease the weight on her heart.

Please, God. Please, God. Please let her be all right.

Tears of frustration filled her eyes. She stumbled over something. Asia's rattle. Munch picked it up and traced the word's Daddy's Girl.

They walked out into the front yard. Blackstone was saying something about APBs and DMV records.

"I'll check with the neighbors," he said. "Maybe someone knows something."

"No," she said, gripping his arm. "Let's not waste time. Take me to my work. I stashed those papers I was telling you about in my car."

When they got to Happy Jack's, the shop was closed. The lot was unchained, but it didn't matter. Her car was gone. For the second time in as many hours, she felt the sickening sensation that she had been ripped off and there was nothing she could do about it. She turned to Blackstone.

"The feds must have towed it. Can you get in their impound lot?"

Blackstone tucked in his shirt and hitched his pants. Munch had the feeling that he was stalling. "Not easily," he said. "Was this all you had?"

"No," she said. "Take me to my place. I have some numbers I can call." She'd also been wearing the same dirty uniform since yesterday and wanted to change.

"Let's go," he said.

On the drive to her apartment, she told him everything she could remember about what she'd seen on the missing papers. She described the lists and the frequency of Tux's name, the pictures of James talking to the man in the suit—how James had been with Sleaze when he visited her at her work. Blackstone was particularly interested in the FBI memo and its exact wording.

It was almost seven when they got to her apartment. She unlocked the front door, swung it open, and flicked on the light.

"Nice place," he said.

She kicked off her greasy work shoes before she crossed her threshold. "You sound surprised."

"No, not at all," he lied.

She let it go.

"Who are you going to call?" he asked.

"A mutual friend." Munch dialed the number of the Snakepit. When the bartender answered, she asked for Deb. Deb answered the phone shouting.

Munch pulled the phone away from her ear. "Hey."

"You comin' up or what?" Deb asked.

"I'm looking for Lisa," Munch said.

"Whatcha want with that sweathog?"

Munch lowered her voice. "She ripped me off."

Blackstone raised a questioning eyebrow. Munch turned her back on him.

"You should know better than to trust that cunt," Deb said. "She's only out for herself."

"I'm finding that out."

"I feel sorry for the kids," Deb said. "Fucking meal tickets, that's all they are to that bitch."

"And now the baby," Munch prompted.

"Yeah, right. And first chance she gets, she dumps the kid off with her ol' man."

190

"Her ol' man?" Munch asked.

"James."

Munch pinched the bridge of her nose between her thumb and forefinger. "Asia is with James?"

"Yeah, he's on his way up here."

"When's he due?"

"Tomorrow sometime. He's driving shotgun with Tux."

She covered the mouthpiece and turned to Blackstone. "We need to go to Oregon."

He started to say something, but she silenced him with a finger. To Deb she said, "You gonna be hanging out for a while?"

"I'll be here," Deb said.

Munch hung up and then turned to Blackstone.

"We?" he asked.

"You wouldn't get very far without me," she said.

"All right," he said.

"That was easy."

"We both want the same thing, right?" he said.

"Yeah," she said, feeling guilty. The catching of Sleaze's killer had slipped on her list of priorities.

As if sensing she was holding back on him, Blackstone asked, "What did Lisa take from you?"

"Huh?"

"You said Lisa ripped you off."

"Yeah, well, it's just kind of a figure of speech, you know? It don't mean nothing." She noticed herself slipping back into street vernacular. "She owes me, is all I'm saying."

"Owes you what?"

"An explanation."

He seemed to accept that. "I'll call the airlines and check on flights."

She pulled out her phone book, set it next to the phone, and said, "I won't be long." She left him to go change and pack a bag.

"When we get to Canyonville," he called through the closed bedroom door, "you can tell people I'm your cousin."

"I don't have any cousins." She opened her closet and pulled out a duffel bag. This was not only her first trip out of state, but it would be her first time on an airplane.

"Tell them I'm your boyfriend," he said.

"Oh, yeah, right," she said. "That's even more of a stretch." From the back of her closet she pulled out her black leather motorcycle jacket, her once sacred "leather." Through the door, she heard him speaking on the phone, repeating back times and numbers, then saying thank you and hanging up.

"Why?" he yelled to her.

"You might as well have COP stamped on your forehead," she yelled back. She pulled on a pair of jeans, a black T-shirt, and then her old Frye boots. Shaking out her coat, she laid it out on the bed. Her leather was personalized by a Levi jacket with cut-off sleeves that fit snugly across its back. She had sewn on Harley-Davidson wings across the lower back and a uniform name tag from her first job over one of the front pockets. To the left of the lower buttons there was a round patch with an embroidered coiled snake on it and the legend: DON'T TREAD ON ME. The jacket smelled rank, she noticed, probably always had. It was against the code to wash a cutoff. She put it on and joined him in the kitchen.

"You look about five inches taller and twenty pounds heavier," he said.

"It's attitude," she told him, tying a red bandanna around her forehead.

"The first plane we can catch to Medford leaves tomorrow morning," he said, showing her the flight information.

She called the Snakepit again. When Deb came to the phone, Munch announced, "I'm coming up."

"That's great. When?"

She consulted his notes. "Eleven-fifteen tomorrow morning."

"We'll be there. How long can you stay?"

"Till the weekend for sure. So your ol' man has been in L.A.?"

"He's been everywhere. I can't wait for you to meet him."

"Yeah, me either," Munch said. She hung up the phone and turned to Blackstone. "They're going to meet me at the airport."

"They?"

"Deb and another friend of ours, Roxanne."

He wrapped a hand around her wrist. "I don't have to tell you that I don't want you screwing up the bust by warning your friends."

"All I'm asking for is a chance to get them out of there," she said.

He nodded. "We'll have to see how deeply they're involved. I can't promise you total immunity."

"Look, have a heart here. You're looking for a murderer. Guys who shoot cops. The worse thing these broads do is smoke a little reefer and party with bikers. Why fuck up their lives by busting them?"

"And if they're involved?"

"No way," she said. "You don't know them like I do." She hoisted her duffel bag.

"You all ready?" he asked.

"Where to now?"

"I want to stop by the hospital, and then we'll go to my place."

She knew that there was no question that one of them would be sleeping on a couch.

The next morning, they parked in the large covered structure attached to the terminal. They were still an hour early. Blackstone excused himself to use the phone. Munch headed for the airport gift shop, which had a section full of Disneyland memorabilia. She selected a Mickey Mouse watch. Then she went to the card section and found a birthday card appropriate for a young boy and took them both up to the counter.

"Do you gift-wrap?" she asked the elderly woman behind the cash register.

"No, dear."

"How about these?" Munch asked, holding up a packet of hair ribbons.

"They cost a dollar each," the woman said. "Rather expensive for gift wrap."

"That's all right. Price is no object." She thought about Mrs. Scott's criticism about how Munch didn't practice fiscal responsibility.

"Is this for your son?" the cashier asked.

"No, but he's the next closest thing. He's my friend's son."

"How long since you've seen him?"

"Almost a year," Munch said, leaving out the part about going to jail and kicking heroin.

The woman made change and helped Munch tie the bow around the watch case. "That looks great," Munch said. "Thanks."

"Have a nice vacation, dear," the woman said.

Blackstone was still on the phone. "I'll pick up the tickets," she told him. He handed her a wad of cash. She handed half of it back. "I'll pay for my own."

She got in line and watched the people ahead of her go about the business of buying their tickets and checking their luggage. By the time it was her turn, she had the routine down.

"Two round trips to Medford, please."

"How many bags?" the ticket agent asked.

"Just our carry-ons," she said, feeling like an old pro.

"Smoking or nonsmoking?"

"Smoking."

"Aisle or window?"

"Window."

"Thank you for flying the friendly skies."

"You're welcome." It wasn't until after she left the counter with the ticket folder clutched in her hand that she remembered to breathe.

Blackstone joined her. "All set?" he asked.

"How's your partner?" she asked.

"Stronger, they say, but still out."

Another half hour went by and then a stewardess announced that they were now accepting passengers. Munch and Blackstone got in the cattle line and allowed themselves to be swept aboard with the other travelers.

Their seats were towards the back of the plane. As she made her way down the narrow center aisle, she remembered an episode from *The Beverly Hillbillies* when Jed and his family took their first flight in an airplane. They thought they were on a really fast bus when the plane taxied for takeoff. The studio audience laughed with delight, because they all knew what was coming. She promised herself that when the plane left the ground, she would yawn with boredom.

They took adjoining seats, stowed their bags, and fastened their seat belts.

The plane rumbled as it taxied down the runway picking up speed. She glanced at the other passengers, looking for signs of distress. A few clutched their armrests and closed their eyes, but for the most part her fellow passengers were calm. The plane left the ground with a lurch that made her stomach flop. She casually looked out the window and opened her mouth wide.

Once they were in the air, the stewardess demonstrated what

everyone should do in case of emergency. Munch listened intently, straining against her seat belt.

"Your first flight?" Blackstone asked.

"That obvious, huh?"

"Most people ignore the safety instructions," he said.

"Seems to me that this could be the most important part."

"You've got a good point there."

The stewardess finished her spiel and all the passengers settled down to wait. Munch watched out the window until clouds obscured the view.

An issue of *National Geographic* was stuffed in the pocket of the seat in front of her. She pulled it out. The cover art showed the chain of evolution with the classic series of drawings beginning with an ape on all fours and ending with an upright man: the ever-popular *Homo erectus*. Deb would have fun with that one, she thought. The accompanying article, written by an anthropologist and entitled "The Communicators," was interesting.

The author's theory was that humans had evolved to become communicators. The article went on to list the supporting evidence. *Homo sapiens* have over a hundred muscles in their faces, she read. That was more than any other animal, even chimpanzees. Humans have very little facial hair, the article also pointed out. This is so that the facial expressions can be read more easily. *Homo sapiens* also have relatively fragile skin, no fangs or claws, and are weaker than any other animal of comparable stature. In other words, if humans didn't communicate, they were screwed.

Munch thought about how bikers had jumped the evolutionary boat with their beards, leather clothing, chain belts, and buck knives. Still, there was something about all that dark power that was very seductive.

Blackstone was working a crossword puzzle. She looked over

his shoulder and said, "Three down is *Avon*. The clue is 'The Bard's river.' That's gotta be Shakespeare."

Blackstone made a small snort of amusement as he filled in the squares. "You're just full of surprises, aren't you?"

She felt her mouth twitch into a smile.

Before leaving Los Angeles, Blackstone had also called his connection in Canyonville. As the plane taxied down the runway, he thought about his brief conversation with Tom Moody.

"Where are you calling from?" Moody had asked as soon as Blackstone identified himself.

"A pay phone at the airport."

"Yeah, that should be okay. What's up?"

Blackstone filled him in on what had happened to Alex, how he had come to identify Munch Mancini as the woman from the morgue, and when their flight to Medford was arriving. Moody apologized for not having anyone available to pick him up at the airport.

"The feds are stonewalling us," Blackstone complained. "We're taking a lot of heat for the officer-involved shooting. I know it ties into the case they're working up at your end, but a lot of shit is being swept under the rug."

"Yeah," Moody said. "Things are heating up here. They brought in reinforcements this morning. What does your source at the Bureau say?"

"That sort of dried up," Blackstone said.

"I'm not surprised," Moody said. "Those G live by their own rules—they get kind of spooky when they're moving in for the kill. Don't worry, I've got my own way in. I'll explain when you get here."

22

Blackstone and Munch spent the three-hour flight going over the ground rules of their partnership. On arriving in Medford, Blackstone would avoid Munch and her friends.

"Not even a 'How are you,'" she warned.

"What's wrong with that?" he asked.

"They'll know you're a cop. It's that in-your-face, too-cheery, direct-eye-contact thing. Total giveaway."

"So you want me in the background."

"As soon as I find out anything," she said. "I'll call you. Deb doesn't have a phone in her house, so it will have to wait till I can get to a pay phone."

He gave her Moody's number. "Call me either way," he said. "Just so we keep in touch. If things start getting hinky, let me know and I'll pull you out. Don't take risks, just gather information."

The plane made a wide turn and began its descent. She looked out the window and took in the breathtaking landscape of green mountains laced with wisps of clouds. They landed with a bump and she held her breath as the plane seemed to struggle to stop, the engines screaming in protest. She realized she was clutching Blackstone's arm and released him, but not before he gave her a you're-not-so-tough-after-all look. It occurred to her that the old her might have felt embarrassed by that exchange instead of secretly pleased that he noticed.

They busied themselves unhooking their seat belts and grabbing their bags from the overhead compartments. She, her duffel bag. He, a monogrammed leather carryall.

The Medford airport seethed with travelers in heavy coats and scarves. She spotted Deb and Roxanne in the queue of people waiting for the passengers to disembark. Deb's brown hair hung loose to her waist. The silver bracelets on her wrist jangled as she waved. Roxanne hung back a bit, almost as if she preferred to stay in Deb's shadow. Blackstone pushed past them without a backward glance.

The three women hugged each other fiercely, mindless of the other people heading for their destinations. At first, Munch thought Deb had two black eyes. But on closer examination she realized that she was just seeing very dark circles, like smudges of charcoal, under her friend's blue eyes.

Even inside the airport, it was cold. She stopped at the bathroom to pull on a second pair of jeans over the pair she was wearing. When she emerged from the bathroom, Deb nodded approvingly. "You look good, partner."

Roxanne said nothing.

"I got sober," Munch blurted out.

"Yeah, I did that once," Deb said. "Terrible accident." Roxanne and Deb laughed. Munch realized that they had no idea what she was talking about.

"No, I mean on purpose. I haven't had a drink or a drug for eight months."

"Must be about time, then." More laughter—sounding toxic and jittery.

She wanted to ask them if they'd been drinking, but realized that was a stupid question.

"Well, come on then," Deb said. "We got an hour-and-a-half drive to Canyonville. I hope you brought money." She looked at Roxanne and the two of them laughed.

"Or we ain't getting out of the parking lot," Roxanne said.

Roxanne and Deb led the way. Up ahead, she noticed the crowd part with angry mumbling. She turned to pinpoint the cause of this reaction and saw a trio of black men in the nucleus of the mob. The three were dressed in long coats and superfly hats. She realized that they were the only black faces in the airport.

"Boy, did you make a wrong turn," someone in the crowd said.

"You ain't in Kansas now," another voice chimed in.

The air was close with the threat of violence. Munch looked at her companions, but they were oblivious to what was unfolding. The black men regrouped, forming a circle so that their eyes pointed out to every direction. They spoke quietly between themselves, faces impassive, eyes never leaving the crowd. She could only imagine what they were saying to each other. Were they as surprised as she to find hatred flourishing in this remote place? Or worse, were they not surprised at all?

She wanted to say something—to protest—but she didn't. It wasn't really her business, was it? She hurried to catch up with her friends. The scene haunted her as they left the terminal. If blacks were treated this badly in a public place, what must it be like for Boogie? Maybe Canyonville was different.

Tux's rusty white Ford pickup was parked at an angle in the parking lot, taking up two parking spaces. The doors weren't locked. Roxanne opened the passenger door and invited Munch to climb in. The door panels were missing, as were much of the inner mechanisms. Pieces of wood held the windows up.

Deb had to open the door to pay the parking attendant with the five-dollar bill that Munch dug out of her pocket.

"We better get gas, too," Deb said.

"The gauge reads half-full," Munch said.

Deb laughed. "Oh, shit, that hasn't worked since he's had the truck."

Munch fished out a twenty and handed it to Deb. This was going to be an expensive vacation, she realized. She sat between her two friends. The upholstery was stiff with cold and ripped in the middle of the seat. It pinched her butt, even through the layers of her jeans. She knew it was no accident that she was seated in the middle. Next time she would jockey for a window seat.

Deb pulled into a gas station and came to a lurching stop at the self-serve pump.

"What's the story with you and Lisa?" Deb asked as she filled the tank.

"I was all set to take Asia and Lisa up and split on me."

"Sounds like we need to have a word with that cunt," Deb said, finishing with the pump nozzle and screwing the gas cap back on.

"I'll be happy to just get the baby back. By the way, what was your ol' man doing in L.A.?" Munch asked as they got on their way.

Deb snuck a sideways look at Roxanne. "He had business there. I'm not supposed to say what."

Roxanne looked out the window.

"What kind of business?" Munch asked.

"Club business. He's a Gypsy Joker," Deb added proudly.

Munch whistled. "I thought the Angels killed them all off."

"Not all of them," Deb said. "The Oakland chapter relocated up here."

"Welcome to the country," Roxanne said.

Munch drew her coat tighter.

It took Blackstone two hours to complete the journey to Canyonville in his rented sedan. The town had one main street ending in a truck depot. On this boulevard were two bars, the Snakepit being one of them. There was also a market, a Western clothing store, and a tattoo parlor.

He stopped at a market, noting that it offered ammo and live bait for sale in addition to produce. A sheepskin-lined suede coat displayed in the window of the shop next door caught his eye. He wished Moody had warned him how cold it was here. His gabardine sports jacket wasn't getting the job done.

As he walked inside the market, customers and staff alike viewed him with interest.

"Can I help you?" a large woman behind the counter asked.

"You got a pay phone?" he asked.

"Sure, honey." She directed him to the back of the store. "Anything else you need, don't be afraid to ask." He pulled out his notebook, found Tom Moody's number, and dialed it. While the phone rang, he glanced up at the bulletin board over his head and read the flyers posted up there. The first one warned of a Jewish banking conspiracy. The second invited him to discover the truth about his Aryan heritage.

Moody answered his phone, "Sheriff's Department."

"It's me," Blackstone said. "I'm in town, at the market, freezing my ass off."

Moody chuckled. "I'm just two miles west of you," he said and went on to describe a yellow house with a white Jimmy parked in the driveway. "I'll be waiting."

"Anything new on the—"

"Let's talk in person," Moody said, cutting him off. "I'll see you when you get here."

Moody, like most resident deputies in small towns, operated out of his house. His was a one-man show.

Blackstone followed the directions he'd been given and parked in the street. Moody's house was a simple one-story building on a half-acre of land. The area between the road and the house had been cleared of shrubbery. Two large fir trees dominated the back yard. Blackstone stepped carefully through the mud to reach the front porch. A portly man in uniform answered his knock.

"You must be Blackstone," the man said, gripping Blackstone's hand briefly. "Moody, here." The deputy guided Blackstone inside and bade him sit. The front room of the house was similar to cop shops everywhere—a desk piled high with paperwork, a bulletin board full of composite sketches and photographs. The smell of coffee brewing wafted in from the kitchen.

Moody wore a dark brown uniform with light brown piping up the leg. A silver star hung over his left pocket; his name tag above the right. When he sat, his pantlegs hiked up to reveal dark brown Wellington boots. Blackstone eyed the footwear enviously, feeling the cold dampness creeping through his socks and loafers.

Moody pushed aside the Stetson hat resting on top of his desk and fished out some paperwork. It was the copy of the FBI firearms alert memo. "Like I told you before, I called them in three weeks ago and told them where all those weapons were. They got all the pay phones trapped and traced," Moody said, staring at Blackstone with bright blue eyes set in a ruddy face. As he talked, he constantly smoothed the thin strands of his white-blond hair. His gun belt was all but lost under his prominent gut. "They really have a hard-on for this one," he added.

"You seem to know a lot about what's going on on the inside," Blackstone said.

Moody shrugged and lit a cigar. "I got my sources." He opened his desk and pulled out the photograph of Jonathan Garillo. "This guy might have been around," he said. "I can't be sure. All these hippies look alike after a while. But there's something familiar about the eyes. I think he wore a beard when he was up here, and he didn't have that messy hole in his head. You say he had the number to the Snakepit in his wallet?"

"That's right." Blackstone poured himself a cup of coffee. "My, uh," he paused, struggling with the word to use to describe Munch. He hated to call her a snitch, but "concerned citizen" didn't quite cut it either. "The Mancini woman, Munch, confirmed the link between Garillo and local individuals. She also had physical evidence that tied together the feds' case, the stolen weaponry, and your resident bikers."

"Had?" Moody asked.

"There was a complication," Blackstone said.

Moody nodded thoughtfully. "So you want to clear your homicide," he said, running his hand over his scalp.

"That's part of it," Blackstone said. "I also want to vindicate my department."

"And you don't trust the feds to have your department's best interests at heart?"

This time Blackstone laughed. "That goes without saying."

"Where do you want to start?" Moody asked.

"The Mancini woman is going to check in with us when she can get to a phone," Blackstone said.

"You gave her my number?" Moody asked.

"Yes."

"That might have been a mistake," Moody said. "The feds have traps on all the pay phones. Speaking of which, let's find out what they're up to."

"You going to talk to your source?" Blackstone asked.

Moody chuckled again. "Something like that." Moody took Blackstone down the hallway of his house. After passing one bedroom, Moody unlocked the door to a second room. Blackstone was stunned to find an array of sophisticated electronic equipment. Two out of three reel-to-reel tape recorders slowly revolved. A shortwave radio set crackled. Another table was covered with Teletype machines and an electronic typewriter. Moody even had a videocassette recorder.

A red light mounted in front of the third tape recorder lit. There was a click as the machine came to life and its reels began to spin.

"Voice-activated," Moody said proudly.

"Whose voice?" Blackstone asked.

"Why don't we find out?" Moody said, sitting before the tape recorders. "Let's see what our government servants are up to." He twisted a volume knob and voices filled the room, familiar voices. They heard chairs scrape and throats clear.

"*How was your vacation, sir?*" Blackstone recognized Claire's distinctive voice.

"*Wonderful,*" a man's voice answered. "*What's the latest?*"

"That's the boss—the director out of Sacramento," Moody

explained. "He came up this morning. They've been waiting for him to get back. He wanted to be in on the raid."

"*We're set for tomorrow night,*" Claire's voice answered. "*Bolt reports that all the principals will be gathered for their monthly meeting.*"

"*What about the money?*" the director asked.

"*Brian Tuxford is driving up from Los Angeles with the cash. We expect him to arrive around midnight and then it's a go.*"

"*How about the L.A. end of things?*" the director asked. "*I understand there was some trouble down there.*"

"*Nothing but. We've kept a lid on it,*" she said. "*I had the woman who screwed up things for us at the morgue remanded into custody.*"

"*What about the shooting incident?*"

"*For now, the LAPD think it was one of their own. The human rights activists are up in arms. That should keep them busy for a while.*"

"*What really happened?*"

"*Willis shot a cop. Tuxford obviously decided that it went against his interests for Willis to be taken alive.*"

"*What about that homicide dick? Blackwood?*"

"*Blackstone,*" Claire corrected.

"*Are you sure he won't make any trouble? I've heard he's pretty sharp.*"

"*Oh, he's very clever,*" Claire said. "*Just ask him.*"

Moody and Blackstone heard guffaws. Blackstone's grip tightened on the pen in his hand.

"*Keep me informed,*" the one Moody identified as the director said.

They heard sounds of doors opening and shutting, feet walking.

"Bolt is the code name of their snitch," Moody explained.

"How did you bug their headquarters?" Blackstone asked.

"They set up shop in the Motel 7 on the interstate. I've had those rooms wired since I took over here," he explained. "I like to know what's going on in my town." He lit a cigar and then pointed it at Blackstone to emphasize his words. "I might have been born at night," he added, "but it wasn't *last* night."

"What do you know about Brian Tuxford?"

"He's the treasurer of the Gypsy Jokers. Goes by the moniker Tux. Drives an eighteen-wheeler."

"Treasurer, huh? Sounds like the feds have been holding off their bust so they can catch him with the dope and the money."

"Yep," Moody said. "Bigger money, bigger bust. Looks good on a congressional report."

"Meanwhile, all those weapons have been circulating."

"They'll probably leave that part out," Moody said.

The red light blinked to life. Moody held up a hand to quiet Blackstone. "Wait a minute, there's more."

A new man was speaking.

"Does the director know how you manage to be so au courant on the situation in Los Angeles?"

"That's gotta be Vanowen," Blackstone said, recognizing the agent's Ivy League arrogance.

Claire laughed. *"Director Hadley has never been one to concern himself with details that he'd rather not know. He thinks it keeps his hands clean."*

"But really, Claire," Vanowen's voice went on, *"a cop? Did you have to sleep with the man?"*

"It wasn't the only way," she said, *"but it certainly was the quickest. He considers himself quite the catch—big man on campus. I know how to play that type."*

Adrenaline coursed through Blackstone's body, causing his legs to shake. He sat down heavily, lest he fall down. Moody watched him with concern.

"*Well, I suppose the situation called for drastic measures,*" they heard Vanowen say. "*Talk about Murphy's Law.*"

"*Desperate times call for desperate actions,*" she said, then laughed. "*Don't be such a prig, Jared. I'd do it again gladly. It wasn't a totally unpleasant experience.*"

The shaking that had begun in his legs spread to his torso. The back of his neck burned with embarrassment and impotent rage. Moody looked at him sympathetically. "Well, at least she gave you that," he said.

"She used me," he said, stating the obvious.

Moody patted the top of his head. "I told you they were like that," he said. "They use people and throw them away when they're done."

"Not this time," Blackstone said, thinking furiously. "I've got to make some calls to Los Angeles." Despite the shock of Claire's betrayal, things were beginning to fall into place. He pulled out his notebook and listed the facts. Then he turned the page and listed his suspicions. To support those, he needed to fill in some blanks, but he was starting to get the picture.

His first call was to the hospital, where he checked on Alex's condition and learned that his partner was still under, but stable. The second call he made was to the crime lab. It was after their regular hours, but he convinced the switchboard operator to ring Firearms. Jeff Hagouchi answered the phone.

"It's me," Blackstone said.

"You'll never believe what I found," Jeff said.

"Try me," Blackstone said, "you'd be surprised what I'll believe."

"The bullets I retrieved from your unit were an exact match to the bullets that killed that couple in Venice, the Ruiz/Guzman case."

"You're positive?"

"Yes. What's going on? Where are you?"

"Jeff, document everything. Take pictures in front of witnesses. Cover our asses."

"We got more background on Darnel Willis. He was a sniper in Vietnam, got to liking it too much. He tried to re-up but the Corps turned him down. Since he's been a civilian he's racked up quite a sheet, mostly violent crimes: aggravated assault, weapons charges, rape. He joined the National Guard as a weekend warrior before his jacket caught up with him. They booted him last month."

"Let me take a wild guess. This was in Kern County."

"You got it. The same armory that was hit."

"I'm reasonably certain Willis was our freeway sniper as well as the shooter in the Ruiz/Guzman murders."

"This just about closes your homicides, right?" Jeff asked.

"Not quite," Blackstone said, looking out of Moody's window. It was getting dark. "There's still some loose ends. On the freeway shooting, remember how I said there would be two of them? The driver and the shooter?"

"Yeah."

A large logging truck swept down the road, its air horn blaring as it negotiated a blind curve. "I'm thinking we're looking for a truck driver. I'm following a lead from . . . a source. I believe the accomplice, the driver, did Willis in L.A."

"Not a cop?" Jeff asked.

"No, we're clean on this one. The trick will be to prove it. I'll check in with you tomorrow." He hung up before Jeff could ask him any more questions.

23

Roxanne slipped a Rolling Stones cassette into the jerry-rigged eight-track and turned the volume all the way up, rendering conversation impossible. The drive from the Medford airport to Canyonville took over an hour. By the time they got to Deb's house, it was raining heavily. Large logging trucks barreled down the freeway outside her door and made the walls shake. The wood-burning stove in the main room threw one-sided heat on the three women seated around the kitchen table.

"So you put down?" Deb asked.

"Yeah," Munch said.

"That's good, partner," Deb said. "I always told you to get off the dope, didn't I?"

Munch watched Deb shake four Benzedrine tablets onto the glossy back cover of an *Easyriders* magazine. She folded the thick paper over the pills and used the back of a spoon to grind them into powder. Munch couldn't take her eyes off the process.

Deb then took a razor blade and cut the powder into four lines. "You got a bill?" she asked.

Munch reached into her wallet and pulled out a crisp one-dollar bill. Roxanne took it from her and rolled it into a tube.

"You didn't want any of this, did you?" Deb asked.

"No," Munch said. "I didn't even know you could snort whites."

Deb drew a deep noisy breath through her nose to clean her sinuses. "Oh yeah. It's a little harsh, but it works."

Roxanne went first, expertly inhaling the two lines set out for her. Her eyes watered. Deb took the bill next. She poised over the speed, but stopped when Boogie burst through the front door.

"Look who's here," she said to her son, folding the magazine over the drugs and concealing the rolled-up bill in her hand.

"Hey, Boogieman," Munch said, holding out her arms.

Boogie ran for her. He put his head down and barreled into her chest. She caught him up in a tight embrace and kissed his flushed cheeks.

"Are you still my ace boon coon?" she asked.

"Say it," he said, "the whole thing."

"You're my ace boon coon," she recited, touching his forehead. "You're my pride and joy." She poked his belly. "You're an ugly little sucker," she said, now tweaking his nose, "but you're still my boy." He laughed his distinctive belly laugh.

"It's good to have you here," Deb said, watching the exchange. "What took you so long?"

Munch felt a lump form in her throat.

"It's my birthday next week," Boogie said, tugging on her sleeve and demanding her attention.

"I know," she said. "That's why I'm here."

"Honey," Deb said, "get Mama her T-bird. This calls for a celebration."

Boogie went to the refrigerator and fetched his mother her wine, getting himself a Mountain Dew. He brought the wine to Munch first.

"See there," Deb said. "That's the man I raised. Guests first."

Munch stared at the bottle for a long moment. "No thanks, Boogie. I'll take one of those sodas."

"So this is like a test," Roxanne said, "you being here and all."

"I guess maybe it is," Munch said uncomfortably.

"You still smoke, right?" Deb asked, pulling out a Baggie of bright green pot.

"No," Munch said. "Nothing. I don't use anything anymore."

Deb turned to her son. "Boogie, go get mama her pipe." Boogie ran into the bedroom. He held his arms out from his sides and made zooming noises.

"You don't mind, do you?" Deb asked, holding out the joint.

"I'll just sit by the window," Munch said, scooting her chair away from them. Deb and Roxanne had both shed their coats as soon as the fire got going, but Munch had yet to thaw out. She cracked the window open six inches. Cold rain blew in.

Boogie returned with a short-stemmed pipe.

"Honey," Deb said, "why don't you go to your room and play. Mama and her friends need to catch up." She waited until the boy was out of the room and then opened the magazine back up. With the bill up her nose, she paused and said to Munch, "I'm real proud of you. That dope was killing you." She snorted up the whites, unrolled the bill, and licked it. She offered Munch her bill back. Munch waved for her to keep it.

Boogie came back into the room and set his empty soda can on the table. "I'm hungry."

"You want a sandwich?" Deb asked. "Munch?"

"Yeah, thanks."

Deb took down jars of peanut butter and jelly and cut four slices from a loaf of misshapen bread.

"Is that homemade?" Munch asked.

"What was your first clue?" Roxanne asked, the weed pinched between her fingers.

"I got chickens in the back, my own vegetable garden, we even hunt for our own meat," Deb added. She looked at her son. "Boogie won't eat venison unless I sneak it in on him."

"Aren't you having any?" Munch asked, seeing that Deb had only prepared two sandwiches.

"No, but you go on."

Boogie and Munch ate their sandwiches while Deb and Roxanne passed the bottle of wine. When Boogie finished, Deb grabbed his coat.

"Honey, I want you to go over to Stella's for a while."

"Aw, Mom," Boogie said. "I'm sick of going over there."

"I want to show Munch around."

"Can't I come?"

"Yeah, Mom," Munch said. "Can't he come?"

Deb shot Munch a dirty look and then turned to her son. "You'd just have to sit in the truck when we go in the bar. Wouldn't you rather play with your friends?"

"We won't be gone long, Boogie," Munch cut in. She knew Deb wasn't the kind of mother to let her kid sit in the car while she sat in some bar. That was one thing Deb used to say she'd never do.

"How long is not long?" Boogie asked.

Munch produced the present she had brought him. "Open it."

He ripped through the meager wrapping and then squealed when he opened the box. "All right!"

"What do you say?" Deb asked.

"Thank you."

Munch strapped the watch on his wrist and pointed to the hour hand. "When this points to the three"—she pointed to the minute hand—"and this one points at the six again, we'll come back."

"Okay," he agreed and walked out the door, his eyes never leaving his new treasure.

Deb stood up. "I want to show y'all something, wait here."

She walked off in the direction of the bedrooms. Roxanne turned to Munch. "Are you still writing poetry?" she asked.

"Not lately. Not since I got sober."

"I liked that Christmas one you wrote."

"'Twas the Night Before Kicking'?"

"Yeah, that one."

"I'll mail you a copy," Munch promised. "So what have you been up to?"

"I was in Alaska," Roxanne said, "working the pipeline."

"How was that?"

"Cold and shitty."

"And now you're here." A gust of cold rain blew in the window. Roxanne met her eyes. "Yeah, right. Now I'm here."

Deb returned to the kitchen, preceded by a three-foot Pinocchio marionette that she held suspended by a wooden crossbar. The puppet did a jerky dance.

"Took me three nights to put this sucker together," she said.

"You made that?" Munch asked. "I'm blown away."

Roxanne finished the last draught of wine, carefully removed the bottom ring of the cap, and put the bottle in a box of similar bottles. Deb returned from hiding Boogie's birthday present, picked up his empty soda can, and put it a plastic crate marked for cans.

"Deb—"

"Deborah," she corrected, standing by the sink.

"Sorry . . . Deborah. Are you happy here? Is this what you want?"

"Sure," Deb said, covering her nostrils with the tips of her fingers. She took a deep breath, removing her fingers halfway through and noisily sucking in any particles of drugs left in her sinuses. "Ahh," she said.

"How about Boogie?" Munch said.

"What about Boogie?"

"Is this what's best for him? I mean, you're out here so far away from everything. What if something happened? You don't even have a phone."

"Don't worry about that," Deb said. "Out here we all take care of ourselves. It's all them other people what has to worry."

"Like who?"

"Anybody who fucks with us, that's who." Deb grabbed her coat. "C'mon, I'll show you around."

The Snakepit was just how Munch pictured it. The only difference between it and the hundred other dives she'd been in was the songs on the jukebox. As the three women entered, Johnny Paycheck was singing "Take This Job and Shove It." Merle Haggard followed with a song about drinking. According to him, the reasons to quit didn't outweigh all the reasons why.

Roxanne and Deb took seats at the bar. The bartender automatically set them up with shots of whiskey and beer chasers. Munch asked the bartender where the pay phone was and for three dollars in change.

"I've got to call the probation recording," she explained to her friends.

"Good thing you remembered," Deb said.

Roxanne downed her drink. "What about that?" she asked.

"What about what?" Munch said.

"Pigs. You still hate pigs, right?"

Munch fingered the scar on her cheek. "Not really. I used to think they were the enemy, always hassling me, always busting me. I used to think that if they'd just leave me alone, I'd be okay. Now I realize that they rescued me."

"By locking you up?" Deb asked, scowling.

"I needed to be saved from myself," Munch said. "I was my own worst enemy."

Roxanne nodded and took a drink of beer.

"Make your call, already," Deb said. "I got some other shit to show you."

"Good," Munch said as she walked to the pay phone. "Because I didn't come all the way up here to see a bar." If she wanted to watch people get drunk and stupid, she didn't say out loud, she could have stayed in Los Angeles.

She called Tom Moody's private line. When a man answered, she said, "Hi, I'm trying to reach—"

"You've got the wrong number," he said and hung up abruptly. She called once more and this time the phone just rang. Great. Wonderful plan so far.

She returned to her friends, both of whom now had two empty shot glasses apiece sitting in front of them.

"Everything come out all right?" Deb asked.

Apparently Deb had forgotten what Munch had gotten up to do, she thought as she slid into the next bar stool. "Yeah, everything's just peachy." She caught the bartender's attention. "Can I get a Seven-Up, please?" He nodded and filled a glass from one of the nozzles above the ice bin. She turned back to Deb. "So who was Sleaze supposed to have snitched on anyway?"

216

"You don't want any part of that," Deb assured her and then ordered another round.

"I don't want to know a lot of things," Munch said. "Who even told you that he was a snitch?"

"James, wasn't it?" Roxanne said.

Deb looked skyward for a second, her lips glistening with whiskey. "Yeah, come to think of it. It was James." She lit a Kool. "When you were in the can, Tux called. They should be getting in tomorrow night."

"James and Asia still with him?"

"Yeah, he says she's really getting on his nerves, crying every two seconds. I told him she was probably teething and to put some Southern Comfort in her bottle. Remember when we used to do that for Boogie?"

Munch squirmed with a hot flash of guilt. "I remember. Did you tell him I was here?"

"He didn't give me a chance. We'll surprise him, huh?"

Moody hung up the phone and told Blackstone, "That was your snitch. She's at the Snakepit." He showed him the digital readout of the phone number on a box attached to the phone. "I couldn't talk to her without tipping our hand. That pay phone has a tap on it, but I didn't give them enough time."

"Let's get over there," Blackstone said.

Ten minutes later they pulled up across the street in Blackstone's rental sedan. The bar was built low to the ground, the exterior wall covered in layers of dark brown woodshake. The entrance was a saloon-style double door. There were no windows.

"This place got a back door?" Blackstone asked. His breath fogged the windshield. He cracked the window and blew on his hands. He thought about the sheepskin-lined coat he'd admired earlier and wished he had bought it when he had the chance.

"You want some coffee?" Moody asked, producing a thermos.

"Yeah, thanks."

Just then, three women exited the bar. He recognized the women instantly as the two who had met Munch at the airport. One of the women was tall and blonde; she moved with her shoulders rounded and her head bowed as if uncomfortable with her height. The second woman had waist-long brown hair and wore an abundance of jewelry: large rings on each finger and silver bracelets from wrist to elbow. Munch exited last, looking none too pleased.

"That's her," he told Moody without turning his head.

"The little one?"

A large logging truck barreled down the road, spraying slush as it passed. Munch's eyes widened, and she froze in midstep. Blackstone was reminded of a doe caught in crossfire. He also knew he'd put her there and that if anything happened to her he'd have a hard time forgiving himself.

Silver Girl pushed out to the street first, followed next by Blondie, and then a reluctant Munch.

"You recognize the other two?" Blackstone asked.

"Oh sure," Moody said, unscrewing the thermos cap. "Biker chicks, they live out on Miller Road by the nickel mine. The one with the brown hair and bracelets has been in town for almost a year. Name's Deborah. She's got a little boy. Tuxford's been dicking her and parking his rig at her house for the last few months. Blondie's only been here a few weeks."

"Roxanne," Blackstone said. "The Mancini woman mentioned her."

He watched the trio of women interact. Munch didn't seem

to belong with the other two. To begin with, she didn't stagger. Her complexion showed signs of life, whereas the other two women were pallid. Not a huge surprise, knowing as he did that she had come from sunny California, whereas the other two subjects were more or less local girls.

No, it was more than that. He watched her pull her coat tighter and duck her head against a chill wind that had come up. The other two women just laughed, their coats swinging open. They were drunk on their ass, he realized.

Roxanne and Deborah jostled each other as they hit the street, leaning their bodies forward and letting their feet catch up to them. Their voices carried as they laughed and swore. Deborah spit and viewed the street suspiciously, as if daring unknown adversaries to come forth. Roxanne followed Deborah's lead, though her bravado was less convincing. Munch drew her mouth into a tight line.

They all came to a stop when they reached a rusted white pickup truck. Munch held out her hand to Deborah, who shook her head adamantly, sending her long hair flying. Munch stood her ground. Blackstone realized that she was demanding the keys to the truck.

"Good for you," he said. As if hearing him, she turned and looked directly at him. Her face remained impassive, but he was sure she had seen him. At least she knew she wasn't alone.

"She sees us," he reported, his hand on the door handle.

Moody held him back. "She's all right. Besides, we've got company."

"Where?"

"Blue van coming up the road."

Blackstone snuck a look in the rearview mirror. "Feds?"

"Ah, yep," Moody said. "Things should heat up now."

24

Boogie was waiting on the front porch, staring at his new watch, when the three women got back to Deb's house.

"Look," he said excitedly, "it glows in the dark."

"Aren't you cold?" Munch asked, opening the door and ushering him inside.

"No," he said.

Deb and Roxanne stumbled in five minutes later. Deb howled. Roxanne imitated her. Munch rummaged through the pantry and the refrigerator. "I'll make dinner," she said, finding eggs, onions, and potatoes.

"Sounds good to me," Deb said. "You sure you know how?"

"I'll manage."

Boogie and Roxanne took seats at the kitchen table. Deb wandered off to her bedroom.

"So what did you do today?" Munch asked Boogie as she washed the potatoes.

"Practiced."

"What?"

"Pitching. I'm on the Little League team."

"Your mom says Tux is coming back tomorrow night." She chopped onions. "Is that a good thing?"

"I guess," Boogie said.

"Does he play ball with you? That kind of stuff?"

"He takes me on trips," Boogie volunteered, "and when we see other people we pretend he's my daddy. He calls me son."

"Oh," Munch said, "that's nice. Why don't you go wash up for dinner?"

After Boogie left the room, Munch turned to Roxanne. "What's the deal with this guy and Boogie?"

"What do you mean?"

"You don't think it's weird for a Gypsy Joker to be hanging around with a little half-breed kid?"

"I guess he has his reasons."

"That's what I'm thinking," Munch said, trying to conceal her unhappiness.

Deb came out of the bedroom carrying a rifle, some rags, and a can of cleaning fluid. She set everything on the kitchen table. While Munch watched, Deb deftly broke the weapon down to three parts: the wooden stock, the steel barrel, and the trigger mechanism.

"Oooh," Roxanne said sarcastically, "Tuxy's coming home, better clean his rifle. She does everything but wipe his butt."

Munch knew her friend prided herself on being a "good" ol' lady. Deb would tell you that it meant respecting your man and standing by him. Maybe she believed that. Munch always thought the biker version of being a good woman translated more to like, "Shut up and eat shit." It wasn't quite as romantic when you looked at it that way.

"This is my gun," Deb said defensively. "I thought I'd take Munch out shooting tomorrow."

Munch broke eggs into a frying pan and scrambled them as they cooked. "That sounds fun."

Deb picked up the trigger assembly. "Only something's wrong with it. The trigger won't pull back."

"You want me to look at it?" Munch asked. "Roxanne, watch the eggs, will you?"

Roxanne stood unsteadily, lurched to the stove, and took up a one-eye-at-a-time vigil over the frying pan.

Munch picked up the trigger mechanism and studied it for a moment. "Here's your problem," she finally said. "The spring has slipped off the stop here."

"Can you fix it?"

"Sure. I just need to pop the spring back in place."

"I knew there was a reason I liked having you around," Deb said as she unscrewed the cap on another bottle of wine.

Munch handed her the working trigger and Deb slid it back into place.

"Up here," Deb said, as she wiped down the rifle's barrel-mounted scope, "we believe in being self-sufficient. We can live off the land if we have to. And between the meat we hunt and the food we grow, we're totally organic." She paused to take another sip of wine. Boogie came back in the room and leaned against his mother.

Munch looked out the window and asked, "Which one is the Thunderbird tree?"

Boogie thought that was the silliest thing he ever heard. "Thunderbird tree," he echoed. "Ha-ha."

Munch cast him an adoring look. You had to love a kid who got your jokes.

* * *

The next morning Munch and Boogie were up first. The bus for school, he explained, stopped right outside the door. She made him pancakes and brewed a pot of coffee. Deb awoke around nine and stumbled into the kitchen smoking a Kool.

"Smells good," she said, clearing her throat.

"About time you got up," Munch said. "I thought we were getting back to nature today."

"Nature will wait," Deb said. She hugged her son. "Good morning, baby."

Outside, the bus driver sounded his horn. Boogie grabbed his book bag and ran out the door. Deb waved from the doorway, flashing some leg out of her open bathrobe. She laughed as she shut the door. "Gave him a thrill. He don't give door-to-door service to every kid, I'll tell you that."

Roxanne groaned from under a pile of blankets on the couch.

"Come on," Deb said, kicking the cushions. "We're all taking a hike. Munch wants to see some country."

"You go on without me," Roxanne mumbled. "I'll just hang out here."

When breakfast was over, Deb called Munch outside to help her load two heavy twelve-inch-square wooden crates into the back of the truck.

"Be careful," Deb said. "This stuff is fragile."

"What is it?"

"I'll show you in a bit," Deb promised, sliding her rifle into the gun rack behind the bench seat.

They drove south. Signs on the road indicated that they were heading for Grants Pass.

"Where are we going?" Munch asked.

"Just a mite farther."

They drove for twenty minutes, then turned off the paved highway.

"Now I'll show you some country," Deb said, grabbing her rifle as she got out of the truck. Munch slid out on her side.

They set off through the forest. Deb carried the rifle slung casually across her back; the webbed sling crossed her chest. Munch trailed behind, negotiating around thick brambles of blackberry bushes. With each step, the soft, wet blanket of pine needles underfoot released a fresh scent. The cold invigorated her. She decided that if she lived up here, she would quit smoking. It would be too much of a sacrilege to fill her lungs with anything but this clean fresh air. "I see why you like it here," she said.

They hiked down a narrow path through the dense forest. Deb pointed out black deer droppings. Ferns curled out from the hillside. The path led to a waterfall that fed a pond large enough to swim in. She scrambled after Deb down the large boulders that surrounded and trapped the water. Numerous paw and hoof-prints were embedded in the surrounding mud.

"Taste some of that," Deb said when they'd reached the water's edge.

Munch crouched and cupped some of the cold water in her hand. It was surprisingly sweet.

"We've got the world to ourselves here, don't we?" she said, looking around at the uninterrupted vista of forest and sky. "This is God's country."

"Plenty of room for you," Deb said. "What's keeping you in Los Angeles?"

She had to think a minute before she answered. What *was* keeping her there? "Well, for one, I'm still on probation. I've also got a pretty good job."

"You could get a job up here," Deb said. "They're always hiring at the logging camps if you're willing to work. Especially you, once you tell them you're a mechanic. Can't you get your probation transferred?"

"I don't know if they'll do that to another state and all. I've also got these meetings that I go to."

"Do you have to go to them?"

"Yes and no. Listen, Deb, there's another reason I came up here," Munch said.

"Shhh," Deb cautioned. "Did you hear that?" She slipped the rifle off her back.

Munch listened, but all she heard was the water tumbling over the rocks. "What?"

A deer broke free from the bushes and looked their way. He was a buck. Twin-forked spikes of antlers sprang from his head. His eyes were large, brown, and unblinking.

Deb took aim.

Munch yelled "Shoo!" The deer bolted, bounding gracefully on his thin legs.

Deb fired twice. The first shot threw the deer's head back, the second tore his throat out. He crumpled to the ground.

"Why'd you have to do that?" Munch asked.

"You always want to avoid a body hit," Deb said, misreading Munch's question. "It can ruin the meat. I've seen where the bullet nicked the intestines and dumped shit all through the stomach." She took off towards her kill. Munch followed reluctantly.

"Now what?" she asked when they reached the animal. His eyes were still open. Blood from his throat wound soaked the ground.

"This is good," Deb said.

"Why is that?"

"When you dress the carcass, one of the first things you do is cut the jugular and let the animal bleed out."

"What's the other first thing?" Munch asked.

"You slice open the belly and roll out the guts. To preserve the meat, you got to get it cooled down as quickly as possible."

She looked at the fallen animal. It had to weigh at least eighty to a hundred pounds. "How are we going to get it to the truck?" she asked, not relishing the idea of dealing with the dead animal.

"We'll bind its legs together and pole-carry it. C'mon, where's your imagination?"

While Deb tied together the deer's hooves with some twine she had in the truck, Munch found a branch long enough and strong enough to support the animal's weight. Together they half-dragged and half carried the dead animal up to the road and slung it into the back of the pickup truck.

Deb started the motor.

"Now where?" Munch asked.

"Same place we're going tonight—for the party."

"What party?"

"It's Friday night."

"Of course." *Like one day is different than another,* Munch thought. It wasn't like Deb worked a straight job or anything.

"And Tux is coming home," Deb added.

"So where is this party?"

"At the clubhouse."

"I don't want to go to a Gypsy Joker clubhouse," Munch said. An unescorted female visiting a biker's stronghold was ill-advised. She should know.

"You don't have to worry," Deb assured her. "They know who my ol' man is and they respect him. You'll be safe."

"But right now we're just dropping off Bambi, right?"

"Well, there is one other thing I promised Tux I'd do before he got back," Deb said. "Besides, I thought you were so hot to get your hands on Asia."

"I am," Munch said.

"So quit your bitching."

The clubhouse was closer to Grants Pass than Canyonville, Munch soon learned, and would require an additional twenty-minute drive. Deb shoved a Leon Russell cartridge into the eight-track and cranked the volume up full bore. Fifteen minutes later, they turned off the paved highway and headed up a narrow, deeply rutted dirt road.

"Is it much farther?" Munch yelled over the music. "I've got to pee."

Deb pulled over. "Go ahead. I need to stop here anyway."

"Check out this boulder," Munch said as they both got out. "Doesn't it look like a big old turtle?"

"I guess so." Deb reached for one of the boxes in the back of the truck. "Give me a hand."

Munch grabbed one of the wooden crates and together they shimmied down the embankment.

Munch found a bush to squat behind while Deb unpacked the contents of the boxes. Each crate held two olive drab steel ammo boxes. Deb slipped open the latches and removed Styrofoam packing. The Styrofoam fell away to reveal cylinders of black cardboard, each the size of a small aerosol can. One at a time, she carefully slit the tape wound about the cardboard wrapping.

"What are those?" Munch asked.

"Grenades," Deb said.

"Lovely," she said, "just fucking lovely."

"Don't worry," Deb said, "they're not the kind that go boom."

"What other kind is there?"

Deb held up the gray can with the yellow stripe for Munch to read what was written there: No. 35, WHITE SMOKE, HC GRENADE. Beneath the words there was a military insignia.

"That makes me feel much better."

"Give me a hand with this stuff, will you?"

"You sure I'm not going to blow off some fingers? I might need them later."

"I know what I'm doing," Deb said. She dumped out the contents of a backpack on the ground. Several pieces of pipe started to roll away. She collected them and stacked them beside her. Next to these she placed the other contents of the backpack: a box of dental floss, a hammer, and a pair of scissors. The sleeves of pipe were large enough in diameter to accommodate the spoon end of the grenades.

"Check this out," Deb said, unwinding a thin strand of dental floss from its plastic case. She hammered the sleeves of pipe into the ground at the base of several trees. Then she slipped a grenade into each pipe and ran dental floss from the top of one grenade to the other, tightening the floss until it stretched taut. "When I'm ready to set it, I'll pull out the pin. If someone or something trips the string, the grenade pops out of this sleeve and goes off. Instant alert."

"What if I just cut the string?" Munch asked.

Deb unwound additional strands of dental floss. "We'll run a second line in the opposite direction, making it spring-loaded," she explained. "You cut the one side and it releases the tension."

"Ah," Munch said, understanding. "Then it pulls out the grenade from the other side."

"Exactly," Deb said. "Not too shabby, huh?"

"Oh, yeah," Munch said. "Just great. I guess a simple No TRESPASSING sign is out of the question, huh?" She didn't ask just who they were so anxious to be warned of, but it wasn't hard to figure. The weed from the other night had been green and still damp—obviously grown locally and recently harvested. "What's to stop a deer from tripping the line?"

"It's a risk we have to take," Deb said. "In 'Nam, pigs set off perimeter alarms all the time."

She said it like she was talking from personal experience, Munch noticed. Had she always been so full of shit?

"Give me a hand," Deb said. "I promised my ol' man I'd do this yesterday. We got word that the Forest Service was going to clear-cut this section last week. Had to do some hurry-up harvesting. Now our south flank is exposed. Can't have that."

They worked a moment in silence and then Munch said, "So what's the deal with your ol' man?"

"Like what?"

"You said Tux takes Boogie on road trips."

Deb didn't look up, but Munch saw that she had stopped working. "Pretty nice of him, don't you think?"

"Almost too nice, don't you think?"

"What are you saying?"

"I'm saying that he isn't doing it out of the goodness of his heart."

"How do you know? You haven't even met him."

"I've met all your ol' men."

"He wouldn't hurt Boogie."

"Using him for things he doesn't understand is hurting him. Having a man who doesn't really care about him call him son will hurt him. Can't you see that?"

Deb flinched. "Why'd you come up here? To preach to me?" She set up two more trip wires. As a finishing touch, she used a stick of camouflage grease to make the white dental floss disappear into the surrounding foliage.

"I came," Munch said, "because I care about you two. I don't want any more friends of mine getting hurt. You need to get out of here. Come back to L.A. with me."

"Why would I want to come back to the city when I have all this?"

The two women climbed back up the hill.

"How about for the sake of your kid? You used to put him first."

"I still do, but I got a life, too." Deb climbed up to the hood of the truck, whistled, and waved her arms. A minute later, two bikers materialized from behind a bend in the road.

"We felled a buck back there by the swimming hole," Deb told them. Then she made introductions. One of the men went by the name Spider, the other called himself Count. They sized Munch up as if she were the carcass in question.

"You coming back tonight?" Spider asked as he and Count lifted the deer from the back of the truck.

"Yeah," Deb said, "and I'm bringing friends."

They grunted, which Munch took to mean, "That sounds great. Look forward to seeing you."

The two women headed back down the hill. Munch watched the two men grow smaller through the sideview mirror. "How'd you know those guys would be there?"

"They always have sentries posted," Deb explained. "You see? It's perfectly safe here, so cool it. You sure it was worth getting off dope if it meant you'd have to turn into such a poop butt?"

"Yeah, I'm sure. How about you? You were going to be different, remember? You were going to be the best mom ever. Remember that?"

"Shut up," Deb said. "Just shut up, okay? God, woman, it's like I don't even know you." They drove for a few miles in silence and then Deb said, "This is about Sleaze, isn't it? I'll miss him too, you know."

"Didn't sound that way on the phone."

"I guess I was still pissed at him for snitching."

"Don't say that, you don't know for certain."

"Why do you think he got it in the throat?"

"Did Lisa tell you about that?"

"I don't talk to that cunt," Deb said.

"Then how did you know about—?" She stopped in mid-question. The answer was obvious. Deb knew about Sleaze's throat wound because she had heard about it from another source. She sure hadn't read about it in the paper.

"Look, let's just drop it, all right?" Deb said.

"Fine. If you see a pay phone," Munch said, "let's stop. I've got to call my PO's recording. I've got a funny feeling that she's going to want to see me."

25

Blackstone and Moody spent the morning going over the transcripts of all the conversations that the feds had had since moving into Motel 7. The two cops were seated in Moody's front room. Blackstone was wearing his new suede coat with the sheepskin lining. He'd also bought a pair of cowboy boots and a hat.

Moody explained that his sister-in-law in Portland was a court reporter. He sent her the tapes, which she then transcribed and sent back to him. Moody had pulled out the copies of dialogue that he felt would be of particular interest to Blackstone after the L.A. detective revealed his theory.

Three weeks ago, Blackstone learned, the bikers had suspected that there was a leak within their organization. Moody's bugs not only picked up conversations within the motel room, but when the feds played back recordings from their eavesdropping, those could be heard as well.

Moody dug through his records until he found the transcript

of a recording made two weeks earlier. "This was when things started to go sour for the feds. Their informant was in danger of being made," he said as he handed the file to Blackstone.

Blackstone opened the manila envelope and found neatly typed pages inside. He began to read. The conversation was between Special Agents Jared Vanowen and Claire Donavon.

J.V.: They think they have a snitch.

C.D.: Then let's give them a snitch.

J.V.: Who?

C.D.: Someone they already don't like. It will make them more inclined to believe that he's betrayed them.

J.V.: Sounds like you already have someone in mind.

[Sounds of paper dropping on desk surface.]

C.D.: They call him Sleaze. Last week he took a quantity of methamphetamine from the lab at the clubhouse.

J.V.: Perfect.

Sleaze? Blackstone thought. *As in Sleaze John?*

The red light in front of one of tape recorders lit up, signaling an incoming message. Moody turned up the volume. "This is your buddy Vanowen's room," he said.

"*We're going in tonight, as soon as Tuxford arrives,*" Jared Vanowen's voice said. "*We'll approach from the south.*"

They heard papers rustling. Blackstone assumed that it was the sound of a map unfolding.

"*The Forest Service just did a three-acre clear-cut,*" Vanowen's voice continued. "*This will make an excellent staging area, with only a hundred yards of woodland left to traverse before we reach our objective.*

They heard a chair scraping across the floor.

"Does Bolt know we're going in tonight?" Claire asked.

"Yes. I warned him to keep his nose clean. I reminded him that we'd already gone way over the line for him."

"How about his people in Los Angeles?"

"All set. They were moved to a safe house last Tuesday. They'll be taken to the orientation center later this week—after the bust goes down."

"I hate having to offer these scumbags deals," a new voice chimed in.

"We can't make our case without him." Claire's tone was authoritative. *"Be grateful he was willing to roll over."*

"Instant new identity, home, and job? They never had it so good."

"Did you tell him I retrieved the packet?" Claire asked.

"Why should he have peace of mind?" Vanowen said. The agents in the room chuckled.

Blackstone and Moody heard doors opening and closing. Another minute passed and then the tape recorder stopped revolving.

Moody opened his desk drawer and removed a cigar box. Inside was a revolver. "You might be needing this," he said.

Blackstone pinned his gold shield onto the lapel of his jacket, making sure that the badge hung straight and wasn't bunching the suede.

Moody handed him a holster to go with the gun, and Blackstone strapped it around his waist. Moody's private line rang. He answered it while eyeing the digital readout on the attached box.

"Moody."

"Finally," Munch said. "Is Blackstone there?"

"Just a sec, darlin'." Moody handed Blackstone the phone. "It's her."

"You okay?" Blackstone asked into the phone.

"Just great. I can't talk now. Meet me tonight. I'll walk down the road towards the nickel mine. You know where that is?"

"I'm sure I can find it. Five o'clock?"

"Yeah. But wait for me if I'm late." She hung up.

Blackstone relayed the gist of the call to Moody, who filled a thermos with coffee and said, "It's going to be a long night."

26

Boogie was playing in the front yard when they finally got back to Deb's house. "C'mon, Boogie," Munch said, grabbing the boy's hand. "Show me your room."

"Okay," he agreed as they walked out the door, his eyes never leaving his new treasure.

She spent fifteen minutes with him, not knowing what to say. He answered her questions with monosyllabic answers. She showed him how to tell time and he seemed to catch on quickly. He'd always been a bright boy. "You know, Boogie," she said, "if you ever wanted to come visit me or stay with me, you can."

"I know," he said without enthusiasm.

There was so much she wanted to explain to him. "Some people are idiots," she said.

He giggled at the word.

"And some people are just full of hate. You have to be better than them. Do you understand?"

He tucked his head to one side and scratched the side of his face. "What time is it now?" he asked, holding up the watch.

She saw that it was almost five. "Time for me to take a little walk." She hugged him. "I love you."

He squirmed. "I love you, too," he echoed.

"I'll write you. Would you like that?"

"Sure."

She smoothed hair back from his forehead. "I'm going to take a walk. When I get back, maybe we can play a game."

"Okay," he said, rubbing his ear on his shoulder.

She hit the road outside of Deb's house at a jog and didn't slow down until she was past the bend and out of sight. Ten minutes later, a station wagon rolled up next to her and stopped.

Blackstone was sitting in the passenger seat, wearing brand-new Western-style clothing. The fat, balding guy driving introduced himself as Deputy Moody and invited her to get in. She noticed after she was seated that the back doors had no inside handles.

"What did you find out?" Blackstone asked.

"I know who put the mouth on Sleaze. It was James. Lisa's James. James was the guy riding shotgun with Sleaze the last time I saw him."

"So you believe this James was involved in John Garillo's murder?"

"He's as guilty as if he pulled the trigger himself. Sleaze was set up. John was a lot of things. But they killed him for something he didn't do."

The two cops exchanged looks, as if an earlier conversation was being continued.

"What?" she asked.

"I believe Darnel Willis shot John Garillo," Blackstone said. "But he wasn't alone. Someone was driving."

"Tux?"

"What makes you say that?" Blackstone asked.

"C'mon, he's in this up to his eyeballs. What's our next step?"

"*We* are doing nothing. The FBI is going to raid the Joker club-house tonight," Blackstone said, "as soon as Tuxford arrives."

"You shouldn't tell her that," Moody said.

"No, I think she's all right. Besides," he said, "she won't be talking to anybody until it's all over."

"I won't?" Munch asked.

"No, we're pulling you out of here. It's too dangerous."

She thought about the clubhouse. From what she had seen, it wouldn't be an easy place to take. Did the FBI know about the trip wires that Deb had set up only hours ago? She sighed. Sleaze was dead and there was no bringing him back. Whether or not any of her old friends would approve of what she was about to do was irrelevant. That whole line of thinking was part of her old value system. She was a new person now, a self-supporting citizen. How many more months would she waste carrying yesterday's banners?

"I've got to go up there," she said. "There's going to be a baby up there."

"What baby?" Blackstone asked.

"Her name is Asia. She's an orphan. Her mom died a couple months ago. Sleaze was her daddy. Tux and James have her with them. They'll all be at the clubhouse tonight."

"What's your connection to this kid?" Blackstone asked.

"I'm her godmother," she said, the lie coming easier with each telling. "I promised I'd give her a good home—you know, some-where safe." She paused, tried to see outside. Her breath fogged the window. "I'm not leaving here without her."

"I don't know how all the laws concerning orphans work," Blackstone said. "That'll have to be handled at a county level."

"That's not good enough," she said.

"What did you have in mind?" Blackstone asked.

"I'll go to the party at the clubhouse tonight. Deb says that the brothers up here know Tux is her ol' man and we'll be safe. I'll grab the baby and split before the bust goes down."

"That's your whole plan?"

"No. There's one other thing we need to do. Sleaze was killed because the Jokers thought he was an FBI informant, right?"

Moody looked out his window, but Blackstone looked directly in her eyes. "Right."

"The FBI pays their informants, gives them new identities and lives, right?"

"Yes."

"A slice of that pie should go to Asia. Wouldn't that only be fair?"

"How do you propose to make that happen?" Blackstone asked.

"The same way they operate," she said. "A little bit of trade, a little bit of blackmail."

Moody turned back around. "I think I like this girl."

She massaged her throbbing temples. "There's no way they're going to make it up to that clubhouse without shedding a lot of blood. There's trip wires everywhere, I spent the morning help-ing to set them up. They're connected to illumination grenades. You say the feds are mounting a raid? That means they've set up local headquarters. I think it's time you paid them a visit."

She outlined her plan to them. The two cops listened, their faces breaking into wide smiles. They even added a few touches of their own.

Moody turned the car around. "You better get back to the house," he said to Munch.

She bent her head and clasped her hands in front of her.

"What are you doing now?" Blackstone asked.

"Calling for backup," she said, and went back to her prayers.

Munch, Deb, and Roxanne left for the party right after dinner, just as it was getting dark.

Boogie was dropped off at the neighbor's house.

The three women drove for thirty minutes, turning when they reached the dirt road leading to the clubhouse. Munch spotted a few familiar landmarks, like the turtle-shaped rock.

The truck bounced as it maneuvered over deep ruts, exposed boulders, and ancient tree roots. She pictured the damage a car would sustain trying to climb this road. It wouldn't get far before it bent tie rods or a rock punctured its oil pan. They came to the place where they had hiked to the waterfall and shot the deer. She recognized the blind bend up ahead and knew the sentries were close.

"What happens if we meet someone coming down?" Munch asked, noticing no turnouts or shoulders in the narrow road.

"Then somebody will have to put it in reverse," Deb said. She and Roxanne laughed at some inside joke. "Of course, scooters always have the right of way."

They crested the last bend in the road and Munch saw twenty Harleys parked in front of a two-story wooden hunter's lodge. The sound of rock 'n' roll carried from inside the building. Ten-foot-tall stalks of marijuana, some with roots still intact, hung upside down under the protection of the roof's awning.

Deb parked the truck. "Let's go inside and get us some antifreeze."

Roxanne laughed. Munch shivered inside her coat.

"You sure we're going to be safe?"

"What's the matter with you?" Deb asked. "You were the one

who always led the charge and it was always me holding back. Now you're a big wussy."

"A lot of things are different," Munch said. She got out of the truck and looked up. The number of stars in the sky stunned her. She'd never seen anything like it before, how they crowded each other and twinkled. Maybe it was the cold that did it. The fog of her breath was thick enough to blow smoke rings.

"Deborah," she said, wanting to share these wonders, "check it out."

But Deb's eyes were on the five or six bikers drinking beers on the front porch of the clubhouse and shouting encouragement to their brethren.

"The *hawk* is *out*," she exclaimed, her Southern accent kicking into high gear as it always seemed to do around a group of men. The men shifted their attention from whatever was going on around the side of the building and watched the three women approach.

Munch didn't have a good feeling about their scrutiny. She also knew that she didn't have a choice, so she tried to affect an air of indifference. Finally, the men returned to what they were doing.

She saw that they had hung the deer from a tree and were halfway through skinning it. Two men stood beside the carcass with short bloody knives. The hide was peeled back to the rump. One of the men tied a slip knot into the thick rope he was holding and fastened it to a loose hunk of bloody, inside-out deerskin. He tied the other end of the rope to the bumper of a pickup.

"Let her rip," the man with the rope yelled. At his signal, the pickup took off.

"I don't need to see this," Munch said and pulled her friends towards the front door of the building.

The minute they entered the clubhouse, bikers swarmed

around them. The music was loud and discordant. The overhead lights flickered and she heard someone curse about the generator.

A woman with spiky blonde hair refilled the men's mugs from the keg of beer set up on a rough-hewn wood counter. Smoke hovered under the low ceilings of the front room. A pool table was in use in the center of the floor. Three men sat elbow to elbow on an old sofa against the far wall, drinking beer and watching the game in progress.

"C'mon," Deb said, tugging her arm. "I'll introduce you."

"Great," Munch said under her breath. She nodded to each seated man as Deb recited their names: Bull, Insane Wayne, and Bug-eyed Tom. Munch didn't think she'd have any trouble keeping their monikers straight.

"She's looking for James," Deb yelled.

"Oh, yeah, I just remembered," Bug-eyed Tom said. "He told me to take care of you."

"Yeah, right," Deb said, laughing and pushing him away. "Watch out for this guy," she told Munch.

Bull, the one with the Schlitz logo tattooed to his arm, shoved his mug of beer towards her.

"No thanks," she said.

"Drink," he commanded.

She shot a look at Deb, hoping to get some help, but her friend had already turned away.

"What?" he asked, his face growing uglier.

"I'm on penicillin," she said. He grunted, satisfied that he hadn't been slighted. Her declaration also bought her some distance from a few of the men within hearing distance.

Deb passed a bottle of Jack Daniel's to Roxanne. Roxanne tilted her head back and poured. "Hey, easy with that," Munch said.

Roxanne turned to her with glazed eyes. "What?"

Did I look like that? Munch wondered.

The bottle came around twice more, followed by joints. She passed them along without comment. Insane Wayne cut out lines of meth on a mirror. Deb went first, taking the fatter lines. Roxanne took her leavings.

Deb took over the woman-with-the-spiky-hair's position by the beer keg, laughing at some joke, rolling her eyes and pretending the guy talking to her was saying something interesting. Roxanne shouted something, but it was lost in the general uproar. The men bounced off each other's chests like figures in a pinball machine, eyes glassy and beards matted with spilled beer.

Munch knew that if she smoked a little and drank some Jack, the scene before her would miraculously transform. The men would get foxy, their jokes funny. She would feel cool and superior to all those normies—those citizens—who didn't know how to live. The voices inside her head would quiet, give her a break from their nagging.

Was that what she wanted? A break?

She located a good spot by an empty wall to stand.

"You want to play pool?" Bug-eyed Tom asked.

She accepted gratefully; anything to stay busy and not to be such a sitting target. She snuck a look at her watch. Where was James?

Bug-eyed Tom racked the balls and broke them. Nothing dropped. She took her turn and sank the two-ball. Someone jostled her arm as she was aiming for her next shot. She missed.

"All right, then," her opponent said. He took aim and sank a solid. Maybe he forgot that he was stripes. She said nothing. She wasn't about to utter a sentence to him that included the words "your balls." Besides, it didn't matter who won this game. She just wanted out of the line of fire.

Bug-eyed Tom leaned into her, bringing his florid complexion and oddly bulging eye close to hers. His breath smelled of garlic and liquor.

"Why don't you and me go somewhere and get all fucked up?" he asked.

"No thanks," she yelled into his ear. The music was deafening. "Not today, I can't." She raised her hands in frustration, as if to say that the music was too loud and her story was too long to tell.

He turned from her and made a grab at the woman with the spiky hair. Munch took the opportunity to slip away, knowing that if she was out of sight by the time he turned around again, the chances were good he'd forget about her.

She looked for Deb and Roxanne and found them passing a bong. It occurred to her that maybe she had already crossed the line and copped a buzz on all the secondhand pot smoke. She tried to determine if she felt any different. Would she know it if she were high? Probably.

Where are You? she asked. *Still with me? I could use a little help here.*

All around her, the partiers got rowdier and louder. Another half hour went by. She kept losing track of Deb and then Roxanne. Someone turned the music up another notch. She thought she heard the roar of more Harleys arriving, but couldn't be sure. She felt as if her head was going to explode. She needed some fresh air, but to get to the front of the room would require wading through the masses.

What's behind door number one? she wondered, spying one of the doors she had noticed earlier in the back of the room. She fought her way to the corner and tried the knob. It was locked. When she tried the second door, the knob turned, and she pushed it open.

It was dark. She groped for a light switch, found it, and snapped it on. She'd found the bathroom. Well, that was something. Securing the lock behind her, she used the toilet and splashed some cold water on her face. Beyond the shower stall, there was a second door. She conjured up a spatial image of the clubhouse's floor plan. The rooms of the building seemed to be laid out pretty straightforwardly into squares and rectangles, which meant that the door had to lead to the second room. And perhaps, with any luck at all, the second room also had a back door.

Wanting no more surprises, she first put her ear to the door and listened. All she could hear was the thrum of the music booming in the front room. She bent down and peeked through the keyhole. The lights were on in the other room, revealing yellow walls. Freshly painted, from the smell of it. She pushed the door open cautiously. No, not yellow paint, she soon realized, but a residue. She saw the burners, beakers, and scales. This was a meth lab. Were these guys fucking crazy? They shouldn't keep all this flammable, toxic stuff in such a closed-in room.

Munch stepped closer to the table holding all the paraphernalia. Large rocks of meth had been laid out on sheets of aluminum foil to dry. They glistened like Jill's chunk of quartz. Rather pretty, really.

Fortunately, she had never cared for speed. At least that was what one part of her brain said. The other half seemed to be in control of her hand, which was reaching for the meth. It said something kind of funny, really. In a voice that sounded like Deb's, it told her that she could always learn—that eight months was long enough. She drew her hand back.

Maybe tomorrow, she promised to quiet the voices. *Just for today, I won't use, I won't drink, and I won't kill myself. Weren't they all the same thing?*

She started to leave the room when she noticed the infant car seats leaning against the wall. They were the same brand as Asia's. The cushions had been removed and lay unzipped on top of a table in the corner. She felt the skin crawl on the back of her neck. Were James and Asia already here? A row of rifles, like the one Deb owned, was propped against the back wall. She worked quickly to disable them by releasing the catch on the trigger guard as she had seen Deb do and pulling the assemblies free. Using her pocket knife, she popped off all the hammer springs, put the guns back together, and returned to the party.

Back inside the main room, she caught sight of Roxanne, passed out on the couch. Not a good thing, Munch knew. Protection or no, an unconscious woman was fair game in these situations.

She elbowed her way over to Roxanne and shook her awake.

"Wha . . . ?"

"Come on," Munch urged, yanking her arm. "We've gotta go outside."

Roxanne stumbled to her feet, swaying as she did. Somehow Munch managed to get her out to the relative safety of the truck and lock her inside. She returned to the clubhouse to find Deb kissing probably one of the ugliest bikers Munch had ever seen.

She tugged on Insane Wayne's arm, pointing at the ugly man on the couch swapping spit with Deb. "Is that Tux?" she asked.

Wayne squinted and said, "Fuck no. That's Shorty."

Great, she thought, so much for protection and respect—now they were all sitting ducks. She grabbed Deb and demanded the keys. "Time to go home."

"I'm not ready," Deb said and returned to her new beau.

Munch felt a tap on her shoulder and spun around. The good-looking man before her smiled. "Aren't you the mechanic?" he asked.

She regarded him for a moment before answering. He didn't seem to be a skeptic or looking to start a fight. Sometimes the knowledge that she worked on cars for a living had this effect on men.

"Yes, I am," she admitted.

"Would you mind stepping out back with me for a moment?" he asked. "I could use your help. I've got a problem with my truck that I can't figure out and I heard you were pretty good."

"Who told you that?"

"Your friend." He pointed at Deb.

"I don't think I should leave her."

"Oh, she'll be okay," he said, disarming her with a little boy grin. "This will just take a second. You're looking for James, right?"

"You've seen him?"

"Yeah, he's back here."

She followed the guy to a door in the corner that she assumed led outside. It wasn't until they were already across the threshold that she noticed that her escort wasn't wearing complete colors, only the bottom patch that read, NOR CAL. He wasn't a full member, but merely a prospect.

Alarm bells went off inside her head, but it was already too late. The door didn't lead outside after all, but to yet another room—a room full of card-carrying, full-fledged Gypsy Jokers. Her escort grabbed her arm and guided her to a stairway.

She faced him, searching for remnants of the boyish charm she had seen earlier, but all innocence was now absent from his face. The eyes that regarded her now were venal and calculating.

Oh, shit.

One of the Jokers locked the door.

27

After listening to Munch's plan, Blackstone left Moody to pay a visit to Motel 7.

Claire, he knew, was staying in Room 3. He checked his watch right before he knocked on her door. It was almost nine o'clock. She was probably resting. He rapped on the door with the authority bred by ten years in law enforcement.

The door opened. She stood before him with a shocked look on her face. "What are you doing here?" she asked. Her eyes strayed to the badge pinned on his lapel. "I don't understand."

He pushed past her. Dark clothes for the night's raid were laid out on her unmade bed. She closed the door after him. "You might want to sit," he said. "This could take a while." He pulled the desk chair closer to the table lamp, where he knew Moody had planted his bug. "I want three things," he said.

"Should I be taking notes?" she asked, raising an eyebrow.

They both turned when there was a knock at the door.

"That's probably Jared," she said.

"Jared Vanowen? Let him in," Blackstone said. "Everyone's invited to this party."

Vanowen came in. He was as surprised as Claire to see Blackstone there. "What's going on?" he asked.

"The detective was just about to tell me," she said, recovering her composure. "He has a list of demands."

"First off," Blackstone said, "I want you, your department, to clear the LAPD of any wrongdoing in the shooting of Darnel Willis, and I want you to do it publicly."

"I already told you I would, Jigsaw. Is this what this is about? You're going to have to be patient. Trust me."

"Second," he said, ignoring her, "I know the Bureau has deep pockets when it comes to their informants. The man you set up— the man who was killed because of the lies you fostered—left behind a little girl. Her name is Asia Garillo. I want a trust fund set up for her."

"He was warned," Vanowen said.

"Shut up, Jared," Claire snapped.

"You can make the check out to Miranda Mancini after you square things with her probation officer. Be creative. Tell Olivia Scott that Mancini helped you with your case."

Claire arched an eyebrow, but, to her credit, faced Blackstone coolly. "You said there were three things."

"I want the credit for tonight's bust of the Gypsy Jokers to go to local law enforcement. You'll thank Sheriff's Deputy Tom Moody for his excellent police work."

She visibly paled. He'd hit a nerve.

"I won't ask you how you came to your conclusions," she said. "The obvious question is: If we don't do as you ask, what then?"

"I'll go public with all that I know."

She said nothing. He could almost hear her gears spinning. She was a bright girl. It wouldn't take her too long to realize that she was out of options. Finally, her posture slumped.

"All right," she said.

He checked his watch. A little under ten minutes had passed since he'd knocked on the door. Jared started to say something, but she quieted him with a hand signal. "I'll give you what you want."

"Do I have your word?" he asked.

"Would that suffice?"

"Sure." He lifted up the table lamp and showed her the bug. "If we don't have trust, what do we have?"

She smiled then. "You're very good. Have you ever considered a career with the Bureau?"

"I don't think so," he said.

"Did you want to accompany us on tonight's operation?"

"You don't know it," he said. "but you need me and my team."

"Your team?"

"Yes, I have a guide to lead us up the mountain. She was up there earlier with one of the biker women and knows where the trip wires are."

"Trip wires?"

"Connected to illumination grenades as of this morning. Your teams would be sitting ducks. You were planning to go up the south side, weren't you?"

"How do you know that?" she asked, and then looked at the lamp. "Of course." She looked at the telephone, then back at him. "All right, fine, let's bring her. What's one more? This whole operation has been a circus from the get-go."

"I know," he said. "I was part of the dog and pony act, remember?"

She actually blushed. That made him feel a little better. He didn't think she could fake a blush.

"Was it all an act, Claire? Was deceiving me amusing?"

"The hardest part," she said, smiling almost playfully, "was memorizing all those chess moves."

He shook his head in disgust. This was all a big game to her. The phone by her bed rang.

She answered it with a curt "Donavon." By the third "uh-huhh," the color had drained from her face. "You've got to stop them," she told her caller. "Well, try."

"What's up?" Blackstone asked.

"We've got problems," she said. "Our support team got their orders scrambled. They're out of radio contact and going in now."

Blackstone jumped to his feet. "You're going to have a blood-bath."

Claire worked frantically over a portable shortwave radio. "Team Alpha, abort, do you copy?"

Static filled the hotel room. Blackstone grabbed his hat and ran for the door. He could only pray that they'd get there in time.

"Did you bring us a woman, prospect?" a big fat biker with Prez over his pocket asked.

"I sure did," Munch's escort said.

"Do you have hair on your ass, prospect?" the prez roared.

"Fucking right," the guy responded.

Munch looked around her, searching for an avenue of escape. She didn't know where this guy was going with this line of questioning, but she didn't want to be there when he arrived.

"Show her."

The prospect pulled down his pants and mooned Munch. She looked out into the sea of impassive faces before her, trying to catch some sympathy. But any eye contact she made was returned with dead, cold stares. She remembered the article she had read on the plane about Communicators and man's evolution as such. Judging from the raw emotions emoting from this crowd, she was in serious trouble. The prospect pulled his pants back up and walked over to her. He held out a handful of Quaaludes.

"Here," he said, "it'll go easier for you if you take these."

She stared at the pills for a long time before replying, wondering if this was how God was choosing to answer her prayers.

She used to love Quaaludes.

Maybe this was the only help she could hope for. If she took the offered pills, they would render her unconscious and then perhaps whatever these bikers planned to do to her body would be easier to live with after. The FBI would find her when they conducted their raid, but that was still hours away.

She heard Ruby's voice in her head saying, *We don't use no matter what.*

"I don't use drugs," she said, but the words came out too softly for anyone else to hear.

"Prospect," the prez's voice thundered out. "You showed her yours, right?"

"That's right," the crowd murmured.

"Now tell her to show us hers." The prospect reached up to Munch's belt and pulled the tongue from the buckle.

It's up to You, she prayed. *I've tried to do my best, but there's no way I'm going through this sober. If this happens, I'm getting drunk.*

And then she saw him. James. Their eyes locked in recognition.

"Wait a minute," he said. "This has to be voluntary." Then to her. "Is it?"

His question stunned her, but she recovered quickly. He had given her an out. "No," she said, fastening her buckle and pushing past the prospect. "It's not. It's definitely not. No."

She walked as quickly as she could without running, somehow sensing that if she ran, if she showed fear, they would descend on her like a pack of hungry wolves and tear her life apart. James escorted her from the room, saying loudly to his brethren, "We need to talk, darling."

Laughter followed. James leaned over and whispered in her ear, "What are you doing here?"

"Where's Asia?"

"I dropped her off." He glanced back over his shoulder.

"Dropped her off where?"

"With Deb's neighbor, the broad who always watches Boogie."

"How could you do that?"

"She's—"

"I'm talking about Sleaze. How could you set him up like that?"

James stared at her without expression. "You better get out of here while you still can."

Munch found Deb still on the couch in a clinch with her Prince Revolting and yanked her to her feet.

"Come on," she said, "we're leaving. Now. Give me the keys."

"What's the matter with you?" Deb asked. "You're no fun at all anymore."

Munch half dragged, half pushed Deb back to the truck. "We're getting out of here."

"All right, all right," Deb agreed sullenly. "What are you all mad about?"

Munch looked at her friend, realized she didn't have a clue. "Just get in the truck."

They drove down the dirt road as quickly as she deemed safe and then a bit more. She had to use all her concentration to keep them from sliding down the bank. *How do people do this drunk?* she wondered.

"Where are we going?" Deb asked.

"I'm taking you home, then I'm going back to L.A."

"I love you, man," Deb said. "You're my sister. I'd die for you. You know that."

"What does that mean?" Munch asked. "You say that. But it doesn't mean shit. You leave me for the first man who wags his dick at you."

"I don't need to be hearing this shit," Deb said. "Not from you."

Roxanne lifted up her head and said, "Yeah, pardon the fuck out of us."

"Another country heard from," Munch said.

Deb slumped over and rested her head on Munch's shoulder. "I'll miss him too, you know."

Munch put a protective arm around Deb's shoulders. "I know," she said. "I know. Let's get out of here." She rounded the blind bend in the road. Her foot hovered over the gas pedal, planning to floor it as soon as the road straightened out.

When she came around the corner, she hit a wall of chrome and blinding headlights. She slammed on the brakes. The pickup fishtailed and skidded. Nothing she did with the steering wheel made a difference. Deb and Roxanne slid under the dash. The eight-track player came loose, fell down at her feet, and jammed against the gas pedal. The truck leapt forward, then made a crunching thud as it smashed into the grille of what she now realized was the front end of an eighteen-wheeler.

Deb pulled herself up from the floorboard and peeked over

the dashboard. Something in the way she said, "Uh-oh," made Munch's blood run cold.

The angry man swinging out of the cab of the semi looked like a cross between a pirate and a lumberjack. It had to be Tux. He was just the type Deb would go for—that both of them used to go for—rough and ready. A dark goatee accentuated the angles of his jaw, a gold loop dangled from his right earlobe. He was a big man, well over six feet tall, and not happy at all.

"What the fuck is going on here?" he said. "And who the fuck are you?"

Deb's head popped out the passenger window. "Hi, baby," she said. She released the door catch and tumbled out. "I've missed you so bad."

It was just then that the first grenade lit up the sky.

28

Two more grenades went off, turning night into day. The stars disappeared under a haze of white smoke. It smelled like the Fourth of July.

Tux grabbed Deb's coat sleeve and shoved her roughly into the cab of the eighteen-wheeler. From his waistband, he pulled a gun and pointed it at Munch's face. "Who the fuck are you?" he asked.

She held her hands out, palms facing him. "Easy. I'm Deb's friend."

They turned when they heard sirens approaching up the highway. Overhead, the first faint beats of helicopter blades could be heard.

"It's over, Tuxford," a loudspeaker announced. "Drop your weapon."

Tux reached forward and grabbed Munch, using her body as a shield as he backed towards his truck. A spotlight from overhead shone down on them. He dragged her with him as if she were no more substantial than a rag doll. Her feet barely touched the ground.

"Drop your weapon," the disembodied voice repeated.

His grip around her chest tightened. He gave her body a jerk that pushed the air from her lungs. They had made it back to his semi. She felt his body twist as he made ready to climb aboard.

Above the sounds of the helicopter and of screeching tires, Munch heard a familiar sound. It was a cross between a *thunk* and a *plink*—the sound of the thick bottom of a bottle connecting with a skull.

She and Tux fell together. The weight of him crushed her, but somehow she managed to push him off and roll away. Deb stood on the running board of the truck, a green Thunderbird wine bottle clutched in her hand. Her eyes glowed with excitement.

"I can't tell you how long I've wanted to do that," she said. "He really was an asshole, wasn't he?"

"Put your hands over your heads," came an almost hysterical scream. Men in dark parkas and ski masks streamed out of the surrounding woodlands. One of them jerked Munch's hands behind her and then pushed her to the ground. Another found Roxanne in the pickup. He dragged her out and dumped her next to Munch. Deb received the same treatment.

Blackstone pushed his way into the melee and pulled Munch to her feet. "You all right?" he asked, brushing her off.

"Yeah, I'm fine."

Agents cuffed Tux where he lay and dragged him off, still unconscious. Deb and Roxanne were shoved against the front of the pickup. "Hey, go easy," Blackstone said. "Save it for the guys up there." He pointed up the hill.

Moody emerged from the sleeper portion of the cab carrying four burlap bags. He opened one and pulled out a stack of bills.

Claire Donavon, in full SWAT attire, jogged up the road. "I'll take those," she said. She motioned for two similarly dressed agents to take over. "Thank you for your help."

"Sure, darlin'," he said.

She walked over to Blackstone, casting a wary glance at Munch. "What's the situation?"

Munch told them both about the meth lab and how she'd disabled the weapons. "You got about twenty guys up there," she said. "About six women. Everybody is pretty loaded. I don't see how they have anywhere to go, either."

"All right," Claire said. "We'll set up a barricade at the bottom of the road and flush them out with chopper teams."

"What about your informant?" Blackstone asked.

"He'll just have to sit tight," Claire said. "What are you going to do now?"

"I'm going to take a statement from Tuxford when he comes around and then I'm heading back home."

"Will I see you in L.A.?" she asked.

"Only when it can't be avoided," he said. He grabbed Munch's arm and led her to his sedan. "What are you grinning about?" he asked.

"I'm just glad that part of it's over," she said. "Let's go get my baby."

29

"The baby is over at Deb's neighbor's house," Munch told Blackstone as they got on the highway.

"Why don't we go over there now? It might take a little while for Tuxford to come around."

She giggled, still high on adrenaline. "Wasn't Deb great?"

"Yeah, she really came through for you."

"What's going to happen to her now?"

"Moody's going to handle that part of the case. For tonight he's just going to question her and let her go. We'll both put in a good word for her in our reports."

"Thanks, I appreciate that."

They pulled up in front of Stella's house. The TV was on in the front room. Just then, the door opened and Stella herself emerged. Her feet spilled out the sides of rubber flip-flops. Something squiggled in her massive arms, dwarfed by the flesh of her wobbling biceps. The bundle in her arms let out a familiar cry.

Munch ran to where the woman stood and held her arms out.

"I can't get her quiet," Stella said, handing over the baby.

"She'll be all right now," Munch told her. Asia clutched her shirt with surprising strength.

"You picking her up?"

"Yeah, I sure am."

"The guy who dropped her off said he'd give me twenty dollars."

Munch opened her wallet. She had exactly twenty dollars left. This fact shook her. Ruby always said that That Old Boy Upstairs gave you exactly what you needed and no more than you could handle. The exact change was one of the more definite signs that Munch had ever gotten from Him. He sure went to a lot of trouble to make His point.

She handed over the money. Stella returned to her television. Munch grabbed her duffel bag from Deb's house, leaving Boogie a note saying that she loved him.

Munch, Blackstone, and Asia returned to Moody's house. Moody provided pillows and blankets. Munch slept on the couch with Asia nestled in her arms while Blackstone interrogated Tux.

When she woke the following morning, Blackstone told her that he had booked them an earlier flight home and to collect her things.

"What about the rest of the Jokers?" she asked.

"They were taken into custody at three this morning. They've being shipped to Roseburg. That was the closest town with a big-enough jail."

"Was anybody hurt?" she asked.

Blackstone laughed. "The feds had their hands full getting half of them to wake up to be arrested."

On the drive to the Medford airport, Munch held the baby in her lap. "How soon will I get the money?" she asked.

"Within the week," he said. "Don't worry, they won't screw us around."

"Tell 'em I want my car back, too."

"Already handled. It'll be waiting for you at the airport. What are you going to do now?"

"You mean with the rest of my life or when we get back to L.A.?"

"I meant your immediate plans."

"I'm going to church."

"To give thanks?" he asked.

"Nah, I did that already. I need to get this kid baptized." She didn't explain how a baptismal certificate was as valid a form of ID as a birth certificate. Or how to keep things simple, she planned to list herself as the mother.

Blackstone smiled uncertainly. "That's nice. I didn't know you were that way. Religious, I mean."

"There's probably a few things you don't know about me," she said.

"I'm sure."

She decided to keep him guessing.

30

Blackstone went straight to the hospital from the airport. Alex, he soon learned, had regained consciousness that morning and was alert and responsive. When Blackstone entered Alex's private room, he found his friend fast asleep.

"Hang in there, buddy," he said quietly.

Alex opened his eyes and studied his partner. "Who the fuck are you supposed to be?" he asked. "The Marlboro man?"

"How do you feel?"

"All right," Alex said. "Except there's this goddamn phone that rings all the time and then when you finally answer it, nobody's there."

"You just get your rest, all right? Don't worry about anything else. It's all taken care of."

"Hey, Jigsaw."

"Yeah?"

"We got the guy, am I right?"

"That's right, buddy."

"Tell me again. Who did what?"

"Tuxford was the driver of the freeway hit on Garillo. Then Tuxford turned around and did his partner, Darnel Willis, after he saw the guy had gone crazy and was shooting cops."

Alex's hand went to his bandage.

"And this Willis guy was the sniper on the freeway, am I right?"

"You're getting the picture. He also did the couple in Venice, thinking he was popping Garillo."

"And Willis hit Garillo, because Garillo was an informant."

"But not really. Tuxford and Willis were just led to believe that. The feds set Garillo up to divert suspicion from their real snitch."

Alex brought his arms up in frustration, trailing wires and IV lines. "So who was that?"

"Garillo's brother-in-law, James Slokum. And now Slokum, Lisa, and her kids have been relocated. You know how big the feds are on their protected witness program."

"Yeah, all that cloak-and-dagger shit." Alex picked at a bandage on his hand. "So they knew these crazy shitheads had those weapons all that time and didn't stop them?"

"That's the rub."

Alex yawned. "I think I need to sleep now, Jigsaw."

"You do that, buddy."

The next day, an article appeared in the *Los Angeles Times*—fourteen short lines on page twenty above an ad for the new Ford Station wagon:

The FBI disclosed today, following a month-long investigation, that a large cache of military weaponry stolen from the Kern

County National Guard Armory was recovered. Large quantities of methamphetamine and marijuana were also confiscated in the early morning raid of the Gypsy Joker motorcycle gang's clubhouse in southern Oregon. Working closely with the LAPD and the Josephine County Sheriff's Department, the federal investigation discovered evidence that a member of the same smuggling ring of outlaw motorcyclists was responsible for the shooting death of felon Darnel Willis earlier this week in Venice Beach. Detective Alex Perez, also wounded in the shooting incident of October 24, is out of intensive care and doctors are guardedly optimistic that he will make a full recovery.

Blackstone clipped out the article and taped it to his wall. He noted that there was no mention of the cash.

Epilogue

Three days before Thanksgiving, Happy Jack told Munch that she had a visitor.

She looked up from the tune-up she was performing on a Ford Pinto and saw Roxanne emerge from an aged but clean Buick.

"What's up?" Munch asked.

"I've got twenty days," Roxanne said.

Munch saw her clarity of eye, the glow in her cheeks, and knew she was speaking the truth. "That's terrific."

"I saw how good you were doing," Roxanne explained, "and I thought maybe that program of yours would work for me. I mean, if you could do it—" She stopped in midsentence, embarrassed.

"It's okay," Munch assured her. "I know what you mean. What happened up north after I left?"

"The cops took us to jail. I was cut loose the next morning. Deb was charged with receiving stolen goods. She's got a new old man, by the way."

"There's a surprise," Munch said.

"Some con she met at the courthouse. He took her and Boogie to Belgium."

"Belgium? Why Belgium?"

"No extradition treaty."

"I hope she makes it," Munch said. "I hope we all do."